FRANCESCA CATLOW loves t[...]
heart of Suffolk, Catlow has tr[...]
with her French husband and, [...]
children. Of all the places she's been it is the Greek islands
that have captured her heart. She visits as often as family
commitments allow. The Little Blue Door was Catlow's first
novel – written during the lockdown of 2020 while feeding
her baby in the early hours.

To stay up to date please visit www.francescacatlow.co.uk.

T: @francescacatlow
F: @francescacatlowofficial
I: @francescacatlowofficial

For trigger warnings visit:
francescacatlow.co.uk/trigger-warnings/

The *Little Blue Door Series* in order:
Book 1: The Little Blue Door (2021)
Book 2: Behind The Olive Trees (2022)
Book 3: Chasing Greek Dreams (2023)
Book 4: Found in Corfu (2024)

Related Standalone:
Greek Secret (2023)

Behind
The
Olive
Trees

FRANCESCA CATLOW

Gaia
Fenrir

Published in 2022 by by Gaia & Fenrir Publishing

ISBN 978-1-915208-04-0 (paperback)
ISBN 978-1-915208-05-7 (ebook)

British Library Cataloguing in Publication Data
A CIP catalogue record for this book is available from the British Library
www.gaiaandfenrirpublishing.co.uk
Cover design by Andrew Davis
https://www.andrewdavisdesigns.co.uk/

This book is dedicated to my mum. We have spent hours talking about this book and she inspired the initial idea to write it in the first place! I know it wouldn't have happened without her. I'm so grateful for her time, support, critique and love.

I would like to thank my editor, Debra. I'm so happy to have found you! Your support and help are much appreciated.

I would also like to acknowledge Lesley. Thank you for your help, and checking anything I needed when I couldn't be in Corfu myself to check things. You can find Lesley here: www.corfuselections.com

A big thank you to Noula and Danielle at San Stefano Travel for supporting me and my books. Also, for organising customised day trips around Corfu for my research. You can find them here: www.san-stefano.gr

There are so many wonderful people and places in Corfu. I want to thank them all just for being there, but with a special thank you to Manthos restaurant in Agios Stefanos for supporting the books alongside San Stefano travel.

Chapter 1

I hadn't been back. Not since finding my mother passed away in the living room the year before. But I knew I needed to go back to the house. I needed to visit my brother's grave. The tiny wooden cross at the bottom of her garden where my father – the bastard who murdered him – put his fragile little body. I'd been avoiding it, but with everything that was going on, everything that was happening, I needed to go. I had to go. I wanted to connect with the memory of my mother before everything changed.

Gaia had suggested she should be the one to go with me. Just the two of us. She'd spoken quickly, saying that she would be better than her dad, because she understood the loss better, because she had lost her mum too. I couldn't disagree with her. There was no way I'd want to. I felt privileged that she wanted to be there for me.

Not long after coming back to Corfu to live with her and Anton, we had stayed up talking about it all. About our lost pasts. Ant had felt unwell that night and had gone up to bed, while Gaia and I finished watching a documentary about

1

NASA. Something was said in the documentary about making their mother proud. Little did that astronaut know what they had started in our home. Gaia had muttered something about wishing she knew what would have made her mother proud. Then, there we were, in our shared loss. I had been lucky to have Grandmama as a stand-in mum while I was growing up; my "mama". Gaia told me how it had been for her for the last few years, verging on womanhood. How she'd started to struggle even more than when she was younger. She was close to her father, but there were times she just wanted to ask another woman what was what, and not her dad. Not that Gaia's grandmothers weren't lovely, but she didn't live with them and they weren't her mother. It had all been made harder by the strict lockdowns in Corfu during the pandemic. Even then we still had to wear masks throughout that winter.

She told me what she remembered of the day her mum died, explaining that her memories were disjointed images and thoughts and that her mother's face was no longer clear in her mind. They'd been laughing and running about their home playing some game, when her mother, Katerina, had collapsed. No matter how much Gaia cried, Katerina wouldn't get up. Gaia confided in me that one thing that stood out in her mind was how upset she had been about being hungry. She had wanted her mum to stop being silly and to get her a snack. It was something she couldn't help but feel guilty about, however much she knew it was ridiculous to feel guilty for being a hungry three-year-old. She hadn't left her collapsed mum even for a moment. For her part, she had just sat playing with her mum's hair, waiting for her to wake up, not knowing that Katerina's heart had failed.

That night, as the two of us sat cross-legged on the sofa, I felt

2

like it was the start of Gaia becoming mine. Just like Anton, she had my heart, but that night she had given me a little bit of hers. The pressure of taking on the role of a mother figure was like hanging over a ledge on a tall building. But the risk of falling was worth it just to be a part of Anton and Gaia's wonderful little life. It was hard to believe that Gaia had been the one to lead me to find my mother. I was more grateful to her than she could ever truly understand. From helping me to piece together my past to accepting me into her future.

As we pulled up in front of my mother's old, peeling, blue door. I clung to the leather steering wheel, my knuckles frozen by the air con. Each breath was shallower than the last, leaving my shoulders lightly pulsing with each miniature heave.

'We don't have to go in. We can go home if you want to.' Gaia pushed her thick, dark hair off her shoulder to look across at me.

'No. It's time.' I pressed the engine button to turn off the car. It wasn't as fancy as Anton's Mustang, but I'd got myself a convertible too – a white Mini. Just like Anton with his car, Gaia had been the driving force behind the choice.

Our feet crunched along the dry ground and the air was filled with the hum of insects. It was as if nothing had changed. As though I'd open the door and Liliana, my mother, would be there, with her blonde, flyaway hair in a neat bun, and a blue dress to match her eyes, and bustling from living room to kitchen to find me things to eat and drink. I wasn't sure what felt worse – missing my grandparents and knowing exactly what I was missing, or missing my mother without having had the time to really get to know her. Only knowing a slice of what had been taken from me before her brain tumour had taken her.

A bougainvillea plant had grown like a weed in the past year, up and over the top of the door. There weren't many flowers yet, only a few little dark pink blooms were beginning to show. I was no longer sure if it had always been there or it had just got a lot bigger with no one to tame it. I put the key in the door, but it wasn't locked. As my fingers pressed the tatty little door, it began to slip away from me, drawing me in. It let out a long creak like a high-pitched yawn, and cracking noises, as though it had been sleeping since my mother left. Inside, there wasn't the burning heat I remembered. Being early May, the house hadn't had time to turn itself into a little oven like it did in the deep summer months. Or at least it had been like that the summer before, when I had found my mother.

Everything was how it had been. Mum had never had anything on display. The fact that the sideboard was empty made no difference to the look of the house. It was the same small, dark room with two old chairs and not much else.

'I've never actually been in here. When we used to help Liliana with fruit picking, we stayed outside and she'd bring us drinks in the garden,' Gaia said, running her hand along the fold-up dining table. It was the table Mum had pulled out for us to eat kleftiko, slow-cooked lamb, the only proper meal we had ever had together. Closing my eyes, I took a deep breath; I could almost smell the onions and herbs.

'This is going to sound like a strange question, but does it smell like cooking to you?' Gaia asked.

As my eyes opened, they focused on her, wondering if she were pulling the thoughts straight from my head. A small line had formed between her neat little brows. The herbs and onions weren't figments of my imagination. The smell was as real as the inquisitive fourteen-year-old leaning forward with her nose, sniffing, wrinkling it, searching for an answer.

'Yeah, I guess it does.'

We looked at each other and started edging towards the kitchen. Sure enough, the oven was on, with a large red pot inside. Gaia folded her arms across her daisy-print crop top and sat into her hip, shaking her head.

'Do you think someone is here? Who could be here?'

'I don't know. Shall we look upstairs?'

Gaia's head snapped round to look at me, and the corner of her mouth slowly lifted at the prospect of nosing around. The house was a one-up one-down. There wasn't much to nosey at.

I led the way up the stairs, bunching my white maxi skirt in my fists so as not to trip on the steep, wooden steps. I'd only been upstairs once before, just after my mother had told me the truth about my father. How he had kidnapped her and told her I was "better off without her". I'd taken myself off to the bathroom, when really all I had wanted to do was run away from the truth of my past: that my father had kept my mother captive up until his death. With each step the lump in my throat seemed to grow, almost suffocating me. In that moment, I wanted to believe that the aroma downstairs came from my mother's cooking, that I would pop my head round her bedroom door and there she would be.

Her room was as bare as when she was alive, only now there was an open holdall under the bed, spewing clothes, and a sleeping bag on top of the mattress.

Gaia squatted down and pulled the clothes from their poor hiding place.

'What the– There must be a– I don't know the English,' she said.

It was rare for her to get stuck on a word. Her English was so good, and even better since I'd been living with her and she was using it every day to talk to me.

'Squatter?'

'Yes! Squatter. Shall I ask the neighbours? I know most people from when we lived near here.'

Chapter 2

I agreed to let Gaia go and interrogate the neighbours. I knew I'd have had a hard time stopping her. She bounded down the stairs, shaking the house as she went. I took my time, edging back through the living room to the kitchen to stare at the big red pot under the dim glow of the oven light. The more I looked at it, the more irritated I became. How dare someone come and live in my mother's house without my permission, and touch her things? It didn't matter that there wasn't much there. Everything inside the drawers and cupboards had been sent to England before I knew I'd be coming back to live in Corfu. That didn't matter. It wasn't the point.

I kept shaking out my wavy hair with my hands in an attempt to stop it sticking to my neck. Little sweaty curls kept forming at the nape of my neck. It was hot in the kitchen with the oven on, but I think it was the upset that was making me hot and bothered.

I made my way outside through the back door to look at Phillip's tiny grave. I walked past the patio to the end of the small garden where the little wooden cross had been half knocked down with no one to care for it. Just to the left of it was another beautiful bougainvillea that had also become wildly out of hand with no one to cut it back or look after it. This one was a little more sheltered from any wind and was beginning to bloom. I reached out to touch the smooth petals and it dawned on me that they were exactly what I needed to have a little bit of Mum and Phillip with me. I could ask someone to bring me a cutting. It was perfect.

With that happy thought lingering in my head, I turned my attention to the ground. It was looking rough and the garden was more weeds than grass – nothing like when I'd seen it last. Looking over it made my brain flit through thoughts I couldn't instantly push away. How much pain does a foetus feel? Was it quick? How did my mother manage to carry on after such a loss? Biting my lip to try and focus on a different pain, I took the little cross and propped it back up, lightly touching the *P. J.* scratched into its worn, damp core. As I did so, a small splinter embedded itself in my skin, making me pull in air between my teeth in surprise. It wasn't too deep. The little shard lay with its head sticking out, mocking me, before it was plucked and kicked out the way a cuckoo kicks chicks out of the nest.

I was crouched down, sucking my finger, when I noticed a slight figure slip into the house through the back door to the kitchen. I quickly found my feet and marched towards the house.

'Can I help you?' I announced, closing the door behind me.

The girl had been looking in the oven when I came in. She jumped up and spun round to face me. She was a rakish, blonde girl with her hair piled on top of her head in a tight, neat bun. Her bright, blue eyes didn't blink. They quickly squeezed into fierce, thin lines. In no way did she look Greek, but she was surely local – from her reddish-brown skin to her black jeans, trainers and hoodie. For me it was already too warm for jeans and a hoodie, and I'd only been on the island for eight months or so. I'd never even seen a tourist in jeans other than to travel in. My ribs felt as though they were squeezing my chest, and we had frozen like we'd been engulfed in sticky amber and left to watch time passing at a much slower rate than it truly was. Suddenly, her eyebrows shot up and she jutted her chin out at me. Standing my ground, I placed my hands on my hips and looked right back at her.

'You need to leave.' There was no gravity or anger or anything really in my voice. It reeled off like a fishing line, thin and loose. The girl's slightly fat little nose wrinkled along with her forehead as she wound her chin back in. I then pointed towards the living room – and so the front door – for emphasis.

From nothing her voice came growling out and then was barking at me, repeatedly pointing from me to the door I was pointing at. The only words I thought I heard at that pace were *bampás* and *spíti*. "Dad" and "house"… but I couldn't be sure of that. That was it. I doubted myself with *bampás*, although "house" might have made sense.

'Go,' she barked in English.

'You go!' Everything fell silent, but when I still didn't move, she grabbed at my elbow, digging in her fingers. She began dragging me along towards the living room. I was caught by surprise, but I protested and pulled at her stubby little fingers, tugging my arm back. Momentarily, I managed to escape only for her to lunge at me with both hands and pull me by my top, ripping the seam near the strap.

As she tried to pull me all the way out of the house, I managed to claw my fingers into the hinge of the little front door and hold on. Suddenly I could understand more of her words, but this time it was all swearing. A screech echoed from my chest as the index finger of my left hand couldn't take anymore and I went hurtling forwards and into the dirt on my knees and palms.

'Shit. You nasty bitch,' I hissed, and spun round to get up only for her to be looming over me alongside the clouds dominating the sky.

'You do not know,' she growled through a heavy Greek accent. 'No coming back!' Her face was locked in a sneer before she laughed at me and went back inside.

I made the decision to wait at the front door for Gaia. When she caught sight of me, she bounded along like a puppy with a smile on her face. As she got nearer she started chatting away, completely unaware of any issue.

'Apparently, it's a girl,' she began. 'Everyone thought you'd already started renting the house. Are you okay? Melodie, is that blood?' She pointed down at my skirt, which had stuck itself to my knee in the fall, pressing the fabric deep into my skin, leaving blood and grit stains on the fine white fabric.

'It is a girl. She came back and just kicked me out of my own house. Literally. I'm going to call the police and have her removed. I was just waiting for you to come back, just in case someone who speaks Greek would be better making the call.'

The girl then opened the door and leant on the frame, her smug little face taunting us. She pointed at the car in the drive, presumably telling us to get in it. Then Gaia went into Greek and the girl completely changed. Peeling herself off of the door frame, she stood straight and still. Gaia was reeling off words like a waterfall, flooding the air with her voice. Her hair whipped about her shoulders as she pointed at me and then back at the house before finishing her monologue with folded arms and sitting into her hip. The girl replied with only a few words and then went back into the house.

'She's going to get her things. She's leaving.'

'What did you say to her?'

'I told her I thought she had no respect, squatting in a dead woman's home. That you owned it and if she didn't leave now, we would call the police.'

'How are you only fourteen?' I wrapped my arms around her. She'd got taller in the past months and was only a little shorter than me. Already well above the Greek average, I wondered if her almost five foot eight would stop there. 'I should've said more. She speaks English.'

'What?' She burst out of my grasp, mouth gaping open and fingers suddenly digging into my forearms. 'What was said?'

'Something like "you don't know" and "no come back".'

A shiver ran from the nape of my neck down my spine and my limbs. 'I think we should go. I'll get your dad to call a locksmith and get this sorted. Come on.'

'Wait. Shouldn't we wait to see if she leaves?'

'No. She might get more violent and I don't want you in harm's way. Let's just go.'

It took almost an hour to get back home to Karousades. At first, we were talking quickly, wondering where the girl came from and why she settled at my mum's. Then, as we passed rows of tall, knotted olive trees lining the meandering road, we fell silent, our eyes caught by the gravity of Corfu. There are gaps where everything opens out into views that easily prise even the most studious driver's gaze away from the road, where the ground tumbles and rolls in all directions with thin, dark-green cypress trees proudly pointing at the clear, blue sky. We let ourselves fall victim to its beauty and no more words were said until we were home.

Anton had been out helping with deliveries and lifting things for one of the elderly shop owners in Sidari. Gaia and I had settled into little routines when he wasn't around, often making dinner together. She'd taught me some traditional ways of cooking different dishes. Everything from *kleftiko* to *stifado* and *marathopitakia*. *Marathopitakia* was something I'd never had before Gaia and Anton made it for me. I loved the golden, crispy pies; the fragrant fennel would fill the house with its deep, liquorice scent. While we cooked, we'd often exchange stories of our day. She'd tell me about schoolwork or about her boyfriend, Finn, and I'd sometimes show her the social media accounts I was working on. I'd scaled down how many people I worked with since moving to Corfu. I still loved looking at the analytics of social media, but I could pick and choose whom I worked with, whose profiles I helped to build. I'd shifted away from anything too corporate and had started to help more local businesses across the island.

That night though, Gaia chatted away. She was back to wondering who the girl was and what she could have been doing in my mother's house, hypothesising everything from a drug den and murderer to just being lost or forgetting where she lived. I quietly laid out the cutlery across the long table. It had eight chairs around it, but mostly it was just the three of us there to eat.

As I turned to face the kitchen area where Gaia was chopping peppers, the front door opened far behind me. I

12

leant as far as I could to see Anton kicking off his trainers, almost knocking over a plant pot, before jogging in my direction.

'I'm so sorry I am late. I know there is much to do.' He stooped over to cup my cheek and briefly meet my lips. I didn't let him settle in before telling him everything about the strange girl. When I said it all out loud I felt the scorching, white tip of anger poking at my belly again. How dare someone squat in my mother's house? How dare she touch her things?

Gaia placed our food in front of us as we continued to talk.

'She hurt you, Melodie-Mou. I cannot have that. We must call the police.' His fingers stretched across and lightly tugged at the tear in my top. I'd meant to change, but I'd been gliding around in a dream since being home.

'No. There's too much to do. She's probably gone now anyway. She was just some stupid kid.' I pulled my top away from his fingers to dismiss his ideas. 'Is there anyone we can call to change the locks or keep an eye on the place?'

'I'll call Basil. He lives only minutes away. If he can't change the lock, he'll know someone who can. Do not worry, Melodie-Mou. We have much more important things to think about right now. Wouldn't you agree?'

Chapter 3

I hated having everyone's eyes on me. But that was the moment I completely forgot about them. All of them. Every last pair of tear filled eyes and sniffing noses were forgotten. I looked up at Anton who was squeezing my hand so hard I thought my fingers and my heart would burst simultaneously. I could barely look him in the eye, for the fear that if I did, we would both break down into tears. He had to bow his head for the Priest to reach and place his crown on his head. Placing a few of mum's flowers on his head as well as mine. I looked him in the eye and a little laugh tickled from his lips. The cry I could feel in my chest switched to a laugh. The overwhelming joy of it all caught and danced in confusion with emotions tingling across every part of me. With our little crowns placed upon our heads, it was official. We were married. We turned to our friends and family, parading for them to see our attachment, there in the symbol of flowers and ribbons joining our heads.

Eventually we were told we could kiss and Anton's palms pressed to my shoulder blades and he pulled me in to him. As though he had forgotten our audience momentarily too, he pressed his lips to mine and I'd never felt happier in my life.

For most of the day I was smiling so much I thought my cheeks would never recover. Being Anton's bride and becoming Gaia's step mother was as close to a dream as reality could possibly get. Everyone was laughing, smiling, clapping and dancing. It was only the moments where I had to be centre of attention that gave me pangs of anxiety; like our first dance where we edged round carefully, as though we were walking along the ledge of a building. Anton's lips had been there reassuring me, lightly pressed to the top of my head. He knew it was what I'd been dreading the most. I had been waiting for the moment I'd stand on my skirt – or worse – for Anton to stand on it, and for us both to go toppling over. It didn't happen. We made it to the end of the dance without any of our, or at least my, usual calamity. I looked up at him with complete relief that we hadn't ruined our perfect day by doing something silly. Anton's silky lips briefly met mine, then he was dragged off by one of his brothers, engulfed by the crowd, the way the sand sinks into the sea's edge.

I'd never been into drama clubs at school, or anything like that. Anything where people would have to watch me. I liked to be the watcher. This was the first time I'd had so many eyes on me so constantly in all my life. I stood still for a moment. Likely for the first time that day. I just wanted to nuzzle inside Anton's white linen shirt pocket and hide from the cameras that kept appearing in my face.

'Here girl, take this,' Maria said, passing me a glass of champagne. 'You can drink my share. You're starting to look a little … overwhelmed.' Her delicate nose wrinkled as she tilted her head to the side.

'Oh, am I?'

'Yes. My hormones make me more sensitive to these things. Plus, your cheeks glowed during that first dance, so unless you're pregnant too…' I rolled my eyes over my champagne glass. '…exactly!' Her elbow then swiftly found my ribcage. 'I think your new mother-in-law wants you, and I better find that husband of mine. I think he is hiding since he tried to eat some baklava off my plate.'

'Melodie! Have you seen Gaia? She and Finn disappeared after your dance, and I wanted to make sure I had a photo. One of them together.'

Athena was poised with her camera as though it were a weapon of war, ready to strike. Every time I looked at her, I couldn't get over how much she looked like a tiny lady-Anton. Not his green eyes. He had inherited those – and his height – from his English father. But her cheekbones high on her face, the thick, dark Greek hair. Even the shape of her brows – although not the bushiness, luckily. Every inch of her face I recognised as the female version of him, more so than Gaia was.

'Shouldn't you know where your new stepdaughter has gone?' she said.

Then a hand appeared on my stomach and a chin planted itself on my shoulder.

'What is wrong, Mum? You're not harassing my bride, are you?' Anton gave a little exhale, and I knew he was smiling underneath it all.

'I'm not harassing the poor girl. I'm sure she gets enough of that from you! Where is my granddaughter? I need a photo. One with her and her boy.' Athena placed her hands on her thick waist, crunching the navy peplum of her dress.

'She's on the beach. Everyone is on the beach!'

He was almost right. The wedding reception seemed to expand by the minute. Well, it didn't just seem that way – it was! We had invited all the restaurant owners – everyone who worked in Agios Stefanos – as well as everyone we had ever met in Corfu, it would seem. People were spilling out on to the beach like confetti. Every tourist was welcomed with open arms too. Mostly being dragged in for a drink to celebrate the occasion.

It was early in the season, the sixth of May, so it was still very quiet in the resort, although we had been lucky with the weather. It was a little breezy now and then, but still delightfully warm. We had decided to have our reception at Waves. The terrace opened out straight onto the beach, only a single step down to grass and sand. At the outer edges of the bay, we'd put wooden lanterns jutting out of the grassy verge, each with a white chiffon bow. Everything was white, tablecloths, chair covers – all with white chiffon bows. Everything except the bougainvillea. We had an archway made and placed on the beach not far from the entrance of the restaurant, and my bouquet too was bougainvillea. Although, it had sprigs of myrtle too; for love and fertility. Not only did I love bougainvillea, but Gaia loved the colour, so her dress was also vibrant pink against all the white.

'I feel like I haven't held you all day,' Anton whispered in my ear, as we watched his mother kicking up sand at the other guests as she marched around the beach, elbows moving faster than her legs, looking for Gaia.

'I know. I'm not used to sharing you with so many people.' I smiled, resting my head against his.

'I love you, Melodie-Mou, sorry, Mrs Melodie Greenwood,'

we laughed. 'Thank you for being my wife.'

'Thank you for saving me, thank you for asking me...'

He briefly kissed my neck, causing a tickle of goosebumps before he was whisked away by yet another English family member who *had* to get him a drink and pat him on the back.

'Mou-mou!' Gaia called out over the music, the little nickname for me that had evolved over the past year. It translated to "my-my", or "mine-mine", which although doesn't actually make sense in Greek, it's sweet across both languages, or at least I thought so. 'You need to get Granny to stop trying to take pictures of me with Finn. She has taken thousands.' Gaia's weight was forwards and her hands were firmly on her hips. Her stance was so like her grandmother's, I couldn't help but laugh. She had her two younger cousins in tow, like little cheerleaders. They idolised every movement Gaia made. If she flicked her hair, they flicked their hair. Both girls were as blonde as their mother and couldn't have been further from Gaia to look at. They had pointed, almost spiteful noses and were as white as newly formed clouds – a complete contrast to Gaia's golden skin and long, dark hair.

'I think it's sweet. She'll want to have lots to take back with her to show all her friends back in Essex. Anyway, there is no way I'm going to try to boss Athena about. No way.' I shook my head behind my glass. 'Why don't you find your grandad? I think he might be the only one to contain her – or better yet, Akis.'

'Why Uncle Akis? Why not Uncle Marty or Uncle Dimi?'

'Yeah, why not Daddy?' The littlest of the two cousins pouted, folding her arms, only to quickly remember that Gaia's hands were still on her hips, and so she replaced hers where they'd been.

18

'Because Uncle Dimi – your daddy – isn't the youngest. Akis is. And just like your little brother always gets away with everything in your house, I know Akis gets away with more than his brothers. Haven't you ever noticed?' I screwed up my face in disbelief that they wouldn't know this already, before taking another taste of bubbles.

All three shook their heads, making a petal from the bougainvillea in Gaia's hair fall out, which was quickly grabbed and pocketed by the littlest cousin. Gaia was only fourteen, but she had changed so much in the past year. She could easily pass for eighteen with her hair done and make-up on. But, in that moment, her green eyes were so wide she looked younger than her age. Almost as though she were a small child who was playing dress-up.

'I think it's because he's the baby,' I clarified.

'He's older than you!' Gaia said, and flicked her dark- brown hair over her shoulder, triggering a reaction in her cousins to perfectly mimic the move. She'd wanted her hair wavy for the wedding day, so that it would look like mine.

'Yes, I know that. But he is still your granny's baby, and he always will be. It doesn't matter if he is thirty-three or one hundred and three. Trust me. Ask Akis for help.'

Then they were all pouting. Gaia decided to give my logic a try and bounded off barefoot to find her Uncle Akis.

The sun was setting into the cool blanket of blue. Each ripple sparkled so intensely making the sea hard to look at; it was simultaneously pleasing and painful on the eyes. I did the rounds before more Greek dancing would inevitably kick off not long after sunset. Anton had assured me that he could do the classic Greek chair dance I'd once seen in Lesvos. It was the one where they balance right on the edge of a wooden chair and step off more blasé than your average cat, and honestly, I couldn't imagine his six-foot-four frame doing anything more than snapping the poor chair into twigs. No matter what, it wasn't something I wanted to miss.

Chapter 4

In making my way to the buffet I was stopped by Basil. In the time I'd spent getting to know Anton, I felt like I knew Basil too, even though we had only been introduced earlier that day. He was one of Athena's friends from school and Anton's godfather. When Anton's family moved back to England, Ant had refused to follow suit and had lived with Basil. He had become almost a second father to Anton.

Basil still lived in Kokkini. Anton had lived with him, his late wife Iolanthe and their son Michail. The village of Kokkini was where my mother had lived. Basil had kindly been the one to change the lock at my mum's for us. I couldn't get over how much older Basil looked compared to Athena and Chris even though they were all around the same age. He was shorter than me, maybe five foot six, with a pointed chin, high, fine eyebrows and weathered skin that showed in beautiful detail each time he had laughed.

'Did Anton tell you?' Basil said.

'I'm going to guess, probably not.' I went to sip my champagne, only to find an empty glass.

'My son Michail is your wedding gift!' Basil laughed. 'Anton, he tells me you want a swimming pool.'

'Wow! That's amazing, thank you so much. Thank you again for bringing the bougainvillea flowers from my mother's house for Anton's buttonhole today. I'm so happy to have a little part of her here with us.'

The music seemed to go up again to what I could only imagine was full volume, making us both flinch, eyes momentarily squinting, as everyone started clapping in perfect rhythm. Athena rushed towards me, then seeing Basil squeezing his cheeks into a pout, she laughed and said something in Greek at him. She dragged me away from him, leaving him to shrug and laugh, while I was helpless in her grip.

After she delivered a firm tap on my cheek, she pulled me to the front of the crowd to get the best possible view. Anton and his three brothers stood to the right of the bar facing out to a growing crowd. The sun was setting in their eyes, making the whole beach and restaurant glow orange like a gold-tinted photo filter. Various waiters from other restaurants circled them, all clapping and ready to set fire to anything that stayed still for a moment too long. All for entertainment, of course. Anton and his brothers were dressed in white linen. At the start of the day, they'd all looked vibrant and fresh. Now they were looking a little like a baby's used muslin around the bottoms of their trousers.

The four men were all so different. There were threads between them, which showed that they were related, but en masse it wasn't instantly obvious. Martin – or Marty as everyone called him – was the oldest and shortest. He was five foot ten and spent his spare time in the gym with his son, that or down the pub. Apparently, he had been that way ever since a very messy divorce not long before the pandemic. His features were so similar to Anton's though. He had the same high cheekbones cutting across his face, and he was the only other brother to have the cat-like green eyes. Dimitri and Akis were built much like Anton, well over the six-foot mark, but Akis was very lean and Dimi had a little gut, as though he were about five months pregnant, and thin rectangular glasses.

The men linked arms and started tapping the ground with their feet. Cross, step, a little tap, another little step, then suddenly a big kick. I touched my fingers to the hollows of my cheeks. I'd never seen Anton dance before. Not like that, anyway. I'd had no idea that he'd been telling the truth about dancing at the reception, not outside of the traditional group dancing. As the music gained in speed, so did the brothers' movements. It was mesmerising. I'd always loved watching the dancing at Zorba's, Little Prince's, and the Greek bouzouki night at Barras, while having a meal on holidays with my grandparents – but watching my new husband and his brothers prance about the floor was a whole new experience. I wasn't one to love the limelight, and I started to dread the idea that someone, likely Athena or Chris, would push me forward.

Gaia came running around them, darting past a flame that one of the waiters had just cultured with some lighter fluid on the floor.

'Here!' she shouted over the music, handing me a plate. I just held it and looked from her to the plate. 'Go on then!' I looked across the floor at Anton's sweaty face. He looked right at me as he did a kick and laughed.

'Come on, Mrs Greenwood!' he bellowed, and then everyone was looking at me.

So, I threw the plate to the ground, sending chunks of it sprawling across the floor in all directions. A wave of cheering followed and *OPA!* bellowed from all round. Then plates were being passed about and people were smashing them in the direction of the dancers. The newly wedded Greek part of me wanted to jump in with as many plates as I could carry. The health-and-safety Brit in me wanted to advise everyone to be careful not to accidentally hit my husband with a plate. I didn't really think it would happen. Plate-throwing like that had been banned for decades, although I knew it still went on. I'd seen it first-hand in a restaurant once. Even so, I didn't think it would happen at our wedding! I'm sure it had been encouraged by one of Anton's brothers, likely Akis or Marty, who had brought piles of plates to hand out. More men had joined in with the dance, and the shards of plates threatened to become more than a bit of fun. The music changed to another, quicker piece of traditional string music. A random man came in, kicking chunks of plate as he went, and placed down four wooden chairs.

'Oh no,' I said to no one in particular, and covered my eyes with my fingers – only to quickly glance between them so I could keep an eye on what disasters were ahead of me. Luckily, someone sensible came darting across with a broom and moved most of the big chunks of plate out of the way in two rounds across the floor.

The brothers all lined up and one by one each stepped onto his chair, then onto the back of it, and successfully tipped the chair over without any of them breaking a neck. My heart was skipping along like pieces of plate in my chest, watching Anton's step onto a tiny little chair. I was amazed none of them ended up across their chair in the splits! Just as I thought it was over, it wasn't. Each chair lay flat on its back – apparently waiting to be propped back up by some miraculous means. Each brother stepped up onto the legs of his chair and shuffled along them with one foot on each front chair leg. It was almost how I would imagine an ageing tightrope walker might perform, shuffling along two ropes for safety reasons. Then, they pressed on the edge of the legs to tip up the chair and try to end by sitting on the now correctly placed chair. Marty managed it perfectly and straight away, which gave us all an idea of what was meant to be done and how. I wouldn't have been surprised if he had spent the past few months with this trick integrated into his gym routine. Dimitri, on the other hand, tipped the chair okay, but went flying forwards with the momentum of it and split his trousers right along the seam and nearly lost his glasses. He swiftly took his trousers off – to the horror and delight of his wife, Lou – causing more hilarity from the guests and his children but mildly bewildering the tourists in the room. After that, Akis and Anton's turns seemed rather uneventful. It took Anton two attempts because he was still laughing at Dimi, but at least he managed it. The plates were properly swept away and everyone began dancing and laughing again. Anton came over to me, sweat dripping from his brow.

'Are you ready?' he said.

Chapter 5

'Ready for what?' I asked, digging my fingers into my waist. Unlike most brides who try to lose weight for the big day, I'd gained a couple of pounds since being with Anton. Eight to be exact. I was still very slim, but I'd regained a healthier curve to my body and more of my hourglass shape. I needed to after the weight I'd lost during the pandemic. Being a part of a family again after the loss of my grandparents meant I was more willing to eat properly and look after myself. 'You're not going to make me dance again, are you?' I lifted half of my face into a cheeky smile. 'I know it's traditional to do lots of dancing, but I've done well not to fall over, I think. Any more and I'm just tempting fate. I'm impressed I made it through the *kalamatiano*, and the first dance.' I laughed and squeezed his hand.

'I know. I was hoping my dance would keep the people happy and be enough to impress you and get you away early.' He raised one thick, dark eyebrow then rubbed his thumb along my cheek. 'I've got a surprise for you. Are you ready to leave?'

'I'd go anywhere with you,' I said, and I meant it. We should have said our goodbyes, but we knew if we started, we would never leave. Instead, I quickly found the silver shoes I'd discarded under the top table earlier in the day and grabbed our wedding crowns. The crowns were my favourite Greek wedding tradition and I didn't want to lose them. Ours were made using wire, vibrant, pink bougainvillea and ribbon that joined them together. They had been handmade on the island. I had been worried about having them placed on our heads with Anton being so much taller than me, but they'd been perfectly made to accommodate his height.

Walking back towards the sand, I looped my arm through the crowns like giant bracelets. Stepping out on to the soft, golden sand underfoot, I hesitated. 'I want to say goodbye to Gaia. Do you think I can manage that at least?'

Anton shook his head. 'I've told her to be good for her grandparents and explained we would sneak away. You'll see her tomorrow. Now come on before someone else stops us.'

'And where are you two going?' Athena called. She and Anton's Dad, Chris, were standing chatting to hordes of family members on the beach.

'Leave it out. Let 'em go enjoy their wedding night,' Chris bellowed, much louder than was necessary for the distance involved. His Essex accent and booming voice carried over the music, making more heads turn and catch us with smiles.

'But what about the last dance? I got money out of the bank ready to pin to them!' Athena slapped Chris's belly with the back of her hand and pressed her eyebrows toward her dark-brown eyes.

'Look, my love, it can't all be Greek traditions. Ant's half English too and he wants to tick off some other traditions, don't ya boy?' He was waving his pint as he spoke, nearly sploshing some onto the cool white sand. Anton's brothers laughed and made comments in Greek. Anton rubbed his brow, hiding a smile before giving an answer I couldn't understand. 'Come on, boys, you know my Greek's useless nowadays!' I'm pretty sure it wasn't. 'Look, you two lovebirds enjoy yourselves,' Chris said. 'We'll see ya tomorrow, yeah? Don't worry about a thing.'

'Have fun little one.' Marty called with a sly smile making Anton puff out a little laugh. He often called him little one. Apparently, he always had as Chris would call Anton *the little one* when he was a baby, and for Marty it just stuck.

I followed Anton along the beach in silence. I grasped his hairy arm between both of my hands as he swung my shoes along in the opposite hand. Footsteps came quickly behind us, kicking up sand in our direction at such a pace my breath caught in my chest, shaking my ribs. Before I could release Anton from my grasp and turn, Gaia had propelled herself onto his back like a little spider monkey. He stumbled forward, unprepared for her, and fell onto his knees in the sand, nearly dragging me with him. Gaia squawked and laughed, then hopped off. She ran around to face Anton, dropped to her knees too, and wrapped her arms about his neck. She looked like a naughty little fairy as she had become more and more dishevelled from dancing, laughing and running. Her pink chiffon puddled around her knees in the sand.

'Love you, Dad,' she said.

'Love you too, Gaia mou. Be good.' Ant kissed her forehead before she stood up and came over to me. Her slim, golden arms wrapped around me tighter than ever before. Strands of coconut-scented hair tickled at my nose.

'I love you, mou-mou,' she announced over my shoulder. She'd never said that before. Suddenly, there was a rock in my throat. I opened my mouth to speak, but had to momentarily hold my breath to stop myself from crying, before managing to continue.

'I love you too, Gaia,' I whispered into her matted locks. With that she ran back down the beach straight to her boyfriend's arms, without even a glance back in our direction. 'Did you hear that? She said she loves me.' I looked over at Anton who was dusting sand off his trousers which now had golden grazes on the knees.

He looked up at me, green eyes shining like jade in the last flecks of setting sunlight. He smiled and shrugged. 'Why wouldn't she? You're perfect.'

We continued in silence again. My mind was throbbing with layers of memories from the day. From our wedding crowns being placed on our heads to Anton's speech – telling everyone how we met and how I was completely intimidated by Gaia – to laughing at Ant's brothers, then Gaia's beautiful announcement. The whole day was surreal. We came to the end of the line of lanterns, then stopped outside Mango Bar.

'Are we having a drink?' I shook my hazel hair out a little and smiled, knowing the beach bar had closed hours before. He bent forward to kiss the side of my mouth. His fingers glanced over the hair that had fallen around my eyes as he tucked it behind my ear. My hair was longer than it had been, making its way steadily down my back. I touched the soft ends for a moment before meeting his gaze.

'I've booked us a room at Delfino Blu for tonight,' he said. 'You're kidding!'

My eyes must have grown to twice their usual size as Anton

chuckled and squeezed my hand. I'd never stayed there before. My grandparents and I had always stayed at Vicky apartments that were almost next door. Occasionally, I'd looked over longingly at the luxury hotel suites, but I knew it was far beyond anything I could afford at the time. I'd been so upset when Anton's family had booked the Margaritas suites that were right next to our wedding venue. They were beautiful too, right on the beach, and each individually designed. I'd really sulked when Anton told me his parents and brothers had booked them because I thought we were going to stay there on our wedding night. He had gone as far as to tell me we would just get a car back to the house and stay there instead. The little fibber.

As it turned out, everything had been perfectly organised. Anton had booked the honeymoon suite for us to spend the night. Like our wedding, everything in the suite was white. It reminded me of the first day I had spent in Anton's bed with its crisp white sheets. It seemed crazy to think that was less than a year ago, and now we were married. With some people, time just fades to nothing. With Anton it was irrelevant. We were happy and no amount of time would change that fact. We hadn't wanted to wait to be together.

The glass doors of our room had been left open. Across the enormous balcony were lots of white chiffon curtains; all had been left untied. Their dance in the breeze lured me out towards them. I held the balcony rail to steady myself in my thoughts. Although it was dark, there was enough light from the tavernas and the moon to see the sea throbbing and tickling the sand. The late-evening air still held warmth from the day, but a fresh breeze occasionally came along to brush our skin, leaving a shiver as though a feather had been tickling at our spines.

Anton passed me a glass of champagne which fizzed almost in time with the sounds of the sea below. The sea still managed to be the dominant noise, even with the wedding reception in full swing further along the beach.

'*Yamas*. To my beautiful bride.'

'Cheers. To my wonderful husband.'

We looked out at the navy sea and sipped the Laurent-Perrier champagne, delighting in the peachy, citrusy bubbles.

I said, 'I can't believe that Gaia said she loves me. I'm sorry to tell you, but I think that was my highlight of the day!'

Anton smiled, pushed his large hand through the hair at the base of my neck and bent down to kiss just under my ear. 'Me too,' he said in a low voice so close to my ear it was as though he were trying to hide in my hair. 'She sat me down two days ago and said she felt guilty. She didn't know what to do about it.' His fingers slipped away and he sat down on the four-poster bed-sunlounger that was on the balcony. His weight made it jolt a little. Carefully, I placed myself by his side.

'Guilty?'

'Yes.'

'What about? Why?'

'About her mother. She told me she was glad we were getting married and wanted you to be her mother. You can tell that from her little nickname, "mou-mou". She's guilty about not remembering her mother and wanting you to be in her place,' he said. His eyes stayed on the sea as stoic as his face. Both sea and man were strong and unwilling to tell their truths on the matter. The distant noise of our wedding reception further along the beach began to die down. I wondered what Gaia was doing in that moment. I could imagine her laughing with her grandparents. Not those from her mother's side. They had declined their wedding invitation.

Anton continued, 'I said to her it's not her fault. She was so young when her mother died. Her mother would only want her happiness. I told Gaia I believe her mother sent you to us.'

'Do you really believe that?' I placed my empty glass on the floor, and Anton eyed the bottom of his empty flute before doing the same.

'I like to think so, yes,' he said. He turned to me and kissed me, lightly at first, then deeper, searching for unspoken words and promises of love for his – our – family.

We began to melt onto the bed, holding each other in a loving embrace. Soon my fingers were fumbling with Anton's shirt buttons, and he pulled at the four buttons on the back of my dress. There we were, warm skin pressing together, wrapped up in the fine chiffon layers of my dress.

For a moment, Anton looked down at me, as still as the stars over his head.

'*Se agapó*,' he whispered – I love you. Then he began to whisper Greek words in my ear, most of which I couldn't understand. I wanted to concentrate on them, but I couldn't. He shuffled me along the bed, slowly. So slowly. He rested on his elbows, his hands tangled in my hair. His breath on my ear was warm against the cool night air. Each word rolling from his tongue was as entrancing as the sound of the sea rolling on the sand.

I closed my eyes and let my fingers trace his spine over the satin skin that held together the strong man inside. I worked my way down, enjoying the feel, then grabbed him and pulled him harder towards me, making him momentarily pause in his monologue. I could hear the smile, almost laugh, on his breath before he continued talking and rocking, slowly gaining in speed, along with my breath and my heart, until we couldn't take a moment more. We held each other, knotted together. Like a wedding knot. Never to be untied.

Eventually, we caught our breath and lay back, naked under the stars. The breeze momentarily picked up, causing the chiffon curtains to lift and swirl, like seven or eight ghosts come to haunt us. Anton disappeared into the apartment and came back with two cotton bathrobes.

'Shouldn't we go inside?'

'No,' he said. 'Let's lie with the stars.'

Chapter 6

After a week away for our honeymoon, we came back to copious amounts of unpacking and unwrapping of presents. Athena and Chris had been staying at the house with Gaia while we were away and it was obvious as soon as we walked through the door that she'd been spoilt the whole time. As soon as Ant put our bags down, he was made to follow after his mother. He was agreeing to everything she said but with a distinct grunt as he lugged himself from room to room. She was pointing everything out to him, from where she had moved things in the kitchen to how nothing was sensibly placed.

She suddenly erupted in English. 'Melodie, when will you take over all this? Organise this man?'

I just shrugged and laughed; she meant well. Gaia had pulled me over to the sofa to ask questions about our time away and to list everything her grandparents had got her, including *a brand-new-absolutely-awesome-cool-new phone*. As she said it, I could hear Anton's low groan from the kitchen.

'What? I hear Katerina's parents got her an iPad.' Athena

sat her weight into her hip, looking at Anton accusingly as if he had omitted key information to help her navigate within Gaia's life.

Ant replied in Greek before Gaia chimed in with, 'Yiayia and Papou got that for schoolwork. Dad won't let me use it for much else.'

'To be fair to ya gran, you didn't really say that before.' Chris, who was sitting on Ant's favourite leather chair, looked up from his phone above the rim of his reading glasses, but only for a moment to watch Gaia clutch her new favourite toy to her chest, as though he might snatch it from her.

'She didn't ask.'

'I let them get away with more because they miss their daughter,' Anton said, fingers massaging his forehead. 'They miss seeing Gaia too since we moved further north,' Anton's voice droned, as he continued to rub his face.

'Well, I miss Gaia more since you won't move to England,' Athena pouted, crossing her arms.

After Athena had finished showing Anton round his own house, she settled down with me and praised me for taking him on. She reiterated what a mess she thought he had been and how in the month after I had left Corfu he had never been so miserable on "the zoom". They were all things she'd told me before, but it was nice to hear them again.

Athena cooked lamb with spinach and feta. The meat was as soft and delicate as the cheese and filled the house with a warm, rustic smell of traditional cooking. Over dinner, Athena and Chris told us that Anton's youngest brother, Akis, had decided to stay on the island.

'I think he's lookin' for a little romance himself. No luck with the girls round our way so he's come to try his luck

35

here,' Chris said. 'Can't blame him. It's obviously lucky for us Greenwood boys. Corfu's where I found ya beautiful mum and where you found the beautiful Melodie.' Chris had finished his food before I'd barely started mine. For a man of sixty-three, he was in very good shape. He liked to walk everywhere. Back in England they had two Dobermanns – Sissy and Dizzy – that he took for long walks. He had been a handyman and his business was now run by Dimi. 'He's got nothing but a job he hates in England. He might even wanna stay.' Chris's dark-green eyes darted towards Athena, who was the first to look horrified by the idea of Akis staying forever in Corfu. Anton's cutlery also dropped a little too abruptly to his plate, and he bit his bottom lip.

'Where is he staying? Does he want to stay here?' As soon as my words reached the ears of Ant he was tutting and shaking his head.

'No, no. If he stays here with us, he may never leave. I love my brother but…'

Gaia soon jumped to Akis's defence, being a big fan of her fun Uncle Akis. Anton promised his mother that when they had left the island, he would of course look out for his little brother and provide him with a bed should it be needed.

Two days later, Akis and Anton took their parents off to the airport while I was left making *thank you* cards on my phone. Well, partly making them. Anton would have to fill in all the words in Greek but at least I had chosen a couple of nice wedding photos for the front of the cards. As I sat at the dining room table, skimming my phone for a nice photo to place on the back, I went to my favourites file and my thumb scrolled a little faster than I meant to. The image left on my screen was the one photo I had of Mum and me. That's not actually true. There are two photos of Mum and me. One from when I was born and the one from not long before she died. There we were: I was looking at the camera, she was looking at me out of the corner of her striking blue eyes. It was a good photo of both of us, really. We both looked happy in our own way. But there was a line between my mother's brows and a question mark behind her eyes. Whenever I looked at the image on my phone, I wondered what she really wanted to say. If she were thinking about opening up to me about her brain tumour or if she were afraid of ruining the moment with the truth. I needed to go back to her house to tidy up Phillip's little grave properly. As things were settling back into normality, I could restart the healing process.

The booming sound of two identical laughs came flooding through the front door. Gaia called to them in Greek with a smile. I only understood *kaló apógevma* – good evening. The rest was lost on me still. I had been trying to learn Greek as best I could. I was able to order food and drinks, but as soon as anyone spoke at a natural pace, I was lost.

'I'd best lay another place then,' I chipped in. Akis came round and gave me the squeeze of a man who had had one too many Corfu beers with lunch.

'How is my beautiful new sister? I always wanted a sister!'

I didn't want to change his beaming smile, so I stuttered over my words and didn't properly answer. I quickly put out some more silverware and changed the subject to find out what they'd been up to. Clearly more than just dropping off their parents. Anton tilted his head and walked round the table without taking his eyes off me. I kept my eyeline low, but I could feel his green eyes honing in on me. Akis, on the other hand, was bounding towards Gaia to steal bits of fresh green pepper.

'Melodie-Mou,' Anton whispered, taking my cheek into the large expanse of his hand, 'are you okay?'

I swallowed my need to have him hold me. The desire to cry and crumple to the floor like a discarded old shirt caught me a little unawares. I bit my bottom lip and shook my head.

'Just thinking about Mum,' was all I could manage to say.

He knew not to press me. He didn't need words to reassure me, just the feel of his thumb skimming my cheek and a kiss before getting up to help Gaia dish up. Akis placed a bottle of Mythos beer in front of me. He opened one for himself with a click, and a mist of vapour left the perfume of cool hops in the air.

'No, thanks.' I pushed the bottle away.

He flopped in the chair next to me to sit at the head of the table and swiftly pushed it back. 'Come on. It'll lift the worry of "giving Anton another child" right off your face,' he said, with a cheeky little grin. His face wasn't much like Anton's. It was narrower with a slightly pointed chin. He had a scar on his right cheek that turned into a dimple when he smiled.

I didn't turn round to see the reaction of Gaia and Anton. I knew Akis would be able to see them, as the kitchen stretched across the back wall of the house. He didn't take his eyes off mine. Maybe he didn't want to see his brother's face. Like me, he probably knew exactly what it looked like at that moment. I could quite imagine the shade of angry red Anton's cheeks had gone. Where there had been the scuffing of feet and drawers being opened and closed in the dance of dishing up, there was now silence. I would put money on Gaia looking between us all and Anton wishing he could reach his little brother to give him a clip round the ear.

I leant forward, placing my forearms and palms along the table towards him.

'Actually, Akis, I went to my mother's old house before the wedding for the first time since finding her dead in her chair, and to my surprise there was a squatter. A girl. So, no. I'm not worrying about whether or not I'm pregnant. I was just thinking about getting over to the house now that we're home. Basil's been keeping an eye on the place. Sorry if I look at all distracted. I am. Anton and I will be looking into having the house refurbished to become one of our rentals. It's just a little hard for me. Finding her and then losing her the way I did.'

Behind me, I heard Gaia exhale a little puff from her pretty, turned-up nose like a satisfied baby dragon. She might as well have said *that told you*.

Anton, on the other hand, came to sit opposite me, leaving Gaia to finish plating up the *moussaka* and salad.

'Sorry, Melodie. I was just having some fun.' Akis shrank down from his six-foot-something frame, leaning his forehead in his hand.

We hadn't told anyone other than Basil and his son Michail about the girl in the house. With everyone arriving at once for the wedding and Basil promising to keep an eye on the place, it had soon been overshadowed.

'Why didn't you tell me? Bloody hell, security is my job. I would happily help.' Akis took my hand and squeezed it.

'Personal security, not houses.' Anton rolled his eyes at his little brother.

'Still bloody security, Ant. You should've told me. I'd have made the time to go over and check it out.'

'Look ...' I let go of his hand and snatched a look between them. 'It doesn't matter now. Let's just eat.'

Gaia placed food in front of us and we quietly chatted. Before anyone else had finished eating, I excused myself, standing up, grabbing the beer I hadn't wanted before.

'You have not eaten enough,' Anton declared. He began to push his sleeves back up his arms like he was ready to argue his point. His Greek accent would sometimes be a little more pronounced when he was tired and I could tell he was getting that way. Akis, on the other hand, had a hint of Essex in his English and I wondered if he did when he spoke Greek.

'I'm just not hungry. You three eat and chat. I just want to get some rest.' I went round the table kissing each of them on the head. Anton caught my fingers in his grasp.

'*Se agapó*,' he said, and kissed my knuckles.

'I love you too.'

Chapter 7

I sat on the edge of our bed. We'd been married for almost two weeks. Everything that was mine became his and everything that was his became mine. I'd been sleeping in that bed for months and had still seen it as his. In that moment, the dark-blue walls felt like their sole purpose was to crush me under the weight of my own questions. Before the wedding I could distract myself from it all, but seeing the photo of my mum again made it all come crashing back. Anton and I had chatted about it on our honeymoon now and then – about everything from the deranged blonde squatter to the bricks and mortar to Gaia being the one to lead me to my estranged mother. Part of it still felt like a dream. Finding my mother when I least expected to and losing her just as quickly. It was on our honeymoon that Anton and I had decided we would turn her place into a rental property, rather than have squatters taking advantage, or having it fall into disrepair. Which it was already in high risk of doing.

The day I had gone with Gaia to the house was supposed to be about healing wounds, seeing my brother's grave and reconnecting with what little I had left of my mother before getting married. I still needed that. Athena and Chris had brought a lot of my things back with them when they came for the wedding. They had all been put in one of the spare rooms. I crept along the corridor, keeping my back close to the wall. Downstairs, the Greenwood trio had all moved to the sofas at the front of the house, and if I edged close to the banister I ran the risk of being seen. I didn't want there to be a big commotion about what I was doing.

Sneaking past the sepia family photo of Anton, Gaia and her mother Katerina, I caught her eyes on me. Anton had insisted on moving it from the living room when I moved in. I didn't mind it being in the house – Katerina was Gaia's mother after all. He had wanted to put the photograph in Gaia's bedroom, but I thought that was too much, so we agreed on the landing. If I were to be completely honest, I was pleased that he had suggested moving it. I didn't want to be the one to ask for it to be in a less prominent position. There's no way I would ever want to take away any reminders Gaia might have of her mother, because I would never want anyone to take away what little I had of mine. Whenever I walked past it though, guilt pangs hit me like little elastic bands as Katerina's eyes so often met mine. I had everything that should've been hers. I tried to avoid her gaze and carried on to the green guest room. The one we did hope would soon have a little baby in it. We would be happy with a healthy girl or boy, but we both thought it might be nicer for Gaia if it were a boy. I'm not sure why really; she wasn't the type to be jealous in that way. I felt quite confident of that. Not that I'd have said any of that to Akis. Neither of us wanted the whole family asking every two minutes if I were pregnant or not.

The room had boxes lined along the mint-green wall at the back. It was used more as an office space since I had moved in. Anton had put a large white desk and green office chair in there for me to do my work. I tucked my skirt around my legs and crouched down to assess the contents of the boxes. I had to carefully and quietly peel back packing tape to see what was inside. Some were things from my grandparents' house. I pulled out an oil lantern they'd bought in Crete when I was five or six. When they got it home, they had filled it with oil to burn only for it all to seep out of the bottom. Apparently, it was ornamental and really shouldn't have been lit. Luckily, no harm was done and it was yet another thing for them to laugh about together. Putting it back, I opened the next box. It had papers that belonged to my mum. It wasn't the biggest box, but it was pretty full. I lifted it, put it on my hip, and made my way slowly back to our room, doing my best to avoid any creaky floorboards and Katerina's dark sepia-stained eyes.

I sat on the floor at the foot of the bed with the box in front of me. It patiently waited to be opened again as I sipped from the beer bottle Akis had given me. Eventually, the bottle was placed by my side and I laid my hand on the box instead – almost as though the box were a pet or a child. The contents were all I really had of my mother. One box of papers and only a few days of memories. I hoped there would be a note or a letter addressed to me, something with advice that I could cherish forever. I hadn't had the chance to go through the papers, as everything had been sent to England before I knew I'd be moving back to Corfu. The timing of everything meant I'd never looked in it until that day.

Inside there were three notebooks sprawled on top. They included the one I had found with her when she died; a little yellow diary with five entries. I'd already read them dozens of times. Most of them were about her deteriorating health. I was pretty sure that the last one – the unfinished entry – related to her wanting to tell me about her brain tumour. She'd written: *I need to tell Melodie the real reason I couldn't leave the island so easily*. Her illness was obviously the reason why she hadn't been able to travel.

I decided to pick up an A4 blue notebook instead. Inside, there were three newspaper clippings, all in Greek, with a photo of a baby. The only thing I could make out was the year. The cuttings were nineteen years old. They were loose in the front with no notes to understand them.

'Are you all right, Melodie-Mou?'

Even with this shy approach, I gasped for air and clutched my chest. Anton's green eyes above high cheekbones peered around the door like a nervous jack-in-the-box unsure when to emerge.

'You arse! You really made me jump!' I hissed air out at him through my teeth as he came to sit by my side. He tried to sit with his legs crossed like me, but his size wouldn't allow it. He reminded me of a dog pacing its basket before managing to settle. Eventually, he got himself leaning to one side with one knee up.

'Are you quite done?' I teased.

'Yes. Now, what are you doing? I thought you needed rest.'

'I just needed a quiet moment. I adore Akis, you know that, but … I just didn't feel much like putting on a face. Sorry.'

'I understand. I've said he can stay here tonight. I didn't want to drive him back to his Airbnb. I had a little thought though. Maybe he could stay at your mum's house. To keep an eye on it for us.' His elbow had found his knee to lean on,

44

and his hand had found his stubbled chin to scratch.

'Maybe.' I looked back at the newspaper articles and handed him one. 'What does this say?'

He squinted at the article. I had only put the bedside lamps on, so the room was filled with a low warm glow from the other end of the bed. 'It is about a baby girl who was left at a small church near where I used to live. The baby had a note in English that said, *Tell God, at least I didn't kill it. Call it Keres.* I think it was the strange note that got the attention of a couple of local newspapers.'

'*Tell God, at least I didn't kill it,*' I whispered back to him. The words hung about my head and dug in like a crown of thorns.

'Keres is a bloody horrid name,' Anton muttered to himself, reading over the article.

'Cerys? It's Welsh, isn't it? I quite like it.'

'No, you're not saying it right. KEEres.' He went on to explain how the "Keres" were death spirits, I guess a bit like a grim-reaper character. In Greek mythology they were goddesses of doom and death. Not a name you would readily choose for a child. Obviously, some cruel joke: perhaps from Adam. The thorns that had been pressing into my head suddenly drew blood in the way of realisations dripping over my skin. It had to be my father, Adam. Surely there was only him around my mother at that time who was so evil.

'You don't think it could have been Adam, do you? Who left a baby there? I mean, how many deranged English people would've been hanging out near Kokkini back then?'

Anton shook his head, 'did your mum mention another baby?'

'No, but that doesn't mean there wasn't one. It's not like we had a lot of time to catch up. It's just a bit strange, isn't it?

45

Why else would she have these clippings?' I picked one up and waved it at him. 'You don't think I have a sister, do you?' As I spoke the words, the realisation that I might actually have a living relative made my heart pick up speed and I could hear my pulse knocking on my eardrums.

'What else is in this book?' he nodded towards the notebook resting on my lap. 'If that is your sister, surely it'll say in there?'

'I don't know. That's as far as I'd got.'

I turned to the first page with writing on excited and terrified at what I might discover. The heading read, *Finding the Truth*, which had been underlined twice with some pressure. I began to read aloud to Anton as he rested his head on my shoulder. I could smell his tropical shampoo and felt a sense of comfort as I began to read through a shaky voice.

'*Last week I planted some blue pansies around Phillip's grave. I don't really know why I hadn't done it sooner. Done something at least. To my horror the flowers just seemed to attract rabbits and it quickly looked dreadful. The rabbits kept leaving their little droppings everywhere and such. Then, yesterday a dog ran into my garden. Probably drawn in by the naughty rabbits digging small holes near Phillip's grave. I saw it through the kitchen window. It was, it was digging up Phillip's little grave. I ran out and got rid of the rotten mutt. I was terrified to look. The idea of seeing his little bones. There weren't any. Not one bone. In its time in the garden the little dog had dug a few deeper holes where the rabbits had started. I don't know what came over me but I dug deeper with my bare hands then a little trowel. There was nothing. Then I dug all around and the only thing I found was dirt.*' I began to read her words faster tripping over them to find out more. '*I need to know what Adam did with the body of our son. I have no one I can ask for help so I've decided to do some detective work and write everything down.* There's a list of things to do, including looking at newspaper articles from around the time.'

I shifted away looking square at Anton. 'This baby couldn't be a sister, could it? My sister? She said the baby was a boy, Phillip. She told me I had a brother.' My hands bounced in time with every word. 'If she thought I had a sister surely, surely, she would have said, right?'

'Melodie, breathe again, yes?' Anton's big hand cupped my cheek. 'There might be more. These are articles about babies, yes. It does not mean it is anything yet. Let's see what else is in her books and see what we think then. Come and sit on the bed.'

He helped me to my feet, before pulling his shirt over his head to show his muscular frame and glowing olive skin.

'Are you trying to distract me from all this horror?'

He didn't answer. He laid himself out on the bed in just his jeans. I sat down, but he pulled me to lie by his side. I held the book up above us. The first few pages were just lists of what to do and what to look up. She clearly wasn't very internet-savvy, and she couldn't read Greek, which meant her progress was slow. My arms quickly began to tire with the notebook in the air above us. I rolled onto my front, madly flicking through the notes. Then I was prodding at the pages again, my finger tracing along my mother's words as her soft voice filtered into my mind.

'Here, look, she says, *Roula at work has been helping me to find copies of newspapers. I haven't told her why and thankfully she hasn't asked. I don't know what I'll say if she does. She's a nice lady* ... Blah-blah-blah ...' My eyes and finger skipped ahead to find the next relevant part. '*If they don't turn up anything I'll have to ask her to help me find obituaries. If I can't find anything*

47

in the papers I'll have to dig the whole garden up. She must have been distraught.' I shook my head at the thought of it.

I flicked across a few more pages as Anton rested his hand on my lower back. The heat penetrated the thin fabric of my skirt, comforting my skin. *'I have found three articles about a baby girl. She has to be mine. The date lines up and a note was left in English. One of the photos has a picture of the note in it. It's very small, but it looks like Adam's handwriting! I have started to write a letter to Melodie, but I think I should wait until I know more. Maybe if I find her a sibling, she'll want to see me.'* I lifted my head, slapping my hands on the book. 'As if I wouldn't have wanted to see her either way. I hate that my stupid father made her believe I didn't want to see her. I'm so glad he's dead. Evil bastard.'

'A sister though?' Anton sat up and rolled onto his side and gave my shoulder the briefest kiss. 'What do you think? What does your tummy tell you?' He only had a half-smile on his full lips. I guess he didn't want to build my hopes up.

'I think I have a sister. I think that baby is my sister.'

His face spread into a wide smile and a laugh in his chest vibrated the bed. 'Me too. As soon as I see that photo, I think – that baby looks like baby Melodie.'

'You're tired. Your English is slipping.' I leant on my elbow and turned to face him.

He muttered in Greek and buried his face in my collarbone.

'What did you say?' I did my best to sound stern which just made him laugh into my cleavage.

'I basically said, let's see if your Greek is as good as my English.' He laughed and kissed my neck. His velvet lips tickled my skin, leaving goosebumps rippling across my flesh.

'Stop,' I said. 'I need to read this.'

'I'm sorry. Akis was not wrong though. I would like another child.'

'I know. So would I! But right now, I need to see if my mum managed to find my sister.'

He flopped onto his back. 'Pass me a book.'

We read out passages that might have some use here and there. Halfway through her search, she had found out about her brain tumour. She'd started to write less, putting it down to headaches. Mum had even blacked out at the supermarket where she worked. That's when tests showed what was going on. She had been trying to find out anything she could from the orphanage on the island, but it was almost impossible. Even her timelines didn't always make sense. In one entry I came across, the month and year she thought my sibling was born was completely different to anywhere else I'd seen in the notebook. Details seemed to jig across the pages, finding their own version of truth in events. It was hard going. Almost like watching her mind unravel and deteriorate between the thin, grey lines of the books.

'This might be interesting. Listen,' Anton began. '*Roula said her nephew took a DNA test. Just for fun I believe. To find out if his family had always been on the island. I'm not sure. Quite a strange thing to do if you ask me. She told me all he had to do was spit in a cup and anyone else who's done the same that's related to him comes up as a match, apparently. It made me think, if I had been adopted maybe I would take a test like that. It's a long shot, but it's worth a try. Apparently, there are lots of companies that do it, so I've sent off for three different ones.*'

Anton looked up. 'Do you know your mother's email address? I think these things are often sent to emails.' He flicked along the pages as I shook my head. Then he paused

49

again. 'Reading here …' He stabbed at the page. Even the A4 looked tiny in his long fingers. '… she took the test and was waiting for results. This entry is a couple of months before you got here, last year.'

I began rubbing my forehead. I felt as though I'd been given some very difficult algebra to understand and rubbing my skull might loosen up the muscles ready for action.

'How can I find her email address? She was using library computers.'

'Forgive me, but as someone not—'

'Au fait?' I offered.

'Au fait with computers, she might have written it down. Maybe we look at the house tomorrow? Or the box tomorrow? It is getting late, Melodie-Mou.'

At some point in our searching and reading, he had made it down to just his fitted, black boxer shorts. 'Take your clothes off, Melodie-Mou. Let me hold you.' He lay back on the bed and his left hand absentmindedly skimmed his toned abs, rising and falling over the tiny hills of his muscles. Then it came to rest under his boxers. I raised an eyebrow in his direction. He raised an eyebrow straight back at me. I began to slip off my clothes under his watchful, emerald eyes. My hair puffed out from the static of undressing and I carefully tried to smooth it back down, suddenly bashful as I wondered how I looked to him.

'You really are desperate for another child.'

'I'm desperate for you,' he said. His voice was low, barely audible. He knelt up on the bed and pulled me to him. I could feel his desire digging into my hip as he kissed my neck. 'Please don't put pressure on this. On finding your sister. You have family here now. You're not alone, we will help you.

Don't forget that.' His words sounded deep in my ear as his fingers dug the back of my neck, massaging and relaxing the tight strings that encased my thoughts. His fingers travelled down, releasing the clasp of my bra. The straps glanced off my shoulders as there was a knock at our door.

We jumped apart. Anton was closer to the edge on his side and he slipped straight off the bed like he was performing some great trick on a slip-and-slide. He hit the wooden floor with such a bang that he was left like an overturned turtle with his feet hanging in mid-air.

'Oh my God! Are you okay?' I quickly crawled over the bed to see if he was all right. He rested his big, brown feet on the white sheets, and as I hung my head over the edge, I could see he was hiding his face in his hands. 'Are you okay?' I demanded. Then I could see his whole belly and chest juddering in fits of giggles. When he moved his hands tears of laughter were streaming down his face.

'Who is it?' he called from the floor.

'Akis.'

I quickly put on my white, cotton dressing gown and Anton let him in. 'What was all the banging about?' Akis asked, folding his toned forearms across his chest. He looked between us, and his high cheekbones – the only part of his face that matched Anton's – lifted as he tried to hide his smile.

'You made me jump. I fell off the bed. What do you want, Akis?' Anton folded his arms too, and pulled himself to his full height, making him stand a good three or four inches taller than his brother. Apparently, Chris, their father, had some Dutch heritage. He always said that's why everyone in his family was so tall. I could never tell if he was joking or not.

'I had a message from Michail about a possible job and a

catch-up. Any chance you're going to Kokkini tomorrow? To see him or Basil? Or your mum's old place? Just wondered if I could get a lift, really.' He removed his arms from his chest and thrust his hands into his pockets instead.

Anton looked at me, so Akis did too.

'That's fine, Akis. We'll be leaving around nine,' I said.

Then Anton ushered him out and carefully shut the door. I turned to walk away, but he caught my hand and pulled me in once more. Without a word, he pressed me against the wall and held my face between his hands as he bent forward to kiss me, his tongue searching my mouth. His hands fell across the contours of my body inside my robe and found their way to my waist. He lifted me up as though I were as light as a dragonfly, whirring above the water's edge on the breeze of his arms. My legs wrapped tightly around his olive-tree torso as we pulled each other in, tightly and fiercely. Our skins fused together, pressed so hard into one another that I wondered whether we would ever be able to part. I clung to the back of his neck as he pulled me from the wall and dipped me to arch my back in a perfect curve as he kissed along my neck and my breasts. When we couldn't take a moment more, he pulled me close again and held me. Rocked me. His face in the depths of my hair. 'I love you,' he said.

I just gasped and squeezed the taut muscles across his back. He carefully laid me back down on the bed and kissed my head.

'I love you too.'

Chapter 8

We'd searched the boxes but hadn't found anything that could've been an email address or a password. At my mother's house every drawer was empty. Even though I knew they should be empty, there was still a part of me that thought we would find a scrap of paper that would turn something up, but the people I'd hired to box everything up had clearly done a good job.

I sat down to sweat in the old armchair near the front door, the one I'd sat in every time I'd been in the living room talking to Mum. My weight came down hard, releasing a stale cigarette smell – there to remind me that it must have been his chair. Adam's chair. My father's chair. Anton was sitting in my mother's seat; I don't think he thought about it. Looking across at him, my mind replaced him with my mother – with her dead eyes that wouldn't shut and her cold hands that wouldn't move. Anton began to fidget, pulling me out of my trance. He was thrusting his hands down the edges of the chair. He pulled out twenty cents, a purple hairband, a pen and eventually a scrap of paper.

'What does it say? What does it say?' I chanted, rapidly tapping my knees.

'MyMelodie321. Sounds like a password to me. Pretty easy one to remember too.'

'I can't believe we found it!'

'Yes ...' Anton looked down at the little piece of paper, gently shaking his head.

'What? What's wrong with it?'

'This is brilliant, yes. But we don't have her email address, Melodie-Mou.'

I flopped backwards into the hard chair. He was right. It was only one puzzle piece that, on its own, told us absolutely nothing.

We wandered hand in hand in the garden so as not to collapse in the heat of the house. I took down the tiny wooden cross my mother had put up for my dead baby brother. Seeing as he was never even there, he was likely in fact an alive baby sister instead. I didn't really know whether to leave the cross there. I held it for a moment, then put it back where it had always been. Even though the house itself was hot, the day was cooler than it had been. Clouds filled the sky like thick, sheep's wool, hiding the sun and leaving a chill in the breeze. We decided that we should extend the house into the garden and add a dining room and another bedroom, so it wasn't a one-up one-down, then rent it out rather than let squatters take advantage. We were still discussing our plans when Akis came bounding around the corner into the garden.

'What's the news?' Akis flopped down onto a white metal chair, making it clang against the patio slabs. He wasn't much older than me, but he seemed like such a child at times. He had actually been successful in England working for his best friend's family business in personal security. On one level I couldn't imagine him doing such a sensible job. But in the same thought, I knew how caring he was. There was also the advantage of height and the Wing Chun he had apparently been doing since he was twelve.

'We're just working out about renting this place.' I waved my arm towards the house behind me. He sat up tall in his chair, suddenly interested.

'How much?'

'You're staying here anyway,' I said, then went back to letting my eyes create vivid dreams across the small rectangular garden.

'Yeah, I mean longer.'

'Really?' Anton and I spoke together, but didn't take our eyes off Akis.

'Here?' Anton continued. 'What makes you want to stay here?'

'It's near the old house, so I know the area, don't I? I've got some friends here. Just for a month or two. Go on, please? I need to decide whether I want to live here again or not. When I went to see Michail, Basil was there and he said if I did want to stay, he would find a job for me. He was asking when you two would go and see him. I nearly asked him if I could stay in your old room, but this would be loads better.' He sat forward on the edge of his chair. A breeze ruffled his hair. It was long around his neck and pushed back. Sometimes he wore it in a tiny bun on top of his head. He ran his fingers through it but didn't take his eyes off me. He knew the decision was mine and not Anton's.

'Of course. That would be very helpful, if I'm honest. With your security skills you can keep the place in check. Don't worry about rent, just pay for the stuff you use. Fair?'

'More than fair.'

A couple of days later and I was no closer to finding my mother's email address. I had even paid an email lookup service just in case they found something, but there was no luck. I stayed in to get some work done on some of the social media accounts I was still managing. I was staring at my screen, editing a photo to send to a client for approval. The hum and whirring of the computer was making me sleepy. I hadn't been sleeping well at night, because of thinking about my sister. Where was she? What did she look like? Had she been adopted by nice people? These questions repeated over and over until I was dreaming about meeting her. In my dream, she was always a baby and I had to look after her instead of having my own baby. My eyelids were gaining in weight and my chin was drooping on my hand when my phone buzzed, diverting my spine to an upward position. It was Akis:

You didn't tell me your squatter was fit.

I couldn't believe she was back again. Irritation flushed my cheeks and I tapped the corner of my phone down onto the desk, scrambling to think what to reply. Then another message came through:

Hot... but bat shit crazy. She said I need to leave. She said this is her house, the "Jones" house. Lol. Who's Jones? Haha

Chapter 9

I replied to Akis with only four words:

Don't let her leave.

I sprinted along the landing and down the stairs. I grabbed my keys but didn't even put shoes on. Without shoes, I'd normally pick my way along gravel and dirt, but I ran without a thought for my feet. Of course Akis didn't know that Jones was my father's surname. To him I had been Melodie Pelletier before marrying Anton and changing to Greenwood. I vaulted my car door, which I didn't know I could do, then I was wheel-spinning out of the drive and dashing across Corfu, praying she would still be there when I arrived.

It wasn't uncommon to come face to face with tourist coaches on the winding roads of Corfu. In fact, there were times it was to be expected. But in all the places it would be awkward to pass them, there they were. I had to reverse three times and one of those times I nearly hit a lemon tree in my haste. The jolly little coach driver found my red face most amusing, I'm sure.

Eventually, I made it to the little door that always seemed to house my biggest emotional fears. I had the same knot in my stomach that I'd had the year before when I went to see my mother for the first time. Suddenly, everything slowed down. Or at least I did. I could feel the pressure in the sky building. Each breath was like inhaling the electricity in the air. A static charge was burning my lungs with each step closer to that tatty blue door. The silly thing always seemed to be the key to my past. A past I had never known about.

I carefully pushed the door open. It wasn't locked. It wasn't even properly closed. There she was. Her face changed when she saw me. She pounced to her feet. Unlike me, she had trainers on and looked ready to sprint away at a moment's notice. I tried to ignore what had happened the first time we met. She didn't know me and I didn't know her.

'Keres?' I held out my hand in that way lion tamers do, directing her away from approaching me while also attempting to subdue. 'Keres?'

She looked at Akis who was sitting in what I'd come to think of as my chair.

I didn't formally acknowledge him, I just pointed in his direction. 'Akis messaged me. He messaged me saying that you told him this was your house.'

She was so young. She didn't really look like how I imagined a sister of mine would look. Her face was round and angelic, nothing like mine or Mum's or Grandmama's. Her hair was loose around her shoulders. Nothing like the last time I saw her. The ends were fine, straight and blonde, a natural golden blonde with dark blonde-brown lashes framing her wild blue eyes. Completely different to my hazel waves and hazel eyes.

Mum's eyes had been blue though. We closely matched in height. Perhaps she was just above my five foot eight. Her athletic frame made her seem taller at least, unlike my hips and bust. She had her arms pulled together, almost cuddling herself, and she was pinching at one elbow. She spoke to Akis in Greek. He just laughed and lifted his shoulders into a shrug.

'Who are you? He says this is your mother's house. I leave before but not again. This is mine,' Keres said.

My hand gravitated to my mouth and my knuckles pressed on my lips. I became acutely aware of what I looked like as I assessed her every move. I'd thrown on a white Nike T-shirt that I'd spilled coffee down that morning, with faded, bobbly, blue leggings, no make-up and no shoes. My face went hot, but a cold sweat lined the back of my neck under my unbrushed hair.

'I'm your sister. I'm Melodie.'

Akis moved so abruptly the wooden chair legs creaked under the sway of him.

'Sister?' they both chimed.

I just nodded and kept my eyes on Keres. She had stopped pulling on her elbow and had become very still and the muscles in her lean arms were visible under the tension of it all. The air in the room wasn't as deadly as it usually was. It was comparatively comfortable. Yet she was going pink and my sweat was making me uncomfortable in my skin.

'You said this was the Jones' house, right?' She didn't agree; she barely managed to blink. 'And you're a Jones?' This time she managed one slow nod. 'Me too, technically. This was my parents' house too. I only found out a couple of nights ago that you might exist, and that your name is Keres. I can't believe you're my sister!'

Keres began to frantically shake her head. '*óchi*, no. I have no sister.'

'My parents were Liliana and Adam Jones, I wouldn't lie, we have the same mum and dad. That's how the house is mine.' I indicated about the room. The frown didn't lift from her blonde brows but she did give a slow nod before her face split away from the wide-eyed creature ready to run. 'I have a sister?'

I nodded and tugged at my dirty T-shirt as though straightening it out might make me more presentable and appealing to her. I was hoping that we could start again after the confusion of before.

'Mum didn't know you were alive, but when she found out, she did look for you. God, that probably makes no sense to you. How much do you know? You clearly didn't know about me ...' I pressed my hands flat to my chest. Almost as though I might be able to press down all the emotion that was starting to pile up. My breathing was coming in sharp little tugs and I could feel droplets forming around the corners of my lashes.

She carefully sat back down. That's when I saw how much she was like our mother. Her dainty frame and her concaved body language. She looked like she might cry too, but she held it in. The only clues were the red tip of her nose and the sudden bout of sniffing. She muttered something in Greek, and Akis gave a quick reply. I'd almost forgotten he was there. 'What?' I looked at him to translate.

'Keres said, "I can't believe he didn't tell me I had a sister". I said, "I didn't know you were sisters so I couldn't tell you." I mean, if you didn't know, how the bloody hell would I know?'

'It's a very long story. I didn't grow up with Mum and ... our father, either. Can we start again? After everything

60

that happened last time, I think we need to start a fresh. I'm Melodie, I'm your sister. I'd really love to get to know you.'

'I am Keres and I very much like to know you.' She spoke with a thick Greek accent, with a soft childlike tone to her voice.

'I guess my first question is, why are you staying here? I thought you'd been adopted. Where are your adoptive parents?' I perched on the arm of the chair where Akis watched everything unfolding as eager as a Labrador near a sandwich. He may as well have been drooling.

Keres hesitated, looking down at her forearms, which encased her body as she continued to clutch her elbows. 'They,' she snatched a breath pulling her chin to her chest, 'dead, in the pandemic.'

Her words were like spears being thrown through my neck, choking me on my own pain. I'd lost Grandmama and Grandpapa – the only parents I had ever known – in the same way. I didn't know what to say to her. I couldn't believe the bonds we already had. In that instant I decided she should come and stay at the house. I tried to persuade her, but she didn't know me. Why would she trust me? I was the one who had shouted at her and said I'd call the police and had changed the locks. I had probably left her homeless for a time. We did talk about it at least, that dreadful first meeting. How she thought I was an intruder in her parents' home and how I thought the same. It wasn't as though we looked much alike other than our height. There was no way we could have guessed we were sisters. We both apologised for the misunderstanding. It wasn't as though it was anyone's fault.

'Why did you leave if you thought the house would be yours?'

I said, suddenly wondering what persuaded her to gather her things and go for a time.

'The girl–'

'Gaia.' She raised an eyebrow when I said the name. I forget what a powerful name it is being the Greek goddess of life and earth.

'She say this is yours and wants to call the police. I wonder if I am in the wrong home, or if you buy it. I have no paper to say mine.' She then went into Greek towards Akis who nodded a lot before replying to her and translating for me.

'She was trying to find papers but there's nothing here. Basically, she'd been trying to work out what to do to claim the house as her inheritance. Then you showed up,' he nodded up at me.

After talking to her about what had happened when we first met, I managed to persuade her to come with me to meet Anton and Gaia for dinner at our home. I didn't want to pressure her, but there was part of me that was sure if I left without her, I would never see her again.

We left Akis still sat in the living room. As I drove us to my home in Karousades, I didn't stop talking the whole time. I told her about our grandparents. I told her about our holidays to Agios Stefanos and other Greek islands through the years. At some point in the journey, I realised I was stalling. I looked across a garden with a rusty old fence where a father was playing with two little girls and a neon-pink football, and I realised I didn't want to tell her the truth about our parents' relationship and the horror of our father. There was no choice though. As soon as I paused to think about it, she asked about them. About him. His side of the family. Who he was. What I knew. She must have already been brimming with questions the whole time, but I had been blocking the conversation with tales of my childhood.

My palms began to sweat when I thought about everything she needed to know. I managed to divert. To bide my time for a little bit longer. She didn't say much at all. Her arms were still wrapped around her waist like a blanket and she only occasionally looked at me while I rattled out any story I could think of that might interest her. As we pulled up to the house, her hand slapped down to her knees and she leant forwards, mouth hanging ajar as she scanned the place. I looked at it then as if through her eyes. I had forgotten how impressive it was, as I'd just adopted it as home. The tall, wide building was modern but with old fashioned quirks. The shutters, frames and doors were all painted a vibrant pink and the walls were whitewashed. But it was big, and perhaps daunting to her.

We arrived to an empty house. Keres carefully pulled her trainers off and neatly tucked them next to the front door. I had no such issue, although I did try to wipe my feet on the mat as I came in. She followed me through the house, talking to herself in Greek as she looked at the sweeping staircase and wide- open square of our home. She edged around the one structure in the centre of the massive space which was actually mostly the downstairs loo and a cupboard or two. While she did a circuit of the house, I put out pittas and dips and sat her at the table opposite me. Then it all came in, the same way wine glugs out of a carafe. I filled her mind with everything that had been pressing against the walls of mine. Firstly, about our father and how he kidnapped our mother when I was a few days old. Then about how everyone thought she'd run away because of a letter he'd sent. I told her how evil he was

63

and how he told our mum that her pregnancy with Keres had resulted in a baby boy who had died at birth. How Mum had been pretty much unconscious through it all as he had beaten her so badly. She nodded as I spoke, carefully tearing off sections of pitta and eating them without making even a crumb of mess. She didn't gasp, or cry, but her eyebrows stayed pulled together throughout.

'I've got some of her notebooks upstairs you can look at. She would have died believing you were a dead baby boy if those rabbits and then that dog hadn't been digging holes in her garden.' Once I let it all out, it was like I was able to breathe properly again. I hadn't really spoken about Adam since my mother had died. To go over it all again almost felt nice. Like accidentally releasing a balloon and watching it float into the rays of the sun; sad, but oddly satisfying. Keres still didn't actually speak. She took a sip of her water and carefully placed it onto the glass coaster.

'Evil? You are sure?' She frowned in a way so like Grandpapa it made me know it was all real. She was real. I really had a flesh-and-blood relative.

'Yes. It was dreadful. She had scars on her face from his abuse. She would have done anything to protect us though.' Then a silence fell between us. Her frown didn't lift. Eventually I couldn't take it anymore. 'So, what about you? Where did you grow up?'

She wasn't very forthcoming, likely intimidated by my over-sharing. It was overwhelming and we were both going in different directions trying to work through the shock. I blabbered on and she was like a watchful shrew taking everything in. At least I found out that she'd lived with her parents in a little house with a garden not far from Athens.

She also had a brother, Andreas.

'Did they adopt you before or after having Andreas?'

'Uh? Oh, me then Andreas. When my parents die, Andreas became very angry. He is only twenty and he made me leave. So, I decide to find my dad and mother.'

'I wish you could have met her. Wait, twenty?'

She nodded, then the front door opened and Anton and Gaia called out to me. I stood up, eager to introduce Keres. With the downstairs being almost completely open, they saw us immediately. Their long legs bounded towards us. Anton was smiling, ready to welcome the unknown guest into his home. Gaia on the other hand recognised the girl straight away and was shaking her head and her hands looked like balled up socks by her sides.

'What's she doing here?' Gaia almost spat, her green eyes clear and narrowed to points like pin pricks.

'This is Keres. She's my sister. I only just found out today.'

'You found her!' Anton dropped Gaia's bag where he stood, and came over to squeeze me and kiss the top of my head. 'I'm so very happy to meet you, Keres.' He stretched out his hand to greet her, something that was slowly making its way back into society's norms.

I looked over at her, hoping Anton's size wasn't too intimidating along with everything else. A pretty smile had made its way across her lips and her cheeks had flushed rose. Her shoulders were back and she'd brought herself as tall as she could to meet his hand, which she took in both of hers. She spoke to him in Greek. Luckily, I actually understood some of the exchange, as she thanked him for welcoming her into his home and there was a compliment in there too. Maybe she said "beautiful home"; I wasn't so sure on that.

The rest of the evening was spent with more bewildering explanations with questions layering in from Anton but mainly from Gaia who always had questions no matter the subject. We begged Keres to stay, but she hadn't brought her bag and she was adamant she didn't want to impose in any way and she suggested that Anton should take her home, which made sense as he could bring Akis back to ours to stay the night while we worked everything out.

Anton didn't arrive back until the early hours, Akis decided to stay at a friend's house in the end so he arrived home alone. When we eventually tucked ourselves into our white sheets, I clung to Anton's body and pressed my face against the safety of his chest.

'You don't mind me bringing her here. Do you?'

'Melodie-Mou,' – I could hear the low vibration of his voice through his chest – 'this is your home, and your family is my family. Of course, I worry how little we know of her. But she is welcome. How did she find your mother's place and name?'

'It must have been the DNA stuff. I can't remember if I asked or not.' I yawned and tucked my face amongst the tiny hairs on his chest. 'I'll ask her tomorrow. Oh shit, I'm meant to see Maria. Do you think she'll be okay to come with me?' I felt him attempt a shrug. 'If she's all right with it, will you come with us tomorrow too, to Agios Stefanos?'

'I would be honoured.'

Chapter 10

Our journey into Agios Stefanos was quiet. Keres spent most of the journey tapping on the door with her index finger and staring out at the olive trees. We took Anton's Mustang with the top down. I suppose it did make it tricky to talk over the tousle of air rushing across the car. Whenever I turned to say something, she was looking across the undulations of the terrain. Or that's how it seemed. Maybe taking her to meet one of my friends was a bit much for our second time meeting each other, but it was too late, we were on our way, and she had agreed.

We arrived to find a heavily pregnant Maria with one foot on Harry's lap being worked with the enthusiasm of a clever man. A man who knows that keeping a pregnant lady happy is paramount. They were waiting for us at Silver Star. I'd messaged Maria to say I had something to tell her. I think she thought I was going to announce our own pregnancy. It felt like everyone was waiting for that news, along with us.

As we walked up the stone steps, Maria snatched her foot from Harry's lap and pressed her hands on the table to support herself as she stood up to greet us. I could see her eyes narrow at Keres. She gave me a little frown and flattened her nose to her face. Not exactly flaring her nostrils, but not far off. I tilted my head at her with a coy smile.

'This is Keres. She's my sister,' I announced. My smile couldn't contain itself to just my painted pink lips. I could feel it spread, like a sunrise, touching all the contours of my face with its rays. This was pretty much the opposite of Maria and Harry. Harry looked to Maria as though she would have some kind of answer to help him understand, while Maria's pretty little face was suddenly full of lines, contorted with confusion. 'Sister?'

Then the story was told once more, this time over strawberry milkshakes under an orange umbrella while Harry continued his work, massaging Maria's swelling feet.

'That's crazy, girl! As if,' she looked right at Keres, 'as if you could just fall on our Melodie's lap, just like that. Wow...' She was smiling, but there was a protective edge to her. She had slipped her sunglasses off the top of her head and covered her eyes while the story had been told. This had left me unable to read her as I might have, and she knew it. Now that she was pregnant, she'd become more protective than a whole herd of elephants. I shrugged, making the thin, blue strap of my dress fall off my shoulder. Anton carefully replaced it with one delicate finger before I'd even noticed it fall.

'We're so pleased for you both,' Harry interjected, without even a glance at Maria. He released her foot and ruffled the tight curls on his head, leaving one protruding above the rest. His round brown eyes fixed on me with a broad grin.

'I am lucky,' Keres interjected, her hand placed over her heart. 'Melodie has welcoming me and I am lucky.'

That was the first time she had given away how she really felt about it all. I swallowed hard before I was able to speak. 'Of course you're welcome in my life. You're my sister. The only family I have left.'

'And what do you call him?' Maria's stubby, swollen finger pointed towards Ant who looked up. He had been happily slurping the dregs of his milkshake before we all turned to look at him. 'And Gaia, of course,' she added.

'You know what I mean. Biological relative. Of course, they're my family.'

'So, Keres, how did you discover your parents were even here?' Maria continued.

Keres opened her mouth to speak, then bit her bottom lip before turning to Anton and saying something in Greek. At this Maria snapped in to perfect Greek. Even I forget she can do this. She'd actually never lived anywhere other than Corfu but in her home her parents only spoke English and Harry was English too. She went to school in Corfu, had dated Greek men before Harry and was half Greek. Keres clearly hadn't expected it though as her head had flicked back to Maria and away from Anton.

'Sorry, what's going on?' I interjected.

'Keres hadn't understood my question, so I asked it in Greek and explained that, like her, I might not look all that Greek but it doesn't mean I'm not.'

'On the internet,' Keres began, 'I find my parents on the internet.'

'Mum had done a DNA test to try and find her,' I said, turning to Keres. 'Which, of course, is all online. We had been trying to find mum's email address to sign in and see if any matches had come up, but we hadn't had any luck.'

69

'Yes. DNA. I know my parents were in Corfu. I come here to look.'

I wasn't sure that Maria was satisfied by the response, but Anton's phone started to ring, interrupting the conversation while he had a quick chat with his ex-mother-in-law about when Gaia was going to visit them again.

Keres didn't have much in the way of clothes. Only one small red holdall since leaving her family home. I wanted to treat her to something, ideally something she liked and therefore chose herself. We walked with Maria and Harry as they went off to see her parents. We stopped in the clothing shop next to the jewellers where Maria worked. The window was elegantly dressed with white linen dresses and chunky necklaces in emerald green the colour of Anton's eyes. Just inside the door, there was a white cotton dress with a puffy skirt and generous pockets. Hanging with it was a rich golden-yellow necklace. It looked like a work of art in itself. A large yellow, glass disc spiralled with gold sat in the centre between fat little yellow and gold beads alternating along the thread. It was somehow loud and ostentatious but beautiful at the same time. I stood holding the fabric of a yellow silk shirt for a moment while appreciating the air con gently blowing my hair about my ears.

'What sort of thing do you like?' I looked over at Keres whose fingers were lightly scanning the soft cotton pashminas on the side wall.

She spun round to face me, her big blue eyes still, with a face as blank as the moon, both familiar and completely unknown.

'Everything here is beautiful. I have all I need.' She set off looking at some dark-green, silky T-shirts further into the shop.

Anton bent forward to whisper into my ear. 'This must be hard for her. From a brother who kicked her out to a sister she doesn't know.'

'Shh, you're very loud when you whisper,' I said, shooting him a look. The loud tickle of laughter followed him as he walked away, down a step or two into another section of the shop. My eyes stayed on his broad, shoulders and tanned arms. It was a warmer day as summer was beginning to set in. Anton was wearing black jeans and a pale blue shirt that was soft and delicate.

'Oi, oi!' called from behind me, and I was hit by a swift pat on my bottom.

'Hands off my wife, Nico,' Anton called from the other end of the shop – without so much as glancing in our direction – before starting to chat away in Greek to the lady behind the counter.

'Melo! Where have you been? Huh? I have not seen you since your big day. Still my saddest day.' Nico pushed up the sleeves of his crisp white top and folded his arms about his chest. He was as slim as ever and was using his big, puppy eyes to look mock-hurt at my recent nuptials. I caught him looking past me and turned to find his eyes were lingering on Keres.

'Oh no! Out you go!' I began to gently shove Nico towards the door he'd just stepped through, catching my flip-flop and stumbling into him a bit.

'No, Melo, don't be jealous. I still love you,' he laughed. His long, thin fingers ran over my hair and I swiped at him to stop.

'Why are you being extra silly today? I thought we were past this?' I stamped my foot as I spoke, not wanting the playful fuss of Nico on a day like today. A day that was meant to consist of bonding with and forming memories with my long-lost sister.

Keres edged forward with a rosy hint in the apples of her cheeks. Her tan was a reddy-brown, not a Greek olive at all. She flicked her golden hair off her shoulder and introduced herself to Nico in Greek. He took her hand and kissed it. Even during the pandemic, I can't imagine Nico would have stopped kissing girls' hands.

The exchange was light and natural on both parts. It was the most animated I'd seen Keres since we'd met. I felt not only astonished, but strangely jealous. Not of her flirtation with Nico, but of his ability to get her to talk and smile. Her rosy cheeks suddenly protruded on her round face. She parted her lips into broad smiles for him. Her second top incisors slanted towards the centre two slightly, completely symmetrical and oddly sweet, somehow adding to the angelic appearance with her fluttering lashes. She leaned her left hand on the glass display next to her, which was full of rings and necklaces. Her right hand sat on her hip.

'Melodie, you do not mind if I meet Nico at eight? He is taking me to Fantasea Restaurant for dinner,' she said. She smiled at me, not as broad as for Nico, but I was pleased even to get a glimmer of what he was getting.

'Of course. I'll drive you if you like,' I said.

'No, I'll pick her up,' Nico said, still looking at Keres.

'How do you know each other?'

'She's my little sister,' were words that quickly brought his long nose pointing in my direction. I only gave him the briefest of information, telling him that Keres could fill him in over dinner. Nico took her number and left us in the shop. I decided to use the interaction to my advantage.

72

'Pick something and I'll buy it for you to wear tonight.' I bounced my hands about at all of the choice in the room. She didn't put up too much of a fight before I had her trying on the green top she had been admiring, with a white gypsy skirt. While Keres was in the changing room, Anton came up behind me and slid his arms around my middle.

'Are you going to try on something nice?' His voice vibrated in my ear.

'No, why? Don't you like my clothes?' I looked down at my fitted blue-and-white striped maxi dress.

'Actually, I very much like this dress.' He squeezed me a little tighter. 'But, I don't know – I like imagining you getting undressed behind those thin curtains shops have.'

'Stop it.' I slapped his hand, but he didn't let go of me. Instead, he kissed my neck as though we were alone at home.

'I am unsure,' Keres announced, as she pulled back the curtain.

Anton wasn't fazed by her appearance. He just placed his chin on my shoulder. I, on the other hand, felt like my skin had been baking in the sun for a little too long.

Keres went on to try on half a dozen other outfits before settling back on the T-shirt. Although it was a T-shirt, it was much more elegant than a regular T-shirt. It was V-neck at the front and the back with a little tie across the back to stop the shoulders from falling down. The material was as soft and creamy as butter, gliding between my fingertips, although when Anton touched the material, he moaned that its softness caught on his mildly rough fingertips, as though his skin were suddenly covered in tiny blades and he didn't want to cut the material to shreds.

Keres's slim build meant the top hung a little low on her. I

73

felt my stomach turn in a protective ache. I knew it was silly. She was a grown woman and I had no claim to, or right to, boss her around. In a sensible frame of mind, I wouldn't even want to. She looked beautiful. I told myself that Nico could be a gentleman when he wanted to and pushed any worries to one side. She told me she had a skirt to wear with it back at our mother's house. As we stood ready to pay, a green faux-opal necklace caught my eye. I looked down at my opal necklace, which had been Mum's, and my opal ring, which had been given to me by my grandparents. Although it wasn't quite the same, I had to buy it for her. I snatched it up and paid.

Anton and I walked hand in hand along the road while Keres walked ahead, typing away on her phone and monitoring it every other second.

'I got Keres a necklace too. I feel bad that I didn't get Gaia anything.'

'Do not be silly. You know she loves you,' he said.

We squeezed each other's hands a little tighter. I looked up at him. His strong, stubbled jaw tilted down towards me. A light smile fluttered across his full lips which made my heart drum in my chest. After so much hurt, loss and heartache, I had become so lucky. I was surrounded by people I loved and cared about.

Keres said about as much on the journey back from Agios Stefanos as she had on the way in. Only this time she was glued to her phone the whole way, only looking up to ask if she could take up the offer of staying with us, as it was nearer to Nico. To be honest, I thought she intended to anyway as when we picked her up, she had put her bag in the boot of the car.

As soon as we arrived back at the house, she started talking;

for the first time she was really talking. Asking questions about Nico. How did I know him? What was he like? I explained that he had pursued me the year before and how we were just friends. When Gaia came back from school, she joined in the Nico talk too. She had her own little crush on him. She gushed about his soft, shaggy, brown hair and how he had recently had the tips lightened. Then they discussed his – apparently "beautiful" – big brown eyes. I didn't like to be the one to say I thought his nose was a bit big in comparison to his oval face, so I kept my opinion to myself. None of it mattered. What did matter was that Keres was talking, relaxing. There was a shift in her body, as though she had begun to forget her fear and relax into just being herself.

Anton had become rather fed up with the conversation early on and had fallen asleep across the leather sofa. I'd become stuck with his head on my lap. Even when I started to really need the loo, I didn't want to wake him, which left me stranded in the Nico talk.

I slowly slipped further out of the Nico conversation so Keres and Gaia eventually went into Greek as I scrolled through my phone. Greek was a lot more fluid for Keres. She became more animated and spoke at a rapid speed. It hadn't occurred to me that language was another barrier that might have been making her feel more anxious around me and not with Gaia.

I looked down at the face resting on my lap and wondered if I were pregnant yet. If I'd be able to tell. My index finger and thumb came together between Anton's eyebrows and lightly parted the soft black hairs. I slowly repeated the action over and over while watching the micro expressions of his sleep. Occasionally, the corner of his mouth would lift a little. I just wanted to kiss it. Eventually, I moved on from his eyebrows and ran my fingers through his thick brown-black hair. It needed cutting really. It was always longer on top, but it was getting a little wild, as was the stubble on his chin. Pushing my fingers through his hair, I began to dream about the child we didn't yet have. If they'd have his green eyes, my hair, his build, my head for statistics, his head for business. If we would have a boy or a girl.

'Mou-mou?' Gaia said.

My eyes snapped up and both girls were looking at me, as though I had done something, or I was meant to say something.

'Yes?'

'I said, Keres wants to show me her new top. Where did you put it?'

I suddenly realised I hadn't given her the necklace. I felt guilt brush over my skin because I hadn't got Gaia anything. Not that she would worry, but I hated to seem unfair. I tried to carefully free myself from Anton's heavy head, but I didn't quite manage it. His eyes opened, slightly bloodshot from the rude awakening. I kissed his forehead and went to the dining table where I'd left the bag.

'Here it is.' I passed her the paper bag. 'I also got you a little necklace. It reminded me of mine. It was our mother's. Our grandparents got it for her. They got me a ring too.' I pulled at the necklace around my throat and then showed her the ring.

'I also thought it would look nice with your new top.' I smiled, hoping that she would understand what it meant to me while trying to talk as though it wasn't a big deal so as not to upset Gaia at all.

'Thank you, Melodie. You are very kind to me.' She threw her arms round my neck and squeezed. Her soft arms were cool against my cheeks. Then she was running after Gaia, giggling and bounding up the wooden stairs, and the moment was gone. I didn't move for a moment. I stood trying to hold on to the memory of the first time my little sister had put her arms around me. A moment I never wanted to lose.

'They're getting along well,' Anton chipped in from his horizontal position on the sofa, without even bothering to open his eyes.

'Yep. We're just one little happy family,' I breezed.

Chapter 11

It was 2.22 am exactly when Keres came tiptoeing through the front door. I had just looked at my phone for the twenty-second time that hour, and I was hovering at the top of the stairs. I did my best to skulk away, but I couldn't skulk quick enough without being heard and she caught me.

'Melodie?' she hissed in my direction, and shone her phone torch at my face.

I felt like I was on some crime TV show and I'd just been caught robbing the place.

'Sorry. I started to worry when it got past midnight.' Her light was still blazing into my eyes so I couldn't see her face. I began to shield my eyes and she lowered the beam of light to my feet. Even then, she was just a mass of orbs and colours in the dark as my eyes had no time to adjust. She let out a puff of amusement through her round nose.

'I come to Corfu alone and find my ways. You have no worry with me.' Then her blurry face leant in and kissed my cheek. I could distinctly smell Nico's overused aftershave on her skin. '*Kalinychta*, goodnight,' she said as she walked in the opposite direction towards her room.

I slid back into bed next to Anton, trying not to disturb him, but a sharp inhale came from his side of the bed then a rustle as he straightened his legs into a stretch.

'What are you going to be like when Gaia is out all night?' he said through a yawn.

'I'll be there behind you, so don't you pretend.'

He let out a sharp laugh and rolled towards me.

'Yes, true,' he said. His hand slipped up my nightie and settled on my bottom before he fell straight back to sleep, leaving me stuck facing him on my side. I couldn't sleep anyway. I still had the smell of Nico's sandalwood aftershave in my nose. Cautiously, I rolled Anton's heavy arm off me and slipped into our en suite. I pulled the little cord for the light over the mirror. In the dim glow I looked so like Mum and Grandmama. Keres didn't. The thought nagged at me, tugging at my earlobe like a heavy earring that's impossible to ignore. I thought she looked like him. Like Adam. I wasn't really sure; I'd never met the man. I had that one photo my mother had given me of them out for a meal when she was sixteen and he was twenty-seven. It was in one of the boxes I'd been raking through. I remembered seeing it. A big part of me wanted to go and look right away, but I knew it wasn't fair to run the risk of waking up the house just to see how alike she did or didn't look to our father. I slipped back into bed, this time unnoticed by the mound next to me who was quietly snoring under his breath.

Keres didn't emerge at breakfast that day. It was a Sunday and Gaia had plans with Finn. She was desperately hanging about to ask Keres how her date went, but in the end she had to leave without getting any gossip. I was also on edge, wanting to see the photo again. Eventually I decided that if I woke her up, it didn't matter. I went to the bedroom next to hers and began to search the boxes. I pulled everything out of every box. Nothing. No photo. I checked behind the boxes, under the bed, under our bed. Nothing. I went downstairs trying to imagine where I might have left it.

Keres appeared on the stairs in just an oversized T-shirt that had Greek writing on it. She thudded down, not looking up from her phone until she reached the bottom.

'*Kalimera*,' she said. Good morning. Her blue eyes darted between Anton and me. She ruffled her hair. It had previously seemed shiny and fine but now it was all kinks and loops whirling around her head. Walking around the curling banister, she didn't come and sit down in the living space. Instead, she went the opposite way, past the little TV nook and straight to the dining room. Tucking her feet onto the chair at the head of the table, she sat, still tapping away on her phone.

'Did you sleep okay?' I offered, as I came to sit with her.

'Yes. Thank you so mutz.' She pushed her phone away and looked at me with a broad smile. The apples of her cheeks were as round as her eyes, making her look like a messy cherub. I could feel some of the tension in my shoulders release a little. We chatted as she had fruit and water for breakfast. Anton came and joined our discussions for a short while before going out to catch up on gardening.

'Go and get dressed and I'll meet you in the bedroom next to yours. Obviously, the one that isn't Gaia's room,' I said.

She grabbed her phone and scurried away, texting again as she went. I knew she wouldn't be ready right away so I went past the kitchen and out of the back door. Anton had removed his shirt and was bending over, weeding at the side of the garden where he was growing courgettes and beetroots and other delicious things. I crept up on him and kissed his lower spine. This resulted in him jumping up and knocking his bottom into my face leaving me falling on my back.

'*Gromto*! Shit! Melodie! You frightened me. I didn't know it was you. Are you okay?' I put my hand out, which he grabbed straight away. Instead of having him pull me up, I tugged him down onto me, laughing. I kissed him and slid my fingertips along the droplets on his spine. 'I'll assume you are okay,' he said into my mouth.

'Love you,' I laughed, then patted his bottom to indicate it was time to move.

'I love you too, Melodie-Mou.'

I didn't say a thing more. I just sauntered back into the house, pleased to have the taste of his salty skin still on my lips and the feel of his firm, damp body in my hands.

I took a right at the top of the stairs towards the bedroom with all the boxes. I could hear a shower running so I knew I still had time to get a little organised before Keres came to explore with me. While looking for the photo of my parents, I'd put Mum's notebooks and papers in random piles across the room, some on the pale wooden floor, some on the desk and some on the soft green pillows on the bed. I began sifting through it all, trying to make sense where at times there was none. It was as though she had had good days and bad days near the end. It made me question if I had met her on the good days or the bad days, and if that's why she hadn't been able to open up to me straight away and tell me the truth about my father's abuse. I reread some of the things Anton and I had already gone through. As I skimmed over the entries in the notebooks, it hit me how sick she had really been, how all over the place she was. Her timeline was constantly off. There was no telling how long she had even been living in Corfu. Not for sure. When she was in front of me, she had said fourteen years. In her notes she was looking for baby Keres, who was nineteen in one moment, then back to searching for younger babies in the next. I clung to her words, her handwriting, letting my thumb run along the smooth paper, and I almost wished I could feel the words on the page like Braille, as though that might help me understand the truth. The notes weren't meant for me. They were meant for her. I was an onlooker without the key to crack the broken code.

The door creaked open and in tapped Keres on her phone, her hair still wet from the shower. She had a near-blinding, neon- orange tube top on with her black jeans.

'Come and look at this,' I said, passing her the article about her.

She studied it in a way that I couldn't. I knew I'd never be able to read Greek or even be fluent. A knot squeezed in my lower belly at the idea of holding a baby in my arms and not being able to communicate with them in their main language, the language of the island. I swallowed, and shook my head to sidestep the idea. I wanted them to have the advantage of two languages; being sad about it was utterly selfish. Hopefully, over time my Greek would improve.

'So, this is me?' Keres turned the newspaper clipping in my direction. Her round little cheeks glowed almost as much as her top.

'It's your name, isn't it?' I gave a little smile and fidgeted around, changing from kneeling on the hard floor to crossing my legs like a child in assembly. Keres looked back at the clipping, lightly holding it with both her hands. Her fingernails were tiny, bitten to almost nothing, with chipped, red paint.

She snorted and a drop of water fell from the tip of one lock of straight hair onto the clipping before she handed it back with a grin of milky-white teeth. I wiped the droplet away as quickly as I could, but it had smudged a couple of the words. I told myself it didn't matter. I couldn't understand them anyway. Keres didn't even seem to notice the little intruder that had blurred the words. She grabbed the notebook nearest her, which happened to be the little yellow one I had found at Mum's feet when she had died. She breezed the pages with her thumb before opening it out to see what was inside.

'This stops,' she said, pointing at the unfinished final entry.

'That was her last entry. It's what she was writing as she died.'

'Oh.' She shut the book with no further questions on the subject. Part of me wanted to tell her exactly what had happened, exactly how I felt, but I knew it wasn't fair to put all of that on someone else if they didn't want to know. I pulled my lips tightly together and smoothed my hands on the cotton of my fitted, navy shorts.

'Read this one.' I picked up another notebook from the cardboard box and passed it to her. 'It says about the DNA test. How she ended up doing them. I'm so glad she did, otherwise I would never have known you were out there and you may not have found her.'

We carried on looking through it all together. Sometimes in silence, sometimes I'd explain the odd thing or read some of Mum's diaries and notes out to Keres, when she struggled to read or understand them.

'Will Akis stay in the house?' Keres asked, as she held what looked like a more legal piece of paper and scanned her eyes along it.

'Well, that was the plan. He's gone to Michail's for a day or two – he's a friend of Anton and Akis. Anton actually lived with him and his family for a time when he was younger. We want to do it up a bit, the house I mean, and rent it out.'

'"Do it up?"'

'Sorry, yes, ermm – to make it better, to improve on it. To renovate it.' She nodded, making more water droplets spring from her ponytail.

'Do you have photos of my grandparents?'

'Of course! Only on Mum's side though. I didn't know about Adam and I haven't gone looking for grandparents on his side.' I grabbed for my phone and began to thumb through as fast as I could to find one from Corfu. Soon enough, I'd found one of the copious amounts of beautiful photos of them. In that particular one, I'd wedged myself between them and they were both laughing. I had a manic smile, all teeth and cheekbones. Mama was elegant in an aqua-blue top with floaty sleeves and Papa was all in white, both with rich golden tans. Keres leant forward and carefully eyed the photo.

'Do you have photo of them at home? At their home?'

'I do somewhere, but I'd have to look on my laptop, I think.'

'Oh. What was it like? Your home?'

I had tried not to think of the old place once it had sold. The last time I had been there, I had lain on the floor with Anton. We'd left and I hadn't looked back. Thinking too much about it made my chest feel tight. The mixture of happy memories versus loss was too strong, particularly after finding out that was where Adam had abducted my mum. There was too much in that house for me to handle thinking about.

'It was just an average home. A village not far from Cambridge. It was nice enough. A good-size garden full of vegetables and rose bushes. It wasn't anything special.' I looked back at my phone and the laughing faces, eyes squinting and creased, mouths as wide as they could go. I could almost hear them.

'Do you have it? Or do you sell it?'

'I sold it. I found it too hard to be there without them there to welcome me in.' My bottom lip disappeared for a moment so I could dig my top teeth into it. 'I just miss them. I'm sure you feel the same about your parents.'

She frowned and tilted her head before slowly nodding, deep in thought.

We stopped for lunch and then we were back looking at the notebooks and exchanging ideas until Anton's head appeared around the door like a disembodied entity looking down on us.

'Gaia will be home soon. I'm making lamb for dinner.'

Of course, Gaia was only interested in what had happened with Nico. I'd avoided asking all afternoon. I didn't fancy knowing. Keres said he'd taken her to Fantasea. She told me about the delicious food and the view across the watery sunset. All of which I knew about in detail as Fantasea had always been a favourite of mine. She'd even shown me a photo that Nico had taken of her posing in front of the sunset with a glass of wine. We got the details of their food-sharing, his romancing her with a flower. I wondered where the flower might be, as she hadn't had one with her when she came back that night. With every detail, Gaia was becoming more and more hooked by Keres's words.

Eventually, I went to help Anton in the kitchen, and the girls sank into the brown leather sofas, rushing through the Greek language, hands flapping about like they might fly away into the depths of their conversation. Little outbursts of giggles rolled around the house as Anton chopped garlic and I clung to him like a safety harness strapped to his waist. He was too tall for me to put my chin on his shoulder so I pressed my cheek to his back instead, and slid my fingers into his waistband. He made a muffled noise of either excitement or embarrassment at the new position of my hands. I didn't let them wander further down. I just enjoyed the embrace and followed his body as he began to chop tomatoes and peppers and feta and cucumber. I rubbed my cheek on the white cotton shirt he'd thrown on but not done up. I couldn't believe how different my life was. Only a year before, I had been living alone in Cambridgeshire surrounded by loss and isolation. Now I had a husband, a sister, and dare I say, a teenage daughter.

Anton turned to face me, as though he could read my thoughts. He looked down, smiling as I slipped my arms under his shirt and left my face pressing against the soft little hairs on his chest.

'I would die without you,' I whispered, and he squeezed my shoulders into a shrug and kissed my head before muttering in Greek.

Then he pulled me away from him, clasping my shoulders with his palms and not his fingers to avoid covering my arms in feta. 'I would die without you,' he repeated my words, and forgetting himself, his fingers found my face. I quickly grabbed at them.

'Oi! Your hands smell of garlic,' I laughed. 'Now my face

will smell of garlic!'

'Delicious!' The madman then licked my face like he was a crazed cat.

A screech erupted from the top of my lungs as I tried to escape him, but he held on, making low groaning noises and threatening to lick again. The muscles in my tummy clenched in hysterical laugher and soon he had me pinned to the floor.

'Stop! Stop!' I managed between exhausted breaths.

'Yes. Please stop!' Gaia called from the lounge.

He did stop. But before helping me back to my feet, his lips found mine, and we indulged in a moment pressed together behind the kitchen counter.

After dinner, Gaia and Keres went to Gaia's bedroom to try on clothes and presumably talk more about boys. I couldn't imagine they had much more they could possibly say about Nico or Finn, yet they kept finding more. Although at least half was just about Nico's thick and apparently very soft hair.

I popped my head into Gaia's room to say goodnight to them both, but only Gaia was lying on her bed with her phone above her face.

'Where's Keres?' My eyes scanned the expanse of the room from the pale-green fluffy stool to the pink walls. The door to Gaia's en suite was open and the light was off. She glanced at me and informed me that Keres had got a phone call and said she was going outside. I said goodnight and went back downstairs to check the garden.

The downstairs space circled the wide staircase and its wide mouth that faced the front door. So, I wasn't sure how Keres could have slipped by unnoticed when downstairs was where I had been. I could feel lines forming on my forehead as I considered that maybe I'd been like Gaia with my eyes glued to my phone. Just as I hit the bottom step, a door closed upstairs.

'Gaia?' I called, but there was no answer. Then the back door opened so I turned left at the bottom of the stairs to be in line with the dining table and the door behind it. It was Anton. As he looked over to me, he tilted his head.

'Why are you frowning? Is there something on me?' He looked down at his shirt, dusting away invisible dirt.

I carried on walking towards him and pointed at the door. 'Was Keres out there?'

He shook his head, grabbed my pointing finger and pulled me towards him for a kiss. 'I thought she was,' I said. 'I'll look upstairs again.'

'I'll meet you up there once I put the dishwasher on.'

So off I trotted, back up the stairs and straight to Keres's door with a light knock. She answered as though she had been standing on the other side waiting for my appearance. She popped her head round the door with a smile.

'Melodie, I was looking for you. I would like to do something nice for you and Anton tomorrow. So I thank you for my stay.'

'That would be lovely – but you really don't have to. I think Anton has to take Gaia to Agios Stefanos tomorrow. She's helping out at her friend's taverna.'

'I take you for lunch?'

'We'll all go for a lovely lunch somewhere and we'll get Anton to pay! I'm off to bed now. Sleep well.'

As she closed the door, I wondered how she might pay for a meal. I'd assumed she didn't really have any money as she had been squatting in our mother's house. Maybe it was a silly assumption to make. She had made her way from Athens to Corfu alone and fed herself while she was here. Perhaps she had a big inheritance. I didn't like to ask, but I also didn't want her to spend money on us if she didn't really have any. Just the fact she wanted to was enough for me. It showed she cared, and wanting to show it was plenty.

It did make me think though, that Mum's house was technically half hers.

Chapter 12

Anton had arranged to see Akis after dropping off Gaia so I made him rearrange with Akis to come to lunch with us instead. That way Akis could make the hour-long journey in his rental car, instead of Anton going all that way. Gaia went off to help her friend, Natalia, with clearing plates and loading dishwashers over the busy lunch period. I think they just liked having time to chat.

Agios Stefanos was almost back to where it had once been. The pandemic had changed things, of course, but it was starting to fill up with tourists more and more. Over the winter across Greece, different restrictions had come back to slow the spread of a new pandemic variant. Just when the world had hoped it was over, restriction came creeping back in. In Greece, if you weren't vaccinated, there were tighter restrictions in place. Many people still wore masks even though they didn't always have to. I did too, if I was going somewhere busy. But in the winter, masks had to be worn everywhere, even outside. Some businesses had struggled to make it through to the other end and others hadn't. Luckily, many had survived.

We parked on the main road through the village and walked along towards the restaurant, which was down a side road that led to the beach. We had decided to take Keres to Waves, where we had had our wedding reception not long before. We turned off the main road to walk down towards the sea. I loved Karousades, and in some parts of the village the sea views were incredible due to the high vantage point, but part of me would have loved to have been even closer to Agios Stefanos, not that it was far at all. I just liked to have all the memories of my grandparents there at my fingertips. We ambled along in silence, my hand wrapped in Anton's. Keres's hand was wrapped around her phone.

'Anyone interesting?' I tucked my hair behind my ear and tilted my head to see her better.

'Friends. In Athens.' She put her phone in the back pocket of her tiny black shorts and took long strides to be in line with us on the road.

'I love the beatz.' She pointed towards the beach and did a little skip. 'I live near the city. Not mutz time at the sea when I was a child. Daddy took me and would talk to me in English. Make sure I am not too bad! I want to be better.'

'Your English is a lot better than my Greek!' I said, to which Anton muttered something in Greek, patted my bottom and Keres snorted out a little laugh, giving Ant a wide smile. 'It's a very hard language!' They both smirked and gave sympathetic nods of reassurance. 'Your English'll get better and better now you're living with us anyway. I hope you'll stay with us for a while. So, your dad spoke English to you? What did he do?'

She stuttered a little and pulled her oversized jumper off one shoulder.

91

'I don't know the Engliss,' she said.

Then Anton went into Greek. I looked up at his face. He was giving Keres a much more sympathetic look than he had given me for my lack of Greek. I turned my attention back to Keres who was pulling her jumper sleeves into balls around her fists.

We arrived at Waves and were seated. Anton and I exchanged wedding chat and laughter with the waiters. I kept glancing back at Keres whose eyes were glazed over towards the sea behind me. Her mouth was stuck in a small smile. Occasionally, she would nod at the conversation and was charming when we introduced her. When the waiters left to serve another table, I reached across and placed my hand over hers. Instantly her blue eyes left the sea and sharply met mine. They softened back to their usual circles of beauty as she slipped her hand away under the table. I quickly tucked mine back to its hiding place on my lap.

'What's wrong? Is it to do with your dad? I'm so sorry if I upset you.' I didn't need to look at Anton to know he felt awkward. He had sat at the head of the table next to us both. He turned his attention to the beach and the sea as though he were unable to hear our conversation across him.

'No. It is all right. I miss him. He worked a lot for us. I did not always see him mutz. The beatz, it is so beautiful. No wonder the tourists like it.'

I looked behind me, resting my forearm on the back of my chair. She was right. Most of the sunbeds across the golden sand were filled with bronzed bodies with noses in books or snoozing the afternoon away in the sun. Occasionally, the heat would get too much for a pocket of people. They'd be up tiptoeing across the sand like it was hot coals, ready for the relief of the foaming sea. I could happily people-watch for hours.

'Do you know what you're having?' Anton said from behind his menu. He held the menu high on his face but I could see the smile rise in his cheeks.

'No, I don't!' I said defiantly in response to his obvious accusation that I always picked courgette and feta balls when having lunch at Waves. I wasn't going to order it, even though I loved the deep-fried courgette balls the most. I scanned the menu for something else and decided to go with a traditional Greek salad instead.

'Where's Akis? We can't order without him.'

'Akis?' Keres sat up tall in her chair and laid her menu flat on the table, resting her hands on the laminated sheet.

'Sorry, I forgot to say! Anton was going to see him today so I said he should come here instead. I hope that's okay.'

Keres nodded then went back to her menu.

Anton checked his phone while moaning that his brother was late for everything, including his own birth – apparently. 'He says he has parked at the beach. That was five minutes ago and it's a thirty-second walk.'

Just as Anton put his phone down on the paper tablecloth, Akis appeared behind him. He put his index finger to his lips to silently shush me before grabbing both of Anton's shoulders and shouting 'Boo!' in his ear. One of Anton's long muscular arms reached over his head and grabbed his little brother pinning his chin on Anton's shoulder. Akis squawked a little like a chicken as Anton fluffed up his previously perfectly set bun. He was quickly released but not before everyone in the very busy restaurant had noticed him. I'm sure my cheeks were as purple as the beetroot dip. Akis and Anton just seemed

93

to think they were funny. After retying the little bun on top of his head, Akis placed himself next to Keres. She had smiled sweetly at the altercation and carefully brushed her hair off her right shoulder as Akis sat by her side.

'Keres, it's nice to see you again. It was a funny one, the last time, hey Miss Jones?' He laughed.

I said to Keres, 'I just realised I don't know your last name. I mean, you said Jones to Akis, which is obviously our biological parents' name, but what's your name? What's your adopted name?' I leant forward on the table, pulling the front of my wraparound playsuit to make sure it hadn't decided to hang open as it sometimes liked to.

Keres pushed her lips forward into a pout and tilted her head like a confused puppy. She looked from Akis to Anton like a damsel in distress. It was Akis who went into Greek to decode what I'd said for her.

'It is Adamos,' she said, eventually.

'Wow, that's so funny! Isn't it? As your biological father was called Adam.' I leant my chin on my knuckles in fascination at the irony of it.

Keres fluttered her bare, dark-golden lashes and smiled with a shrug.

I felt Anton's fingers find my knee under the table. I wasn't sure if he was trying to tell me something or just being affectionate. While I debated what I might be missing in my mind, we ordered our food.

While we waited, Akis told us about his antics while he had been staying at Michail's guesthouse. Michail had had his house and the guesthouse built in his father's garden. Apparently, a rather large gecko had visited them each night. It had even made an appearance when they had a couple of friends over for a barbecue the night before. Then Akis fell asleep on one of the garden chairs and woke up to a crash as the little thing was trying to steal his beer. As Akis spoke, he seemed to take over the whole table. He was a born entertainer and charmer. Each sentence seemed to come along with its own hand action or routine to make us laugh. Anton sat back in his chair. He was used to his little brother's desire for the limelight and had no issue with him having it. Keres sat back too, only her eyes were wide and she was biting her bottom lip throughout most of the story. Occasionally, Akis would translate something in her direction. He was still going strong as our food arrived and nearly knocked the food right off the tray it was on as the waiter came up behind him.

'That was a close one! Wouldn't want to ruin my nice shirt,' he laughed.

It wasn't even a shirt. It was a sleeveless top in a very dark pinky-red which looked rather well worn. He had various lines of tan across his arms from wearing different tops since being back on the island. They were starting to blend and even out, but some were still visible.

'Yes, I know it is hot today, but you could have come in something more than pyjamas,' Anton commented, as my salad was placed in front of me.

I hadn't caught what Anton had ordered, but now I could see it was the courgette and cheese balls. Without saying a word, he put one on a side plate and slid it across in my direction to enjoy with my salad. It was perfectly golden and a hint of mint tickled my nose. The table had suddenly come to life with the smell of oregano and olive oil, with freshly cooked pita bread for good measure. When we were done, all that was left were olive stones.

As we went to leave, Keres called Akis back. 'You forget this,' she said, and passed him his phone with a bowed head and a small smile on her delicate lips.

'Thanks. I didn't think I'd even taken it out of my pocket. Oh well, lucky you saw it. Ta. *Efharisto*.'

We walked up to meet Gaia who jumped straight onto her uncle's back and asked to go and see the local cats. So off we went, past tavernas and the shops to the corner where they could so often be found. She wanted a cat herself, but Anton thought she should concentrate on her studies and that she was lucky enough he allowed her to keep her boyfriend.

We all bent down to coo over a little cat and a kitten, a dark tabby and a black cat with little white feet. They were so affectionate and softer than threads of silk. Each cat rubbed their jaw in turn on any available surface. The black kitten padded along behind the tabby. I suddenly realised that there were only three pairs of knees bent around mine. I looked up to see Keres hovering behind us with a frown so deep it cut two vertical lines in between her eyebrows. As she saw me looking at her, she pulled her lips into a thin smile and relaxed her forehead as best she could.

'Everything okay?' I asked. Which made everyone turn to face her with quizzical looks.

'Yes. They are very cute. They are …' She waved her hands about, not that they were visible – they were hiding in her sleeves again. She said something in Greek.

Anton laughed. 'She is worried about fleas and worms.'

'Oh no! These are the most well-kept strays you'll ever meet! Trust me,' I said, smiling up at her from my little squat on the floor.

She began to edge forward, her lips still pulled into an

unconvincing smile. She cooed at the little tabby and put her hand out. Its little half-black, half-golden nose elegantly sniffed her stubby nails, before rubbing its length along Gaia instead.

'This one is famous,' Gaia began, scratching at the black- and-gold fur of the little cat. 'Natalia told me when we saw her here the other day. Her name is Liana. I remember, because I thought it sounded like your mum's name, like Liliana.'

'Famous?' Akis looked quite serious. The idea of a famous cat had stopped him stroking a little black kitten and made him rest his hands on his knees instead, dark eyes fixed on Gaia for answers.

'Uh-huh, famous. Some tourist saved her out of the river pipe last year. Apparently, he does parkour and he actually climbed in to get her. I've seen it on Facebook too, since Natalia showed me. We went and watched his videos on Instagram. He is really good. He had one video doing these big jumps over at Athens Bar. Everyone said they should name the cat Sam after him, but he chose Liana.'

I wasn't actually sure what parkour was until Akis described it as "free running". Then I knew it to be that sport where people run up walls and jump off things. Akis and Anton seemed to think it was something they could do. From what they described, I had my doubts. Keres sat with us, watching the cats for a time as the men debated their possible parkour prowess, laughing and jumping from place to place. I noticed that Keres wiped the hand that had touched the kitten on her jumper, looking at it in disgust before turning to smile at Akis and saying something in Greek.

Chapter 13

Anton had a surprise planned for me, but I wanted to say goodbye to Keres before we left and to check that she would be okay for the day. She had decided to stay, at least for the time being. Eventually, she came out of her room. She was wearing full make-up – her long, thick lashes were painted black and her orange lipstick matched the neon top she had on again. It almost looked like she was off out dancing for the night as she'd paired the top with her black high-waisted shorts and Vans trainers.

She hovered near the bottom of the stairs and called down at me, 'Melodie, can I speak with you?'

'Sure.' I jumped off the sofa to head up the wooden staircase. 'What's up?'

She edged back to stand under the photo of Katerina, Gaia and Anton.

'I do not want to be a ... telltale, but I think Gaia is smoking.' Keres dropped a purple lighter and a cigarette into my open palm.

Most people try smoking when they're young. Maria and

I used to indulge all the time when we were out drinking. I didn't like the idea, but I knew Anton would want to know everything and now it was on me to tell him.

'I thought I should tell you. I did not want secrets. Not with us.'

I looked up at her sweet, painted-up face. Underneath it all were the kind blue eyes smiling back at me. Apparently, she had found the lighter and cigarette in a bag she had borrowed for her date with Nico. She begged me not to tell Gaia she had told. I thanked her and agreed, before slipping the lighter and cigarette into the back pocket of my white denim shorts.

'I hope you do not mind. I'm out today,' she said, as she typed on her phone and made her way down the stairs.

'Of course, that's fine. We are actually off out too. I was going to check you would be okay without us.'

She didn't indicate when she would be back. She ran over and kissed Anton on both cheeks and then gave me a quick peck, then she slipped out of the door with only the flick of her ponytail as a wave goodbye – leaving me to deal with the cigarette I'd stuffed in my pocket. I caught Ant watching Keres leave with a raised eyebrow.

'What's wrong with you?'

'Nothing.' His eyes snapped to mine. 'Ready to go?' Anton sat up from his outstretched position and threw his book onto the coffee table. 'You're acting like a mother to a sister. She isn't a kid.' He tapped the brown leather sofa and stretched his long arms in my direction.

'No,' I whined, 'I'm not ready. Help me find the bloody photo of my mum and Adam. It's bothering me. Have we got time to have another quick look?'

He rolled his eyes and stood up to help. I ran my fingers

through my hair and ran up the stairs, two by two, the way Anton and Gaia normally would. He chased me, grabbing my hips and pulling me down as we got near the top, then continued to climb over me like a giant spider, legs and arms either side of me until he was at the top first.

'You silly arse.' I watched his long, golden legs dance about in victory. 'I wasn't racing.'

'Yes, you were. Come on, what do I win?' he said, as I continued up the stairs.

'Your prize is helping me find this photo.'

Anton continued to look everywhere I'd looked. Under the desk in the spare room, under the bed, under our bed. Nothing. As I came out from looking in our bedroom for the millionth time, I saw him leaving Keres's room.

'Oi! What are you doing in there?' I hissed. As though somehow, someone would hear us.

'I found the photo.'

The landing in Anton's house, our house, was a U shape. He sauntered back round towards me, waving the photo as though it were a fan. His broad smile displayed his naturally white teeth, perfectly framed by his full, curled-up lips.

'You shouldn't go into someone's room!' I snapped, as I marched to meet him at the stairs.

In an instant his shoulders dropped and his hands fell to meet his sides. 'I didn't. It's our house. It's our room.' He shrugged, completely devoid of any understanding, then passed the photo over for my appraisal.

I sat on the top step studying the faces for answers. Adam's face was round and angelic, much like Keres's, and Mum's eyes were a clear, watery blue. Perhaps paler than hers. It was hard to say really, the photo was over thirty years old and included their wine glasses and bowels of pasta. Anton sat down next to me on the pale wooden step. 'That is quite the frown, Melodie-Mou. What's on your mind?'

'I dunno. It's funny to have a sister and not look that much like her. I just want to connect in some way – any way.'

'I don't look much like Dimitri or Akis in the face. Not all that much anyway. But, we are alike in other ways. You'll find your ways. We don't all get along all the time. Akis was the most obnoxious child. You know, I'm closer to Dimi. It doesn't matter that my face is more like Marty. I still love them all.'

'Where did you find this?' I flapped the photo at him then tapped it on his fuzzy knee.

'Mmm, you won't enjoy the answer. I'll put it back.' He took the photo and began to head towards her room.

Most likely he was right – I wouldn't have liked his answer – so I didn't press the issue. It was too late to worry about it. Instead, I lay back on the cool, wooden flooring of the landing. It was another warm day but still full of overcast blankets of clouds making everything feel sticky and ready for a storm.

Anton stood over my head and then reversed down the steps before positioning himself in a press-up position over me. I could feel his body heat teasing my skin.

'I'm ready to go now,' I said.

We hopped into Anton's yellow Mustang. He didn't let go of my hand the entire way. He changed gear with my hand in his. It was reassuring that I never had to tell him when I needed comfort. He was always just there, ready and willing to love me. I sat twisted in my seat for most of the journey, watching him and chatting to him across the air that rushed past our faces. The muscles in my shoulders eased and my mind began to tiptoe past any questions about the photo. He was right, after all. Keres was nineteen, that funny age of being fully grown but having your whole life waiting to be discovered. She didn't need another mother figure. She needed me to just be there, like Anton's supportive hand. There without expectations.

I'd quickly cottoned on to where we were going: Nymfes. Anton had taken me there once before. It had been a week before Christmas. He had told me that he knew of a place where we could go for a beautiful walk. I'd been moaning that I hadn't explored in a while, so off we had gone. I remember Anton had stopped the car on a narrow road in the middle of nowhere. It was beautiful, but no more or less than at any other point along the road. It wasn't until I got out of the car that I could hear it. Running water. We had to make our way down a path that could never have existed in the UK. Someone would have taped it up and called it condemned. I remember looking at the handrail that was made out of branches maybe four centimetres in diameter all tied together with wire. Then I eyed the stairs – logs laid out at intervals along the slope. I couldn't have been more thrilled at the adventure.

Through the dense trees I could see where the sound was coming from, because the winter trees had lost their leaves, and I could see my way through. A long waterfall was crashing into a small pool of water at the bottom of all the steps. That December day had been perfect – cool and overcast but not cold. I'd already started to acclimatise to fifteen degrees being cool, so we were both in jeans and hoodies. Anton had stayed one step ahead of me the whole way down, holding my hand as we went. At the bottom, there were two benches, both full of graffiti and carved love notes. The water beating down was powerful yet elegant as it tripped and toppled from one rock to another. I'd never seen a waterfall before that point, not of that size anyway.

Anton held me close to his chest as we sat on the bench at the water's edge, only perhaps three feet away from where the liquid was pooling before making its way further along the river. I'll never forget Anton pointing to the ground and asking something like, "What's that?" As we both shuffled our weight forwards to look, the whole bench tipped. Being less sturdy than Anton, I went hurtling forward towards the water. Anton just managed to catch me by the armpit of my hoodie and pulled me so hard backwards to compensate that we both toppled the bench the other way. He held my head to his chest so closely I thought I might suffocate. Then he was kissing my face all over before settling on my mouth. We lay in a tangled mess on the back of the bench that was flat to the ground. 'I love you, Melodie,' he had said. 'Marry me, please.' And we both untangled ourselves and knelt, knees pressed together, as he pulled a ring box out of his hoodie pocket.

I turned my engagement ring around my finger, thinking about that day. Thinking about that moment when the ring was first placed on my finger. I looked down at the square diamond between the dainty rectangles on either side.

Then we were there once more in Nymfes. I was excited to see how it looked in summer. Anton pulled up at the top of the road, where the waterfall had glanced the rocks behind the thick greenery. This time the only noise came from insects. I couldn't hear the same rush of billions of droplets the way I had before.

'You're not going to try to push me off the bench again, are you?' I said.

'No! Let's not do that again. No, we got married this month, and I thought it would be nice to come back here. If you fall in this time, it will hurt more than if you did it in winter.'

We began to climb down, clutching the smooth, thin branch rail for support and doing our best not to catch our legs on any of the metal posts that held the log steps in place. The cascade was nothing like it had been in winter. Only a thin line of water droplets came down from above. I found it fascinating. Now that the water wasn't so dominant, my focus shifted to the hanging tree roots and the wiry vines at every corner.

'I almost feel like there should be monkeys swinging from the trees,' I said.

Anton wasn't sure what I meant at first. He was used to the lush, dense greenery of Corfu. To me it was like I'd stepped into a rainforest.

A piercing blue dragonfly came between us like an arrow and jigged its way to a far-off branch. It was quickly followed by a huge butterfly with a dancing tail. For some unknown reason, I followed it like a kitten, stalking it down into the dry river bed. Anton was close behind, ducking and weaving past branches and wasps.

'Where are you going?' he huffed, as he swatted at a wasp that was darting towards his hair. All the head-shaking made the hair on the top of his head flop forwards towards his eyes. He fiercely thrust his fingers through his hair to keep it in place before marching to catch up with me. He lost his footing a little on a smooth, grey rock – probably because everything was covered in a fine layer of crispy, dry leaves that shattered to dust with every crunchy step.

'Look!' I said, before he got too caught up in slipping on his espadrille, 'a lizard.' I pulled my phone out of my pocket to get a photo.

'It's not the lizards I'm worried about. I'm worried about what eats the lizards.' Then, as though he had charmed it into being, a snake struck. It took the lizard off its rock and down into the undergrowth. Other than a sharp inbreath when the snake actually attacked, neither of us moved. Without warning, Anton broke the spell with an "I told you so" lift of his left eyebrow and folded his arms across his chest.

'It's nature. It's natural. I love snakes,' I stated defiantly to the accusing eyebrow, even though I hoped the snake would leave us well alone.

'I hope you at least got that on your phone.' I shook my head with a small grimace. 'Melodie-Mou ...' Ant caught my hand as I went to walk away and pulled me into his chest then bent forward a little. 'Don't leave me with the snake,' he whispered into my ear.

I beat my fist lightly onto his chest. There was never a day that he hadn't made me smile. I stretched my body to kiss him. Like snakes, his arms wrapped around my waist and his hands slipped into my back pockets to squeeze my flesh. That's when his mouth stopped caressing mine and his tongue vanished from its gentle exploration.

'What's this?' he said, as he showed me the contents of my own pocket. His eyebrows almost covered his eyes in confusion as though he'd never seen a cigarette before.

'I'd forgotten they were in there.' I quickly snatched the cigarette and lighter back and returned them to my pocket. I hadn't had a chance to think what I would say to him about it all. Unprepared, I panicked and started to march back the way we'd come, back towards the makeshift stairs.

'Are you smoking now? Is everything okay?'

My feet wouldn't carry me any further along without telling him the truth.

'Keres gave them to me. She found them in Gaia's bag.' I didn't turn to look at him. All I could do was wait to see what might happen next. I was still enough for the butterfly with a tail to come and almost land on a branch by my side before deciding there was probably somewhere better to be than in the dense air between Anton and me. Then, as though I hadn't spoken, he was walking past me laughing.

'At least she didn't smoke the cigarette,' he said.

Chapter 14

'I told Akis I would bring him these tools to fix the dripping pipe under your mum's kitchen sink. I said I would go over tomorrow, but as we are already in the car, we could take them now. Do you fancy the drive?' Anton asked.

'I fancy you, but I'll happily go for a longer drive.'

We chatted the whole way. I couldn't believe how relaxed he had been about Gaia's cigarette. He was going to talk to her about it, but he wasn't angry. In fact, he was confident it was just a "silly step" on her journey to adulthood. As we opened the door to Mum's, we were laughing about it all. We were always laughing about something or other. I had sort of knocked, but as it was Corfu and technically my house, I just walked in simultaneously. There in front of us was Akis straddled by Keres, both with orange lipstick smeared across their faces.

No one moved. Keres's breath was fast, lightly panting, then she bit her lip. With the make-up rubbed across them they looked like smudgey clowns. Anton's warm hands slipped around my waist and gently guided me backwards out of the doorway before placing his toolbox on the floor in front of me. He proceeded to close the door, put me into his car, took the time to put the roof up and put the air con on all before actually going anywhere. Then we were driving back the way we came with no words spoken. None.

'What just happened? What just happened? Seriously, what just happened?' My voice came out dry in the air con. My hands became rigid, almost cutting the air. Chopping down with every word.

'Two consenting adults kissing. Nothing more.'

'Nothing more? She was out with Nico only a couple of days ago. And not to mention she is, what? Twelve-thirteen years younger than him? Turn the car around now!'

'Melodie-Mou ...' His voice was low and calm, but I could see his knuckles were almost white where he was gripping the steering wheel.

'Don't Melodie-Mou me! She's my responsibility! For God's sake! She is a child!'

'No, she is not, and you are not her mother.'

'What if it were Gaia with some thirty-odd-year-old man?'

He sharply inhaled through his nose. I began to vibrate under the cold touch of the air con, clenching my fists and my teeth so hard I thought my nails might make my hands bleed. Anton didn't say anything. His chest just rose and fell under heavy breaths and his shoulders rounded his body into a deep cave for his soul to hide in.

'What if—'

'Don't, Melodie. We can't control this. I will call Akis later and you can speak to Keres when she returns to the house. Calmly. She might be your sister, but she had a different upbringing. It is not on you to make judgement.'

The rest of the journey we sat silently, with emotions boiling under our skin in the cold box we had created.

It was late when Keres came in. Gaia had already gone to bed without a clue as to the day's events. We sat in the garden with the back door open. Listening. Waiting. I'd poured myself a small glass of ouzo. Anton had one too, both topped up with water from a little dark-blue ceramic jug. Slowly, we sipped at the clear yet potent liquid. It really was deceptive with its still appearance of water and its hardy kick. The aniseed taste warmed my chest and steadied my hand from its constant desire to form a fist. As the front door opened, I jumped up, running to the back door and hurried through the length of the house.

'Can we talk, outside?' I said, and Keres followed me out.

Anton and his glass had completely disappeared. Even with his broad shoulders and tall stature, that wasn't all that hard in his garden. There were a lot of lemon and olive trees as well as the odd outhouse where Anton kept all his gardening tools and old pots of paint. Keres sat with the sun setting under the trees behind her. The sky was blazing a deep orange, making her golden-blonde hair look like it had been set alight.

'I would like some ouzo, please,' she said, pointing to the bottle resting on the mosaic table.

I went back into the house to get a glass; a short blue one came to hand. Pouring some out for her, I decided to add a little more for me. I would have topped Anton's up too, but his glass was as lost as he was. After she had taken a sip, she gave me a smile over the glass. Her wide, round blue eyes were bright even in the shadow of her own face. It was as though she were a newly sprouting poppy, ready to shine in the sun, and I was the field it grew out of, all churned up and broken. Her lipstick was perfectly in place again. It looked as though it had made it through the day completely unscathed. On cue my stomach clenched and gurgled. We both opened our mouths to speak all at once.

'I like Akis. He is a good man. I hope you are good? With me seeing Akis today?' She placed the little glass on the table. A low-hanging sunray passed through some of the tree leaves and through the glass, making a perfect blue light show on the table for the briefest moment.

I didn't really know what to say. I was stuck. Anton thought I should keep my mouth shut and all I wanted to do was ask a million questions. I know how muddled up I had been after losing Mama and Papa during the pandemic and she was so much younger than me. I snatched my glass up and took a short sip before clattering it down on to the table as my words began to tingle in my mouth much like the ouzo.

'I just want you to know that if you ever need to talk about anything, I'm here. I was shocked today. Akis is a lot older than you and I thought you liked Nico. That's beside the point, I suppose. I just … I'm worried about you. I know we don't know each other all that well, but you're my sister. I just want to know you're okay.' I made sure to speak slowly. I wanted her to understand me. I didn't want a language barrier to make things worse.

'Seven years? He is seven years old?' she said, while her left hand batted away a large moth that seemed to be dive-bombing her face.

It all left me with a desperate urge to laugh. Partly at the crazy moth but mostly at Akis being seven years old. 'What do you mean he is seven years old?'

110

'Seven year more than me.'

'Seven years older! Is that what he told you? He is thirty-three. Not twenty-six.'

The moth made a swift exit as Keres tilted her head, making her ponytail whip towards her shoulder. She frowned and shook her head. 'I do not understand.'

'You are nineteen. He is thirty-three. He is fourteen years,' I flashed my fingers ten then four, 'older than you.' I ran my fingers tightly through my loose waves and took a deep inhale of my ouzo before taking another sip. Akis did look about twenty-six, but in fact he wasn't.

Keres sat looking at her bouncing knees. Jiggling one then the other at a rapid speed only to suddenly stop and look up at me. 'I did not know. I was confused. I am sorry.' Her face was very still. She made her excuses and went off to her room.

I relaxed back into my chair, clinging onto the metal arms as I waited for Anton to return. Inevitably, he'd been listening to the whole thing. He couldn't help himself; he was a secret gossip. Right on cue, he appeared like Bigfoot from out of the trees.

'I thought I should give you two some space.' He sat on the white metal chair opposite me with a little clang. I kicked off my flip-flops and put my feet onto his lap. His big warm hands rested on my ankles like a pair of cosy socks. 'I did message Akis. He said she told him she was twenty-five.'

'What?' I snatched my feet from his lap and leant forward onto the edge of my chair. 'You're joking.'

He shook his head and passed me his phone. I read the messages between them – thankfully, they were all in English. When I looked back up many of our little lights had come on around the garden as the sun had started to disappear. The three of us had picked them out after deciding we wanted the whole place to look magical. There were lots of solar-powered lights hidden in trees and pots here and there. To me it looked like a fairy wonderland. 'I don't know what to say. I guess she lied because she liked him. Or maybe numbers in English confuse her.' I passed him his phone.

'Melodie-Mou, Akis would have been talking to her in Greek. I know it's been some time since he lived here, but Mum always talks to us in Greek. I talk to him in Greek. You can trust me that he is perfectly understandable. It's his English I question.' He sat back and gave a small laugh. Not one that I recognised. It was thin and weak, completely unlike him. 'You spoke to the girl. I spoke to Akis. I think he likes her, although he was shocked – you saw the messages.' He scratched his stubbled cheeks with both hands which turned into a whole face rub before he broke. 'Don't give me that look, Melodie.' His hands slapped down onto his knees.

'What look?'

'Your one eyebrow and twisted pout look! That look you do to disapprove. You do it when I forget to put my shoes away.' He looked up to the sky and mumbled in Greek, with his flat palms projecting from his face towards the sky. 'Yes, it is odd for us. But it is not up to us. We must let it run its course.' His face dropped to meet mine. I couldn't believe how handsome he was at times. The lights in the garden flickered all around him like the fireflies I'd once seen in Sidari. Lines had formed in the middle of his brow, but his bones were so beautiful. His high cheekbones caught the glittering light and his green eyes were deep in the late glow of the evening.

'I love you,' I said.

Chapter 15

The drama didn't last long, or at least it was quickly overshadowed by a new one. The next day I woke up to Gaia groaning and vomiting. At first, we thought perhaps it was a twenty-four- hour bug. As the day went on, she improved a little. Keres came into her own, getting anything that was needed and generally being lovely. As the week went on, Gaia vomited on two separate days, both times in the morning, leaving her fragile for hours. It didn't help that she wouldn't then want to eat for the rest of the day. Anton did everything he could to look after her, but I felt something didn't sit right with him and I was pretty sure it was the same question that didn't sit right with me either. Why was it in the morning she was so often ill? Could she be pregnant?

The only good thing that week was that I discovered Keres enjoyed running as much as I did. Anton and Gaia liked exercise like tennis or going to the gym now and then. Which was okay, but neither of them would run with me. That had meant I had only been running once a week at most, sometimes not even that much. That all changed when I realised Keres liked it too. One evening she put her trainers on and announced she was going out for a run, I couldn't get my trainers on fast enough to join her. We went running most afternoons before dinner. We had even carved out a regular route for ourselves which was a four- mile loop. We warmed up in the driveway, then did some road running and went along a dirt track through an olive grove. It was perfect because we could do it in silence or talk about things and it didn't matter which, because we were together for forty minutes or so no matter what else was going on around us.

We chatted more and more about our grandparents. Keres had really made me laugh asking if they were rich because *Grandmama* and *Grandpapa* were different to the English words she had learnt for grandparents and sounded much fancier. I tried to explain how every family was different and how the names were a bit of a traditional hand-me-down in my family. It was one that had worked well for me as there were times I wanted to pretend they were actually my parents, so sometimes I often shortened the names to Mama and Papa so that people wouldn't instantly know they weren't my parents.

On one of our runs, we had even managed to talk about Akis more too. About why Keres liked him. She confided in me that although Nico was handsome and she had liked him at first, she found him pushy. Which wasn't very surprising knowledge. Akis may have been loud and full of stories, but he wasn't pushy. Not in that way. She said that she and Akis had a lot in common too, although I found the language barrier to that conversation a little bit tricky. The more time we spent together, the better her English got. My Greek was improving but at a much slower rate. I was astounded by how quickly her language skills had improved since we had met.

At a quarter past five, Keres was already bouncing by the door waiting for me. I tied up my laces. A week earlier, my trainers had looked pretty new still. Now they were dusty and settling into the shape of my feet. In no time we were on the road and settling into our rhythm, a rhythm that was soon becoming a welcoming comfort and a break from my mind asking me if I were pregnant – or worse – if in fact Gaia might be.

'I've been thinking,' I puffed, 'about Mum's inheritance. It was for any living heirs. You're her living heir too.'

Keres stopped running as we came to the edge of the olive grove, resting her hands on her knees before she quickly recovered. 'I do not understand. Heirs?'

We carried on into the grove but not at our usual running pace. We went at a jog that didn't progress us any more than a walking pace. It just made us sweat more.

'I mean, you're her daughter. You are related to her too. Her will said "living heirs". Obviously, we thought that was just me. But, now we know you're her relative too.'

'So, we share the house?' She did a little hop over a snaking root that ran along part of the dusty footpath.

I nodded. 'I need to look into it, but, yeah. I think you should be entitled to half.'

Keres stopped and wrapped her arms about my shoulders like a boa squeezing me into her. Our bodies were almost glued together with sweat. She kept thanking me and then gripped my shoulders, looking me dead in the eyes.

'Thank you, Melodie. You are a wonderful sister.'

I tried to explain that I hadn't actually done anything, but it was nice to see how grateful she was at being included as a family member. I didn't want her to feel lesser just because our dreadful father had given her away. It was likely the nicest thing he had done for her in truth. But now it was time for her to feel included again. I was going to make sure of it. Our feet soon found their usual steps along the ground at their daily pace and we were back at the house in no time.

After quick showers, we were in the kitchen cooking up dinner together. With Gaia being ill or feeling ill all week, Keres had quickly taken her place as my cooking sidekick and Greek cuisine role model. She had different traditional dishes to show me or sometimes a new take on things Gaia and Anton had taught me. We could move around each other silently going from pot to pan, knife to board, interacting with little chirps and the waltz that happens between the cupboards.

Gaia made her way down the stairs. All things considered it had been a good day. She hadn't been sick and she had managed to eat lunch earlier too.

'Do you need a hand, mou-mou?'

'It's okay. Keres is doing all the heavy lifting. You get some rest.'

Keres carefully placed a tray of *dolmades*, stuffed vine leaves, into the oven.

'I can't smell the dill. Did you remember to put dill in?' Gaia scanned the herb jars across the work top and picked up the nearest one to inspect what it was.

'I do not use dill. Not for *dolmades*. These are chicken and tomatoes.'

Gaia carefully placed the jar down and began to turn away.

'Are you still going to this party thing tonight?' I called back, as I put vegetable scraps in the bin.

'Yeah. It doesn't start until nine.'

'That's late—' I began, but Gaia was already laughing at me.

'You sound as bad as Dad. Chloe does ballet until seven thirty so by the time she gets back and is ready and had her dinner, it'll be nine.'

'Well, your dad must be okay with it and that's the main thing.'

'If only it were down to you, mou-mou.' She gave a small but glowing smile, one that made me aware of my heart in my chest. Then off she went towards Anton who was reading a book on the sofa. She curled up by his side, and he was quick to put his book down to pull her into an embrace. Resting his head on top of hers, he began to talk softly to her. From the distance of the kitchen, I couldn't make out what was being said, or even what language it was in. It didn't matter. They had their own voice between them, one they had moulded after the tragedy of losing Gaia's mum, one I felt warmed to be allowed to witness at such close range. And not only witness. I'd been welcomed into their world in a way that I could never have imagined. There had only been one time that Gaia had kicked off about Anton and me. Really, she was just annoyed at Ant for embarrassing her in front of Finn. It had all been forgiven when I came back from England.

'Don't you find this odd?' Keres nodded towards the pair of them chatting away. I gave an absentminded hum before frowning at her.

'Shouldn't he be cuddling you? Men should put their wife first, no?' She was leaning on her elbows over the kitchen bench in Anton and Gaia's direction but with her head fully turned towards me, and making sure her voice was just low enough not to be caught.

I shook my head and grabbed the cloth to wipe across the

117

worktop. 'I don't think so. I think it's lovely.'

She looked surprised, turning down the corners of her mouth.

'Did you always know you were adopted?' I said.

She slid herself back off the worktop to lean her back against it instead. 'Yes.'

'Well, maybe that's why you find it odd. I guess your dad wasn't like that with you. Did knowing you were adopted create a barrier? What was your dad like with you?'

'He thought I should learn things. It was important. I should learn mathematics and English. His job kept him away most of the time, so I did not always see him.' Her arms had found their way around her tiny frame, giving herself the reassurance perhaps her adoptive father had not. 'What was Papa like to you?'

It felt odd having someone else call him that. A pulse through my bones wanted to say that it was my name for him and no one else could use it. I shook my head and continued to wipe down the surface.

'When I was very little I would sit on his knee and he would play Vanessa-Mae. I don't suppose you know her. She plays violin.' I did a little mime to be sure she knew what a violin was. In doing so, I nearly whipped myself in the face with the wet cloth. Keres covered her face and sniggered. 'Anyway, I would sit and listen to her. Other violinists too. He loved the violin. He would hold me at night when I was frightened and tell me stories until I went to sleep.'

'But, when you were Gaia's age? Did he hold and talk to you?'

We both gazed across at the beautiful pair who had began to watch something on Anton's phone together. I shook my head again.

'No. We weren't as close as those two. They only had each other for so many years though. I like that they're close. I hope when I have kids, I'm as close to them as Ant is with Gaia.'

'Do you think Gaia will not like being a sister? Will she like to share Anton?'

It was something I worried about at times. In theory she wanted to play the part of older sister. The reality might be something else entirely.

'I cannot see her letting anyone else in,' Keres added, as she walked across the kitchen to retrieve a can of lemonade from the fridge. She tapped it on the top before opening it and made her way to the dining table at the opposite corner of the house from Gaia and Anton's secret conversation.

Gaia might be a brilliant role model and caring older sister, but until the situation was there in front of us there was no way to actually know how it might play out. Ant and Gaia were so close that I had been afraid that any child of ours might not have the same amount of space in his heart. I caught my thoughts and stopped them. They were thoughts that had only previously lived in the periphery. Now was the first time I'd allowed them to creep into the foreground and pull my eyes out of focus. Just because Keres had doubts didn't mean I should join her in worrying about something I had no control over.

As I sat down at the head of the table with my back to the stairs, the voices at the other end of the house began to rise. From our position in the house, it was as though they were coming at us from both directions. We couldn't see them, as the under-the-stairs loo and cupboard in the centre of the house blocked the view and meant the sound was impossible to pin down – until I saw that Gaia was on the move, feet thudding along, making the house almost jiggle under the pressure of her footsteps. Keres and I had matching expressions with question marks for eyebrows. Tentatively, I made my way round the stairs to find Ant red-faced, tapping his heel to the ground at the speed of a cartoon rabbit.

'What just happened?' I knelt down on the floor the other side of the coffee table to look up at him on the sofa.

'I said about the cigarette. I said things like "Do not worry", "We have all done these things". You know what she said? She said it was not hers and was annoyed at me for even thinking it could be. All this "how dare you" and "why do you talk like that" ... *pós tolmás, óchi, óchi, den psévdomai.*' He put on a moany voice and chattered his hands like puppets. 'No. Her big reaction says she is lying and feeling guilty. I know it. Anyway, her lying means she is grounded. She will miss Chloe's sixteenth birthday party.'

'That's a bit harsh, isn't it? I know I couldn't understand half of that, but from what I could, it seems a bit much.'

His heel stopped dead and his eyes narrowed in my direction like he had never seen me before, and he was trying to zoom in to analyse my presence in his father-life. After only a moment, he exhaled through his nose and pressed his palms to his face. 'It's too late. I've said this now. I cannot go back on it. She's been too ill anyway. One good day is not a pattern. I don't want her going out.' He paused. 'Am I a dreadful father?'

'No, you're a bloody wonderful father, you silly arse,' I said, and began to crawl round the table to climb into his arms on the sofa. 'Strange though. That she'd lie and be so adamant about it. Maybe she's embarrassed or something.'

Gaia came back down for dinner only to behave as though her father were invisible. She flicked her hair to cover her shoulder whenever he spoke. She did converse with Keres and me. She kept intentionally starting conversations about things that would either bore Anton or annoy him. Mostly about boys and clothes or feeling like it was lockdown all over again.

As soon as everyone had finished eating, Gaia politely excused herself and left. It was as though Keres, Anton and I had been arguing even though we hadn't. She'd left us unbalanced and unquiet in our own minds. Keres made her excuses and took herself off to her room, leaving us alone.

'Walk?' I offered. Anything to leave the cloud of teenage hormones that hovered there in the dining room. We cleared the plates and took ourselves off into the garden.

Chapter 16

We ambled in amongst the trees until we came to the clearing. It was a deceptively large garden and most of it was left in a natural state. It wasn't always an easy stroll as the ground wasn't at all flat. In places it dipped and wove amongst the trees on the way to the clearing, which I sometimes called the fairy circle, although it was more of an oval, really. It sloped up a little, and Anton had put a two-person swing chair there at my request, which looked back towards the house.

We made our way silently towards the chair, only Anton didn't stop there. He carried on into the part of the garden that was most wild-looking. It was the part that didn't really feel like it belonged to us. Or at least, that's how I felt about it. It belonged to bees, butterflies and a multitude of other insects I'd only ever seen during the past year of living in Corfu.

'We're going to get bitten, you know,' I announced, swatting at something bounding past my face.

'I just like the noise here.'

The sound was intimidating. I had always thought that cities were loud. I'd lived in Manchester for a couple of months with a uni friend and it always seemed to have a hum of noise no matter what time it was. It wasn't like this. The further we went into our eco-friendly, natural garden, the louder the noise got. It was the sound of thousands of calling creatures. Most were invisible although it seemed impossible that they would be heard but not seen. Trees that had stood for hundreds of years were held up by the bodies of insects who sang them to sleep each and every night. Although it was more like screeching than singing.

'Ant, I'm only in flip-flops.'

He turned to look at my old, reliable, black flip-flops and nodded. His features didn't change and to most would have been unreadable. Just a handsome face with nothing inside. To me, his lack of expression told me everything. I squeezed his hand in little pulses, then tugged at his arm when I didn't gain immediate eye contact.

'Hey! Look at me!' Letting go of his hand, I pulled at the neck of his T-shirt, pulling his face down towards mine and cupped his chin in my hands. It was still soft from the morning's shave. I ran my thumb over his bottom lip.

'Don't worry. It's a good sign. At least Gaia's well enough to argue. Maybe she's actually on the mend. It was just a very odd tummy thing.'

The curve of his mouth thrust towards mine and his eager fingers dug into my rib cage and then my waist, pulling my body into his. His mouth tasted of cinnamon from the orange cake he'd had. As I relaxed into his embrace, he scooped me up, pressing me firmly to him. I often wondered if this were easier for him – if the chore of picking me up was more comfortable than bending forwards to kiss me. For someone so tall, his posture was remarkable, but I was aware that he spent most of his time looking downwards. His fingers climbed the ridges of my spine, heading for the clasp of my bra and bringing me back to the lust in front of me.

'Stop,' I mouthed into him.

'Stop?' He began to lightly kiss my jawline, freeing my lips to explain myself.

'Not here. Not with all the bugs. Let's go back to the house.'

A growl from Ant tingled through to my chest, as though his noise were mine.

'But there is no one here, and I'm ready now.' He lowered me down until my feet touched the floor. He made sure to be holding me firmly to his body so I knew exactly what he meant. I couldn't help myself but to run my fingertips along it. I looked up to see Ant biting his bottom lip. His green eyes were dark and fierce. I had said no. I knew he wouldn't make another move. Not until it was obvious I'd changed my mind. That knowledge left me with the burning desire to toy with him, like an orca playing with its food before it devours it.

Slipping my arms round his chest, I clung to him, pressing my breasts into him, letting my warm breath settle onto his neck. He made another small groan but still didn't move. My fingers moved to lower his zip to allow my left hand to roam freely. The only movement he made was to catch his fingers in the hair on the nape of my neck before I made my way down to my knees. The ground was still reasonably soft. The grass wasn't fully scorched or dead from the onset of summer. I placed myself with the hidden insects in the dimming light before tasting the length of Anton, causing him to grab the trunk of a nearby olive tree making the leaves flick around above our heads.

'I thought you said no,' he inhaled, gulping back his word.

I momentarily released him. 'I changed my mind.'

That was all he needed. Pulling me up, he kissed my neck, pushing my back against the ancient tree. Its trunk was split into two halves and Anton wedged me into it. Prising down my top, then taking my flesh into his mouth, his fingers found their way between my thighs. I began to tug at my skirt, pulling it up, turning it into a belt before pulling him hard into me. I couldn't help but release a high-pitched cry that rang above the noise of the ever-increasing insects finding mates around us. There, lodged in the tree, Anton took what he had waited so patiently for, pinning me until the volume of my cries was too much. He pressed his mouth to mine to stop me from being heard all the way back at the house – until neither of us could bear a moment more, and with gritted teeth and shallow breaths every muscle in our combined being contracted – and then relaxed.

We stayed momentarily panting, with our sweat dripping across the bark of the tree. Anton kissed me and laughed, whispering something in Greek, before helping me escape from the clutches of the tree trunk.

'Melodie!' Keres's voice called.

Luckily, she sounded like she was still quite near to the house. Anton and I both froze, eyes wide. *Shit*, he mouthed at me, and we began to pull at our clothes, tugging and moving to gain some level of normality over our layers of sweat and lust. 'Shit,' he continued, 'look at me ...'

He did look like he had gone for a run and then fallen down a cliff. His hair was flopping over his forehead instead of its usual neat, gently waxed appearance, and his T-shirt was almost completely wet. Looking over at me, his eyes followed the lines of my body where his body had been and his chest bounced in a low laugh. 'You look just as bad.' He pulled my top up to properly cover my bra as Keres's voice continued to call us with increasing desperation.

'It doesn't bloody matter. Let's just find out what the hell is going on.'

As though it might somehow conceal our frolicking, we ran through the trees hand in hand and down the slope towards Keres who had just appeared at the clearing. It was getting quite dark, but the lights around the garden made navigating easy enough.

'I do not know where Gaia is!' Her voice was high and raspy and her fingers were pressed to her pink cheeks. Then she and Anton both went into Greek. We all knew it would be quicker and easier to find out exactly what she knew – or didn't know – if they spoke in Greek. The three of us jogged towards the house. It was only as we entered through the back door and into the dining room that Keres really looked at us. As she pressed her lips together, I was sure she was doing her best to suppress a laugh.

'What's going on? Where's Gaia?' I edged towards Keres, folding my arms across my chest as Anton sprinted through the house and made his way to Gaia's room. The whole house shook with each leap up the stairs. Keres just shrugged and shook her head.

'I knock on her door. To ask for ...' She pulled out a thin hairband from her back pocket.

'A hairband?'

'A hairband.' She nodded frantically. 'She did not answer. I went in. She was no there. Please, please do not tell her it was me who told you. I do not want her to think she cannot tell me things.' I tried to reassure her as Ant came down the stairs so quickly his feet were akin to a drum roll.

We made our way to the front of the house as he came towards us. He had put a fresh T-shirt on, bright red with black block capitals that read *Limited Edition* across his chest.

'She'll be at the party. I will get her,' Anton said, before kissing my forehead and thanking Keres.

I bounced behind him, demanding that he wait. Demanding he take me with him. He shook his head as he went to grab his keys off the mantelpiece, but I slid my hand around him and got them first.

'I'm coming with you, Anton. She is my daughter too now, and I love her.'

He turned to face me, kissed me on the head one more time and we both went to find Gaia.

Chapter 17

Anton had been knocking at Chloe's door for five minutes before someone eventually came and opened it. The house was a big L shape, and there was a fountain in the middle of the driveway. I didn't really like Chloe, or her dad. I always felt like her dad was talking to my breasts or finding an excuse to touch me when Anton wasn't looking. I'd only met him twice. Once was at a barbecue they'd had. Chloe was becoming more and more friendly with Gaia and Natalia. It was really because her boyfriend was friends with Finn.

It was the dad, Costas, who opened the door. I could see tension between the two men through the car window. I knew I had no choice but to get involved.

'Costas!' I beamed as I came towards him. Without a thought he pushed past Ant, who was head and shoulders taller than he was, then grabbed for my hand and kissed it three times. Instantly, I wished I'd put hand sanitiser in my pocket instead of leaving it in the car. Around him, I wanted to put my face mask back on so he couldn't see me gag.

'Melodie, the beautiful Melodie. What is wrong with this

husband of yours? He is almost accusing me of abducting Gaia!' Luckily, Costa's English was almost perfect. The only oddity was his hint of an American accent instead of a Greek one. He had lived in the USA trying to make it as an actor – apparently – all paid for by a big lotto win. That's what I'd heard. I'd never actually asked though. The information had come from Gaia and I wasn't sure how reliable school gossip was. The only facts I had, were that his wife was American and looked like a bleached blonde Californian model, but she didn't say that much. The idea of Costa as an aspiring actor made sense to me though. He was flamboyant and touchy-feely, the way I imagined all performers to be. I knew he was harmless, but it didn't help how I felt about him constantly holding my hand or rubbing my arm.

'She's grounded. Could you call her out, please. So sorry to be a bother.' I smiled.

'No, dear girl. It is not possible. They are at the back of the garden camping and I promised Chloe I would leave them to it. Come on, Anton, she's just having fun. Why not come in and have a wine instead?' Costas was patting my hand as though it were attached to Anton in some way, and by reassuring me he was also reassuring Ant.

The whole time Ant had been stretching his spine, extending it to his full length. He tilted his smooth chin into his chest, looking all the way along his nose almost to the point of going cross-eyed at Costas, before huffing air from flared nostrils. 'No?' Costas continued. 'Beer then?' Costas began to walk into the house, still holding my hand. I was quite sure he had already had one too many glasses of something because he clearly didn't care that Anton could see him touching me. 'Harper! Harper! We have guests. Pour some wine.'

We both kept refusing the offer, but he led us to a room with big French doors looking out to a perfectly manicured garden of shaped trees, and cherubs spewing water into ponds. Harper appeared, holding two glasses containing red wine, and welcomed us both with a brief air kiss. Her bleached blonde hair was flattened so tightly to her head she almost looked bald as the light reflected off the waxed shafts of hair.

Anton politely thanked her and took a deep swig from his glass. 'Now, where is my daughter?' he said, passing back the bowl-shaped glass towards Harper's thick, purple acrylic nails. Costas's eyes turned skyward over his chubby cheeks and pointed towards the garden. We both looked out into the night, at the cherubs and the pots, then blankly back at Costas and Harper.

'At the back of the garden there's a path. It goes into a big field. The kids have a campfire and tents. If you ruin Chloe's party, Anton Greenwood,' – he beat his finger on Anton's chest, and for a split second I got the feeling Anton might just snap the thing right off – 'I will make sure you regret it.'

Anton's face contorted into something between a smile and a snarl before he began to march down the garden. It wasn't their fault and Anton's irritation made my cheeks flush red. I could feel the heat of them as a breeze rolled in through the doors. I excused myself and put the drink in Costas's hand before my feet were tripping over themselves to keep up with Anton's long legs.

'Stop. Anton! Stop! You can't embarrass her like this. It's bad enough you've just embarrassed me. She doesn't deserve it. Please! You'll just push her further away,' I hissed into the ever-increasing darkness. There must have been over an acre of beautifully watered, soft grass before we would reach the back of the garden where the path was meant to be. 'Listen to me, you arse! Don't be so bloody pig-headed.' I tugged at his arm until eventually he stopped. It was only then that I could hear the distant sound of laughter and music fizzing up on the right- hand side of the lawn. 'Let me go and speak to her. Please. If I'm honest, I think I should check on her, but let her stay. If you want me to get her though, I will. Please, let me be the one to go,' I whispered, still holding his wrist as though Gaia's life depended on it. Possibly her social life did, but unlikely her life did.

Pulling his arm from my grip to rub the length of his face, he muttered something I didn't catch. This was followed by a mumbled 'Fine'. As soon as he had agreed I wished that it wasn't true and I didn't really have to appear out of the bushes into a party of teenagers. We both crept along the path and the sound of laughing teens became ever clearer over the music. Looking past a bush, my eyes adjusted to the firelight. At first, I couldn't find Gaia. There were fifteen or more figures glowing gold and red in the firelight. The night was beginning to take on a chill as I spotted Gaia in a pair of shorts, with Finn's denim jacket over her shoulders. She wasn't facing us. I took one step out from the path and saw she was holding a cigarette in her right hand. Finn pulled her in, kissing her, both of them swaying – clearly they'd been drinking. I didn't want to see this or be involved in breaking up her fun. I knew Anton would have seen the cigarette too and would be ready to jump out from behind me like a crazed Bigfoot, frightening all the children and saying, 'I told you so.'

Chloe had spotted me so I had no choice but to progress. I marched up to Gaia who, intent on kissing Finn, still hadn't noticed me.

'Gaia,' was all I needed to say for her to turn in towards Finn so quickly she caught him with the cigarette across the arm. They both started swearing in Greek, that much I was sure of, before Gaia turned back to me, her eyes wide in the firelight.

'Where's Dad? Please say it's just you, mou-mou.'

'No, he is in the bushes.'

'What?'

'It doesn't matter. The point is, you left the house and didn't tell anyone. Your dad went up the bloody wall with worry, Gaia. He wants you to come home. I persuaded him that I would check on you and maybe you should stay, but I see you're smoking, and you lied about it to him. Now I don't know what to do.' My stomach began to ache with the anxiety of realising that being a mum would never be easy and maybe I wasn't the natural I hoped I might be.

'I wasn't lying! I'm only smoking this because he upset me. I am not even smoking it! It made me cough so I am holding it.' She threw it down to the ground. 'Please let me stay, mou-mou. Can I be grounded tomorrow?'

I didn't know what to say. My eye darted around all of her friends. On one hand they had all smiled and were polite about my arrival, on the other I could see they were talking amongst themselves and I didn't need to speak Greek to understand teenagers. They had all been trusted by their parents. They were all allowed to camp together and have a drink or two. Gaia and Natalia were a little younger than most of them, but they were sensible girls, at least for their age.

'Listen, you promise me not to drink any more booze tonight, and no more cigarettes, and I'll deal with your father. Because I'll bloody well know if you do, Gaia Greenwood. Promise?'

'Yes, yes! Thank you, mou-mou!' She threw her arms about my neck, leaving Finn's jacket to fall to the ground. I made sure she had everything she needed and made my way back to my husband who I could only imagine had a fire twice as hot as the campfire burning in his guts.

It wasn't until we made it back to the car that he even spoke to me. I don't know that he was actually angry with me. It was more about his inability to take hold of the situation.

'I don't know why I have left her there. She lies to me and gets her own way.'

'She promised me—'

'Promised? How can a girl of lies promise things? No.'

'Anton, stop! She is fourteen, almost fifteen—'

'Yes, and might be pregnant and no wonder if she is off smoking and drinking!'

'Stop! This is Gaia. Let her be her age. She has been through so much and she is amazing. She said she hadn't smoked before tonight and I believe her. I told her you'd punish her tomorrow and she has accepted that. Personally, I think embarrassing her was punishment enough.'

Gaia arrived home around ten the next morning. Keres and I decided to go outside to pick lemons to make lemonade. Really, we just didn't want to be involved in any screaming that might take place. Gaia had seemed pretty clear-headed when she came in, and I felt reasonably confident that she hadn't drunk any more after I had left her. If she had, it couldn't have been much. Anton had put together a long list of dreadful chores for her as well as grounding her and banning her friends from coming over for two weeks.

When Keres and I decided it was time to make our way

back into the house, Gaia was sitting drinking a milkshake and reading over her long list of chores, while Anton sat next to her, watching over her. Presumably in case she had any questions. There was no shouting, no screaming. That was the main thing.

'Pinch punch, first of the month! *Kalo mina*! We're making lemonade,' I announced, waving lemons the size of small guinea pigs at them both.

Gaia's eyes caught mine. The corner of her mouth turned up and her cheekbones lifted the shape of her face into a heart. Anton and Gaia both declined to get involved in making the lemonade, but in doing so Gaia used the opportunity to thank me without words. To tell me she was grateful without even a whisper. Anton loved his daughter, but he wasn't a teenage girl and being the only parent for so long sometimes seemed to bring out extremes. In some desperate attempt to find the middle ground, he would often fly off and find no ground at all. As Keres and I made lemonade, I had to explain in hushed tones what "pinch punch, first of the month" meant.

Soon Gaia was outside picking up old fruit off the ground and watering plants as part of her punishment. Keres and I had replaced Anton and Gaia at the table, sipping our triumphant lemonade and scrolling through our phones. Ant had decided to have a lie-down on the sofa after having had almost no sleep the night before. The cortisol levels in our bedroom had been through the roof all night, from worry to anger to frustration back to anxiety, then five minutes of dreams and kicking off of the bedsheets, before he would start all over again. I contorted my body into a side stretch, clicking my spine at the memory of it all.

'Do you hear that?' Keres tilted her head like a dog waiting for the sound to manifest again.

'It was my spine! I didn't realise it was that loud.'

'No.' She got up and started towards the back door. After a few steps, I decided I might as well follow her. I could hear something too as I got nearer to the door. Stepping out into the midday heat left me squinting and blind. The noise was coming from the fruit trees. Keres was marching ahead, then jogging. My feet were hopping every other step to try to keep up.

Hunched over like a toadstool amongst the trees was Gaia, with a bucket half full of rotten fruit and half full of vomit next to her head. She was wearing a fitted, black strappy top and her rib cage was pulsing, with every bone seemingly visible. Between murmured, muddled cries and splutters of coughing, I dropped to her side, ordering Keres to get Anton.

'Gaia mou, how much did you drink last night, honestly?'

'Nothing after you left. I promise.' Her words were said into the dirt and overshadowed by the multitude of wasps hanging around the fruity, sick bucket. I began to frantically rub her back as though that would magically help, my fingers noting every bump of her spinal column.

'It's okay. I believe you. I believe you.'

In no time, Ant was running up to be with us and swiftly took over, scooping her up into his arms and carefully carrying her to her room, leaving me to deal with the bucket.

Chapter 18

It was a Thursday evening and Keres had gone out with Akis. I knew Anton had so much that he wanted to ask Gaia, after more of her on-and-off days of vomiting. He had tried to persuade himself that it was because she didn't want to do all the chores, and even bulimia got called into question before being quickly dismissed as "not fitting the bill". I knew he had been coming to the same questions and possible conclusions I had. He was too afraid to voice them, particularly to Gaia. He had gently tried to edge that way by asking if she would go for a blood test "to see what it might show up". Gaia hadn't been interested.

While Anton was washing off the thin layer of dust that appeared every other day on the cars, I decided it was time I went to Gaia for a chat myself.

'Hey you. Can we talk?' I stepped into her room. Books and papers were spread across her bed. After missing so much school right at the end of term, she'd been left with a lot to catch up on. She quickly piled them back up, put them on her desk and placed herself on the fluffy stool in front of it. I sat on her bed opposite her. I took a deep inhale and held it momentarily, not wanting to ask what I knew I had to ask. 'I am so sorry to ask this Gaia, but I think it's important that I do. Are you ... Could you possibly be ... pregnant?'

'No, don't be insane.' She didn't flinch. Her dark brows fell into thin lines pressing down on her eyes. She began to gently shake her head.

'Okay, you're sure? You haven't even been near any – oh god, don't make me say it – any sperm?' I'm sure my whole face was pink. At least in Corfu I had a year-round tan to damp down any added colour that rose to my cheeks. I hung my head, letting my hair cover my face. This time she didn't answer. When I looked up, her body was still facing me but her face was as red as mine and she was looking to her right. Not looking. Facing to her right, with her eyes tightly shut. Blocking me out. 'Gaia, it's okay. You're almost fifteen. You and Finn have been together for a while. I understand sometimes things happen.'

She had shrunk down, both in weight and in her posture too. There wasn't much of her to begin with and the on-and- off vomiting had left her legs gangly and bony and her high cheekbones were bordering on making her look like a Halloween skeleton. She normally sat tall and elegantly poised. Now her hands were tucked under her legs and her body was curled in on itself.

'Nothing's happened,' she whispered. 'I can't be pregnant.' Her teeth were gritted, but she opened her eyes and faced me again. Her olive skin was sallow; she didn't look like the vibrant girl she had once been. I felt like I could vomit too. Anton could hardly keep himself together each time that he saw her, and whenever he squeezed her tiny body tightly I thought she might snap.

'Come here.' We both stood up and I held her in my arms, pressing my face into her hair. It wasn't its usual satin threads. It hung limp and slightly greasy on her head. 'I love you, Gaia. You're the priority. I think maybe we should go to the doctor's tomorrow. For a blood test.'

'Can I ask a favour?'

'Of course!' I pulled back, holding her shoulders. I could feel the workings of her joints in my fingers.

'Natalia has a book for me. It's to help with a project we are doing together. Could you go and get it for me? Please.'

'Of course I can! And the blood test?'

She pressed her lips together but nodded in agreement. Even she knew her sickness had gone on for too long.

I came downstairs to find Anton chatting on his phone at the dining table. I pulled out a chair, making a horrid screeching noise as I did so.

'Who was that?'

'It was Basil about the pool you want put in.'

'Ooh, my wedding gift. And it's not just me! Gaia wants one too.'

'Yep. He will bring Michail, his son, as he will take over the business soon and so Michail oversees most bespoke jobs. He is one of Akis's friends. They will be here tomorrow to measure and look at the position.'

'Hmm – bespoke, hey? Sounds expensive. Ah, that reminds me. I want to talk to you about my inheritance and my mum's old place. I need to go and get a book from Natalia that Gaia needs. Remind me when I'm home. But, more importantly than all of that though, Gaia has agreed to a blood test!'

Ant crossed himself and came round the table to kiss my

head and my hands, thanking me over and over. Before he could sit back down, I tapped the table, ready to push back my chair, but Anton waved a hand and tapped his finger. Then placed himself next to me at the head of the table to face me on the corner.

'No, no tell me the rest now. I don't want to forget. Gaia can wait for her book.'

'Well, it's just ... Keres is my sister, and the inheritance – at very least from my mum – was for any living heirs. But I think Mama and Papa would have wanted her to have some of theirs too.'

'Okay. So what are you thinking?'

I hesitated for a moment, rubbing my palms along the smooth cool oak.

'Half.'

'You want to give a nineteen-year-old almost half of a million pounds? You do not even know her, Melodie-Mou.'

'Please don't be like that. I do know her. And she's my sister. It doesn't actually matter if I know her or not. It doesn't even matter that she is nineteen. She is a living heir of my mother so she really is entitled to half of the house if we sell it. I know outside of that Mum didn't have much, but why not give her an equal share of my grandparents' money too?'

'You were named in their will. No one else—'

'But they didn't know about her. Or what Mum was going through or that Keres was adopted.' It all began to stick in my throat as though I'd accidentally swallowed superglue and it was beginning to harden. 'I—'

'Melodie, it is not your fault. You did not know what was happening, and Keres was lucky. It sounds like she was adopted by kind people.'

I gave a couple of quick nods, but my eyes were already on the verge of making their own swimming pool. 'We can talk more later. I have other things I want to talk to you about when I'm home.' With that I was up and heading towards my keys and bag. He came up and caught my hand. I hesitated, giving him just enough time to drag me back to him and settle me into his chest. The weight of his arms pulled me into the synthetic but charming smell of washing powder.

'Just think about it, Melodie. It's your money. I don't care what you do with it, but please be sure. She is very young and honestly, I think you need to be careful of her. There is no rush.'

'What does that mean? Be careful of her.'

He turned away, but I demanded he explain himself.

'I just do not feel comfortable being alone with her. I'm being silly. Ignore me.'

'No. What do you mean?'

'Sometimes her lips, they linger too long on my cheek to say goodbye and ... I sound silly. Just ignore me. Go, get Gaia's book. We shall talk later.'

I left soon after.

Chapter 19

Natalia had left the book with the bartender. Which just so happened to be Nico. As soon as he saw me walking up to the bar, his smile changed to a pout and he began to shake his head. His hair was longer and shaggier than ever. He pushed it out of his eyes in such an over-exaggerated way, I had to roll mine. His arm came up at the same time and he clearly squeezed his bicep to impress anyone who was looking. I thought he was a bit of a skinny thing, cute, nice eyes, but not for me.

'Have you come to seduce me too?'

'Hello, Nico. May I please have Gaia's book?'

'No. You tell me why you cannot be more like your sister,' he said.

I had very little patience. None of us had slept properly for ages, I'd got my period two days before and the ache of knowing I wasn't pregnant was enough to make me snappy. Let alone everything with Gaia.

'What are you talking about? Surely we are alike in that neither of us said yes to you.'

To this, Nico actually spat. Not intentionally, but the pop of his lips and the pah noise that shot out of him landed on the wooden bar in front of me. He laughed so hard he didn't even notice. I just waited, with arms tightly folded across my chest.

'I have seen Keres many, many times. Many late nights,' he winked.

I almost wanted to poke his open eye right out. 'What are you suggesting? I don't have time for your lies and nonsense, Nico.'

'I am hurt, Melo. I have not lied to you. Your sister, she is … freak.'

My eyes were shrinking into slits, narrowing down. I didn't know what to say. Was he right? What reason would he have to lie? Anton didn't want to be alone with her.

'Are you winding me up, Nico? Why are you telling me this?'

He shrugged in response. His white, short-sleeved shirt, oversized on his slender frame, scrunched in response to his nonchalance. I darted my eyes about. There were no customers at the bar; they were all sat at tables with drinks and menus in their hands. I decided to sit down on one of the wooden stools. 'What really happened?'

'You want to know?' He threw a tea towel over his shoulder and leant on the bar. As he leaned in, his face was only a matter of inches from mine.

I nodded.

'I took her for dinner and she wants me, she tells me. She takes me back to my car and—'

'Stop. That's enough. Give me the book.'

'You don't look like sisters.'

'Now, Nico.'

He reached behind him and passed me the book. I made my way between the tables towards the street and away from Nico.

I stood holding the book to my chest for a moment before turning round and marching back in. 'How many times have you ... have you seen her, Nico?'

The side of his mouth turned up and he slowly turned a glass in his tea towel.

'Jealous?'

I squeezed my eyes almost shut again and wrinkled my nose.

'Okay, okay.' He held the glass up as some kind of defence. 'I think maybe five times. Mostly late at night after my work. I pick her up at your home. We drive around and ...' He bit his bottom lip and wiggled his eyebrows like a cartoon.

'You know she is seeing Akis, don't you?'

Now it was time for him to frown, for him to seem confused, for him to stop in his tracks. The glass he had been rotating and drying in his hands was suddenly still.

I didn't say a thing more. I went straight home.

Gaia was asleep by the time I arrived at the house. I took the book back down the stairs and left it on the dining table. Keres was still out, I assumed with Akis, but clearly I didn't know anything. Maybe Anton was right and I should think about the money a little more. Mum's house was by rights half Keres's. I couldn't cheat her out of money, especially when she needed it much more than we did. As I went to find Anton, my phone buzzed. It was Harry:

We have a healthy son! 8lbs 4, mother and baby doing well.

I wanted to shout for Anton, but I didn't want to wake Gaia. I ran upstairs to find him sat on our bed, with his face in his hands. I opened my mouth to tell him the news but quickly closed it along with the door. Sitting down next to him, I wrapped my arms as far around him as I could. He didn't move as I stretched around his shoulders.

'She'll be okay,' I whispered in his ear.

At last his hands dropped, knocking my arms away. He crossed himself and looked at me. He almost looked as sick as Gaia. Obviously not as thin, but his green eyes were dull like beaten stones that sat deep in his skull, and shadows fell on his face even in the light.

'You don't know that. She looks so small.' He was barely audible.

The loudest sound was the clock ticking on the wall, counting the painful moments of silence. I took his left hand in mine. He wore his new wedding ring on the left, not how he had with his first wife, not the Greek way, on the right. I smoothed out the small hairs on the back of his hand with my thumbs in an attempt to comfort him in any way I could. 'She is going for the blood test tomorrow. I think she has had a better day today too. She ate more of her chicken.'

'Do you think she is pregnant? I think I might prefer that to the idea of her being ill,' he said. His voice was like a thin line drawn with a ruler.

'I can't be sure, but I don't think so. She told me she couldn't be, but … There was something she didn't want to tell me. I dunno. It's so hard to say. The blood tests will answer that one easily enough.' I pressed my fingers into the hollow under my cheek bones, squashing and contorting my face until I let them drop to my bare knees. 'She will be okay. It's probably just some tummy bug thing. It's only been a couple of weeks.'

'You'd better be right.' A distinct quiver appeared in his

vocal cords that he had been holding back. 'Come here,' he said, and took my hand, moving me across to sit on his lap. I wrapped my hands around his head like a turban made of arms. We softly rocked as the clock kept ticking our time away. Eventually, I remembered the news I had for him.

'Maria had the baby. It's a boy,' I whispered.

Chapter 20

The next afternoon, Anton took Gaia for her blood test and I picked up some roses and took them to Maria who was home already. Before she'd had the baby, she'd told me that Greece had one of the highest rates of C-sections in the world. Many of them were planned. She thought some people used it as a statement of wealth and that others were afraid of natural birth, as many islands don't have neonatal care units if something goes wrong. Planning when and how the baby was delivered took away some of that fear. Maria didn't care about any of that. She wanted to keep it natural and she had been lucky to have it her way. She had said, 'If we were meant to have the baby pulled out of our tummies, we'd give birth from our belly buttons.' That image had stayed with me longer than it should have.

When I arrived at her bungalow, Jenny and Stavros were buzzing about cleaning the kitchen and unpacking shopping. Harry's parents were coming as soon as they could get a flight, now that the baby had arrived. Maria was sitting on a lilac chair in the corner of her living room next to an open window. Her eyes were closed and she was swaying with the lilac-and-white curtains in the breeze. She looked more beautiful than I'd ever seen her, even despite her exhaustion. She wasn't wearing lots of make-up like she normally would, only a little mascara. A very plain, navy button-down dress loosely moved about her body. Perhaps she was humming; I couldn't be sure. All the running around, and feet tapping about the house, couldn't penetrate that room. In that moment, in her space, there was calm. Their little boy was wrapped in a fine, blue sheet as pale as it could be and still be blue. My bare feet crept towards her, and I placed the roses carefully on the white Perspex coffee table. As I did, she opened her eyes as though a light had turned on in her mind and shone straight out of them.

'How are you?' I whispered, almost just mouthing the words. My tiptoeing continued but at a quicker pace to place myself on my knees by her side, careful not to kneel on my white skirt as I hovered over the baby. She didn't answer me. Her round face turned to the boy instead, as he screwed up all his features to fill his face with old man wrinkles, but ones that were ever so sweet.

'This is Noah,' she said. 'Noah, say hello to Melo.' Then on cue he gave an enormous yawn for such a tiny creature.

'He is beautiful, Maria. Congratulations.' I felt overwhelmingly happy for her. Emotions wrapped around me so tightly they began to squeeze at me as though they were intentionally trying to push tears out.

'None of that,' she waved her hand at my face, making Noah squirm towards her. She hadn't stopped her meditative swaying.

Harry came in with water for us both, brimming with ice.

'He's beautiful, isn't he?' he said, with a smile so deep it was hidden at first glance. It wasn't beaming or hugely on show. Instead, it came out in his bones. The smile lifted his cheeks, changing the contours of his face, and his eyes creased in the corners. His lips had no need to pull wide, only one side gently lifted, almost as though he knew he should contain the smile. Pull it back in. Because if he didn't, he might actually burst.

'Yes, he clearly takes after his mother.' I couldn't help but laugh at him and nod as I spoke.

'You're not wrong there,' he said.

Maria sat a little straighter and wiggled her shoulders slightly at the admiration. She told me her birth story, how she'd been pretty lucky and the labour wasn't too long for a first-time mother. Harry piped in now and then to say how proud he was and how brave she had been. They were rather perfect.

'How's Gaia? Any better?' Maria's tone changed. It was lower and her face was pulled into her "tell me everything" look. 'She has lost a lot of weight, and it's not like she had any to lose. Anton has taken her for a blood test today, otherwise I would have brought them with me.' I opened my mouth to carry on, but the sound that appeared didn't belong to me. It was little Noah whose mouth hung open too. Only the noise was high and screeching, a bit like a terrified kitten.

'He needs feeding again,' Maria said, and began to shuffle around.

'I'll leave you to it. I'll be back when you're more settled. Thank you for letting me see you all though. He really is beautiful.'

Chapter 21

I arrived back from Maria's to an empty house. I couldn't stop thinking about when I might be pregnant and about when my mother was pregnant with me. It was all scrunching around in my head and I couldn't stop it. In that moment, I remembered the photo Anton had found in Keres's room, the only one I had of my parents together. Perhaps it was seeing tiny Noah, or that life felt so out of control, either way I kicked off my flip-flops and sprinted up the stairs, heading straight into Keres's room. The desire to study the photo of my mother and have it in my hands again consumed me.

Keres only had a holdall packed with a rotation of outfits. It was stuffed under the bed. She kept the room so tidy it would be easy to think no one had ever slept there. I dragged the bag from its hiding place and quickly found the photo in a side pocket. It wasn't the only thing in there. Underneath was the yellow-gold necklace I'd seen in the shop when I took Keres to get something new for her date with Nico. I clutched it to my chest as my mind vaulted from one explanation to the next. Looking around the black-and-white bedroom with its big print of Audrey Hepburn smoking her cigarette didn't produce any likely answers as to why the necklace was there. I looked at Audrey accusingly. She would know exactly what was going on if she could bloody well talk. Then the door opened behind me. I didn't turn around. I couldn't. I just sat on my knees with my skirt all ruched up around me.

'Melodie?'

'I – I was looking for my photo. I should've asked. I – ' I still didn't want to look round. I'd forgotten there was a full-length mirror in front of me. When I looked up, I could see Keres hovering over me with tears in her eyes. She carefully walked around me and the bag to kneel down next to me, pulling her jeans up as she placed herself in front of me.

'You find your gift,' she sniffed and wiped the skin under her right eye. She took the necklace out of my hands, carefully opened the latch and placed it around my neck, kneeling over me. I looked down at the striking piece I'd admired on our outing. It was a very odd piece really, but I liked it. Carefully, I pulled my hazel hair from where it was tucked into the necklace, freeing it to dance its way down between my shoulder blades. My painted pink lips hung open as my chin stayed pressed against my chest, studying the yellow circle hanging across my chest.

'Thank you.' I coughed as my voice caught. 'Thank you. It's so thoughtful, and I've been so dreadful looking through your bag.' My eyes started to fill too. She had gone and done something so lovely for me, and there I was scrabbling around in her bag like an unwelcome mouse in corn.

'Sorry I am having the photo. I saw it in the boxes when we look through them together. I just want to look at them. I should have asked. The necklace is beautiful on you. It looks nice, with all white.' She smiled. Her fingers pointed across my off-the-shoulder white top and white, ruffled skirt.

I let the corner of my mouth turn up into a smile.

'I know it is a hard time,' she said, 'with Gaia ill, and I am here. In the way. But I am thankful to find you.'

'I'm thankful to find you too.'

'I have been thinking. Maybe I go back to Athens. Or find somewhere. I have been here too long. I think I am in the way.'

'No, please don't go yet! I feel like you've only just arrived. Please! Who would run with me? You can't go! Take some time and think about it.' I nodded harshly and clambered to my feet, repeating, 'Please think about it', before I left the room. If I left, she couldn't argue with me about it. I made it all the way to the bottom of the stairs before I realised I was still holding the photo of our parents. I brought it up from my side to study it, there at the bottom of the stairs.

She did look a lot like Adam, at least the same colour hair and that angelic, round face. He was very pale though, almost porcelain white with rosy cheeks and a cheeky smile. She had lived in Greece her entire life and therefore had a red-gold tan. He had lived on the island, and from what I had gathered from reading my mother's notes, other places beforehand too. Germany, Athens – all over. I wondered if he had managed that deep red tan or if he'd stayed pale. If he had enjoyed the sun or stayed in. It was easier to keep him as a two-dimensional image rather than to start humanising him so I stopped myself before I tried to think about possible answers. I put the photo on the shelf next to the landline. Keres might want to look at it again. And for all that he was evil, my mum was good and if he hadn't been that way, Keres and I wouldn't have even existed. So I left them there, smiling out at the sofas and coffee table.

I was still standing there when Anton and Gaia walked in the door. In my daze, I'd forgotten how dreadful she looked. Her thick, dark hair was pulled into a messy bun, which just made her face look even more drawn. Dark circles framed her eyes, and just looking at her, I nearly gave a small gasp. I managed to divert the sound into a 'Welcome home'. Or at least I hoped I had. Her legs were so thin that her normally fitted black shorts looked baggy around her almost inverted thighs. I think she had put on an oversized T-shirt on purpose to cover the majority of her frail-looking frame.

'How did it go? Come sit down.' I breezed across to my right and sat where Anton would normally sit in the big brown leather armchair. I needed the comfort of almost being swaddled by its delightful hide. Gaia sat opposite me on the two-seater and Anton not far from me on the three.

'It'll be a few days. It's Friday so ...' She shrugged. Gaia was a practical soul. Of course, she knew something wasn't right in her body, but she wasn't going to be a headless chicken or a hypochondriac about it. Anton on the other hand had gone backwards into babying her and smiling when he was around her. Whenever they were together, they soon emulated a patient lioness and an annoying cub. Under almost any other circumstances it would have been amusing to watch, but the underlying reality was too painful. Anton was terrified and being a six-foot-four-and-a-half bashful lion cub wasn't helping much.

'They didn't seem too worried.' Gaia pulled her knees into her chest, curling into a ball like a little cat in the corner of the couch with only her green eyes looking out from around their black lashes and dark circles.

Keres came running down the stairs and asked Gaia questions in Greek, dropping down next to her, and nodding a lot at Gaia's answers. The girls were fast friends, which had made Keres being in the house so much easier. Something was said by Keres that made Gaia frantically shake her head. She latched onto Keres's arm and looked from me to Anton. Then she burst out with, 'Keres shouldn't go. She can't go! Please let her stay!'

I began to shake my head too. 'I think she should stay too, at least a little longer. But the decision is ultimately hers.'

There was a knock at the door and Anton jumped up, tapping at his head and chatting to himself in Greek. He opened the door and more Greek buzz flooded in as he did. Basil and Michail came in with their matching blue polo shirts and dusty, black shorts. As Basil saw Gaia bounding towards him, I didn't need to understand his words; his body language and face changed completely. He frowned and pulled her to him, holding her little face in his leathery hands. His concern was obvious. Gaia just looked down at him, being a couple of inches taller, as Anton explained everything over his shoulder.

Michail edged towards me as Keres and I hovered in the background of the scene that was playing out. 'You must be Melodie. I am Michail. It is nice to finally meet you. I am so sorry to miss your wedding, the one time I go away...'

He was a touch taller than his father, perhaps equal to my five foot eight, with a muscular frame. He looked enough like Basil that I could imagine that when Basil was young, he would have been a handsome man. The biggest difference between the men was Basil's bald, shaved head versus Michail's full head of curly black springs. They had matching almond-shaped black eyes and fine eyebrows.

I reassured him then introduced Keres. Basil came over to me with a sombre smile after seeing Gaia and gave me a kiss on the cheek, before being introduced to Keres. We didn't give the whole explanation of Keres; we just said she was my sister and things quickly moved on. Gaia decided the day had already been enough for her and a nap was in order.

The rest of us followed Anton out to the garden, past the patio and the clusters of well-kept lemon and olive trees, and into the clearing.

'Iolanthe would be so happy, Anton. She would have loved you Melodie, I am sure of it. She worried for this one after Katerina died. Look at him now!' Anton looked across at me lifting half his face in a smile.

'I am a very lucky man.'

'Yes. Much more than you deserve, I fear.' Michail quipped and Anton's instant reaction was to try to flick him. He quickly dodged and they all went into Greek and were laughing.

When they stopped acting like children, they stayed in Greek to discuss the pool. I sat down on the swing chair looking over at them and was joined by Keres. We watched as much debate took place about the position of the pool. They all marched from one spot to the other, waving their hands. Michail held a big black folder and kept opening it to show images to Ant, or to make a note or to write down measurements. The fact the land had a slope to it seemed to be in discussion, based on the way their hands were pointing, and even the gaps between some of trees were measured out, presumably to see how diggers and such would make their way to the clearing.

After thirty minutes, the men were red in the face from the chatting and the midday heat. Basil and Michail were off again but would be back in the coming weeks to start work.

Over the weekend just the four of us spent the entire time together. Gaia started to be able to eat again, and by the Sunday, other than still being thin, she looked healthier and was back to her normal, bouncy self in most ways. Anton began to relax and didn't have the silly smile stuck on his face. I felt like he was ours again, not the hollow cave I'd been seeing for the past week or so.

On Sunday night we all stayed up late. Keres joined Anton and me in sharing a glass of wine to celebrate Gaia's good streak, while Gaia enjoyed homemade lemonade and a chocolate milkshake before bed. It was nice to see her enjoy things again after only being able to handle water and bread for days. We played UNO out in the garden. Keres had never played before which none of us could believe. Once she had the basics down, she had us all in fits of giggles at her vindictive nature. She would slam a card to the table, eyes wild in delight to get one over us, in particular poor Anton. It was the most animated I'd seen her. She was really fitting into our little family unit. We had spoken again about her leaving and I'd persuaded her that if she left, it should only be for a day or two. Luckily, she agreed. I didn't want Gaia to take a bad turn at the idea of Keres leaving again. Apparently, Akis had been asking her to stay with him. I flinched a little, thinking back to what Nico had said. Not that I'd told anyone about it, not even Anton. It likely wasn't true anyway. Nico always wanted to needle me for his own pleasure. Either way, I found it unbearable, the idea of sneaking around or cheating on people.

Eventually, around one in the morning we all decided that

there were too many mosquitos hanging about and we should get some sleep. As soon as I took one step into our room, I pulled my baggy checked dress over my head and flopped down onto the bed.

'I think I've been bitten on my toe,' I said, rubbing my feet together, too lazy to sit up and use my hand.

Anton threw his shirt towards the en suite, where the laundry basket lived, but it just hit the door and slid to the ground. Jumping onto the bed next to me, he made the whole thing jiggle.

'I'll help take your mind off it,' he said, with the silliest grin.

He'd been working in the garden a lot without his shirt on and his olive skin had gone a deep brown from the June sun. He picked up my foot with the itchy toe and placed it on his shoulder, kissing my ankle and along the inside of my leg. He slowed down as he reached my thigh, then glanced along my body to the curve of my neck. Wrapping his arm about my waist, he then pulled me on top of him into an embrace. I'd missed having his attention and affection. We paused for a moment, holding each other before his mouth found the tender skin under my ear. He kissed me, inhaled me, pulled me in, in a way that I could never leave or get enough of. My fingers moved around his tense shoulders, smoothing them, reassuring them, enjoying them.

'I've missed this,' he whispered into my ear, as though he had been reading my mind through his wandering hands.

I pressed my forehead to his and we were eye to eye, so close it was impossible to focus on more than the tiniest detail – the lines of pale and dark green in his eyes, the curve of his black lashes.

'Me too.' Then our mouths met in a deep and desperate

collision, open to each other, unable to hide. We spent time kissing and caressing like when we were first together, exploring each other into the depths of the night. Slowly, we freed ourselves from the constraints of any remaining clothes and drifted across the bed without control as our bodies led us along. One moment my head was hanging off the edge of the bed, as I let Anton's tongue create waves over my skin as powerful as the currents in the deepest ocean, then the next, I was on my knees pulling him into me like I was a siren he would never escape.

We only managed about two or three hours sleep before Keres was knocking on our door. Anton sat upright like a marionette, with someone tugging on the strings. He grabbed a robe and strode to the door. There was some muttering before he turned to me and said, 'Gaia's being sick again.'

Chapter 20

Keres left later that morning. Both sets of Gaia's grandparents had wanted to do something to cheer her up and help. Athena and Chris sent her a new NASA T-shirt from the UK and Katerina's parents came round to see her one morning. I got on well enough with Helena and Vaso, although I knew they didn't like how quickly Anton and I had got married. They'd expressed their concerns. Helena hadn't been able to hold it in. Maybe she was worried I would edge them out. It was Gaia's voice of reason and reassurance that had settled things. All I wanted was family. I didn't want to cause rifts. There would be no point. I just felt lucky to have people in my life I wanted to be with. That was enough for me.

Anton had been very hurt by it all though, much more so than he had ever said out loud. I could just sense a guard going up towards them. Helena and Vaso had invited us over for dinner about a month after we had announced our engagement. I think we both knew the whole time they wanted to say something, by all the little looks they'd been giving each other through the meal. It had been Helena who eventually said something. Only Greek was spoken in their house, which was fine by me. Ant always translated and I was just happy to be included. I didn't know what was said first-hand though. The only plus was that watching people could tell me more than words at times, and I knew that they weren't trying to be hurtful. I think perhaps it had come out that way to Anton at the time though. On the way back, he had stopped the car on a dark road looking over a sheer drop down to an expanse of tall trees, all of which were shadows and silver from the moon. He had squeezed my hand, saying, "You and Gaia are my everything, but you, Melodie, are my true love. I would do anything for you." He didn't need to reassure me. I knew how he felt. I really wanted Gaia to have two sets of grandparents and loved that they visited to make her feel better no matter how they might feel about me.

Other than getting up once to see her grandparents, Gaia slept for almost two days straight while Anton quietly pottered in the garden helping Michail and Basil – that was when he wasn't pottering outside her door. I had managed to spend a little time getting to know Basil and Michail myself, making sure they came in to have lunch. They were so thankful and polite. Michail didn't say much at first – he was so shy – but I soon realised he had a wicked sense of humour, and often came out with little asides in conversation or silly sarcastic remarks. He wasn't much like his father who always seemed relaxed and confident. I wondered if Basil had always been that way or had just grown into it.

On the Thursday, Anton had a meeting with the company in charge of the rental properties about replacing a bathroom suite. I had had a chat with him a few days before about how unwell Gaia was and how she had still been trying so hard with her school work. With that in mind, I said, why not call up the lovely lady at San Stefanos Stray Cats and have a chat about adopting one? Ant wasn't keen so I called her up in the end to see if she thought there was a suitable kitten that needed adopting. I told Anton that there were two to choose from, and when he was done with the rental stuff he was to head over and pick one of them up. I knew it would put a smile on Gaia's face; animals are so therapeutic. Anton agreed even if he had looked like a sulky teenager with folded arms and a huffy tone.

Typically, while he was out, the phone call came about Gaia's blood test. She was looking a little better and had asked for a chocolate milkshake, which we kept taking as a good sign. Although the doctor on the line did speak English, they wanted to speak to Gaia directly or to Anton as her legal guardian. When Gaia got off the phone, she passed it back to me and flopped back down on to her bed, with her arms splayed out as if she were about to be crucified.

'Nothing,' she said. 'They found nothing.'

'Okay. What are they going to do now then?' I pulled her green fluffy stool closer to her bed and sat on it.

'They want more tests. They have now sent one of my samples off to … I'm not sure I know the English. To see if I have eaten something I shouldn't, I guess.'

'Like an allergy?'

'Mmm … sort of.' She began to close her eyes.

I stood up, smoothed the hair from her cold, sweaty brow and kissed her forehead before leaving her to sleep, and made my way downstairs.

The bottom of the stairs was like the mouth of a river opening up towards the front door, with a banister either side. It felt appealing to just sit there like a puddle and wait for my Anton to come home from inspecting the property.

The button on my jean shorts dug into my stomach as I sat all scrunched up. I stretched my legs out in front of me and lay back against the stairs, looking up at the ceiling far above. Eventually, closing my eyes, I tried to empty my mind of any negative thoughts, only to hear the distant retching of poor Gaia. I jumped to my feet and sprinted back up the stairs. The poor girl's head was back in the bin that was by her bed. I ran my fingers through the sides of her hair, carefully gathering the strands away from the chocolate milk that was pouring back out of her. When her stomach eventually relaxed, she was shaking. I helped her fragile body back onto her bed and pulled the sheet up around her. I quickly nipped into her en suite and grabbed a handful of toilet roll and dashed back to wipe her mouth and her brow. By the time I'd finished sorting her out, she was curled into her pillow fast asleep.

As I looked about the room and her en suite, I saw it was not the same as it would normally be. Gaia liked to have everything in order. The shelf above her bed was normally lined with books colour-coordinated to form a rainbow, and she rarely left clothes hanging out of drawers or on the floor. As it was, everything was everywhere. Anton had put her clean clothes away as best he could before she'd asked him to stop being a pain, but something really had to be done. Even the en suite was littered with used towels. I took it upon myself to be useful and started by picking up the towels to be washed. Then I decided I should empty her bathroom bin. In Greece this is done every single day as toilet paper can't be flushed away and is placed in a bin instead. Usually, Gaia emptied her own bin, but I was sure it hadn't been done for at least a day. I carefully removed the lid to tie up the bag. Sticking out of the tissues was a pregnancy test.

Suddenly my heart was audible in my ears. I looked behind me; she was still lying curled up in her bed. I bent down and carefully pulled it out. Negative. She must have been worried she was pregnant too. Yet another thing I had to tell Anton, but I really didn't want him to murder Finn. He was meant to come over later that afternoon. Gaia had been putting him off and putting him off since the party. They hadn't FaceTimed or anything like that. I don't think she wanted him to see how thin she was getting. He had turned up at the door a few times and Anton had sent him away. Each time he had hesitated before doing as he was told.

I pushed the test back into the bin, leaving it unemptied, and quickly washed my hands. Before I left Gaia again, I woke her up and made her drink half a glass of water for fear she might dehydrate if she didn't. I stood over her for a moment. She was a child, only fourteen. I thought of my mother and how she had got pregnant at sixteen with me. Finn was sixteen already and Gaia would be fifteen in a couple of months. Although I knew the legal age of consent in Greece was fifteen, I knew Anton wouldn't be at all happy if he thought too much was going on. I pushed to one side my own feelings about what had happened with my mother and me, and quietly left Gaia sleeping on her bed.

Chapter 23

When Anton came back from sorting the rental properties, he had a car full of things. He'd been to buy a pet carrier before going to collect the kitten and had then got everything anyone buying a cat could ever possibly need. That included scratching posts, bowls and beds. It was only as he brought in the beds that I realised there was two of everything.

'Wait, Anton, why is there one blue and one pink bed? I don't think Gaia would mind what colour you went with.'

'Well, you see, the kittens to pick from were brother and sister. I didn't really like the idea of separating them. Yes? So … I got both. I got two kittens.'

I put my hand to my mouth trying hard to cover my laughter. Anton just let out a deep breath and skulked back to the car to get the cat carrier, which apparently contained two little kittens. As he brought them in, I had a quick peek at the two little creatures meowing and crying in their plastic cage. I followed him up the stairs. I wanted to see Gaia's face when she saw them.

When we entered her room, she sat bolt upright on her bed

at the sound of the kittens.

'What's that?' She was pointing at the carrier, eyes wide and darting from me to Anton, but her finger still remained on the container.

'They are for you. It was Melodie's idea,' Ant said, placing down the carrier and shutting the door. After kissing us and thanking us both through teary eyes, Gaia sat in front of the grey plastic container and carefully opened the door. Neither kitten wanted to come out. They were both still making a fuss and were letting their fur puff out slightly. Gaia used this time to name the pair. The little black-and-white one, a girl, she decided to call Looper, because of a Bruce Willis film she liked, and the boy, which was black all over, would be called Donnie. Apparently, because she loved the film *Donnie Darko*. I thought maybe she was a bit young to have watched it, but I didn't want to ruin the mood by saying that, and I was pretty sure Anton hadn't seen it. I wondered if the same was true of Looper, but I hadn't seen that one.

'Right, I need to put some washing out,' I announced. As I left the room, I remembered that the doctor had called, and we hadn't told Anton. I popped my head back around the door. 'Gaia, don't forget to tell your dad about the doctor.' Then I looked over at Anton. 'See you downstairs.'

When he eventually came down, I was waiting for him in the garden under the shade of a lemon tree.

'I thought you had left me,' he said, putting his hands up to his eyes to shield them from the sun.

'Never.' I outstretched one hand towards him as he came close.

He took my fingers with his and sat down next to me. 'Did she tell you that they are sending some of her blood for a toxicology report?'

'No, she told me allergies. But, to be fair, she did say she didn't know the English for some of it so I guess that was it.' I leant forward so I could twist and face him more.

He let out a faint laugh. 'That is funny. The words sound almost the same. She wouldn't know that, I suppose.'

'How's she doing with the kittens?'

'They have made their way out and all three were on Gaia's bed.'

'I thought they weren't allowed on the furniture.' I looked at him with a raised eyebrow.

He just shrugged with a small smile.

'It was nice to see her a little more animated. She was sick again earlier.' From the corner of my eye I saw his head jerk to face me, before he rubbed at his forehead with his thumb and forefinger.

We sat holding hands as insects of all sizes hurried along around us. Everything was busy except for us. We stayed perfectly still, unchanged, as the moments passed. So still, in fact, that a delightful iridescent green-blue butterfly landed on Anton's flip-flop for a moment before disappearing. After about twenty minutes or so of peace we could hear movement on the driveway followed by a knock on the door.

'It's Finn.' I tapped Anton's leg and scrambled to my feet.

As we came in the back door, Gaia was already making her way down the stairs, quicker than I'd seen her since the weekend. She'd washed and put on make-up too. She looked better but still not well and bounding down the stairs had left her clutching her stomach and taking slow deep breaths. Anton ordered her to sit on the sofa and went to open the door. A demand like that would normally be met with some resistance. Instead, she just shuffled, knees bent, to sit with me on the sofa. I asked her where the kittens were. Apparently, they'd fallen asleep on her bed.

Finn trailed behind Anton, who, unknown to Finn, had quite a pleased look on his face. His cheekbones were high on his face, and he tried to hide his smile by looking at the floor as he moved across the open space, but to me it was obvious. As Finn appeared from behind Anton, I could see why. He held out a large bunch of pink roses. As soon as he was past Anton, and could see Gaia, any hint of bashfulness flew away with Anton's little butterfly friend. Finn's pace changed immediately, taking long strides to get to her. He kissed her head and knelt down on the floor next to her. For the briefest panic-stricken moment, I thought he might propose. Luckily, he quickly slipped onto the sofa next to her. I'd often watched the way he would give Gaia little looks or touch her hand when he thought no one was looking. They were sweet together.

Remembering his manners, he said hello to me and asked in perfect English how I was. He was quite a plain-looking boy, really, with an oval face and long, straight nose with a rounded tip, and pleasant brown eyes that slightly turned up in the corners, but he made the best of himself. His curly hair was shaved short at the sides and left longer on top, the way a lot of the boys in the villages wore it. He would swim most days, according to Gaia. The key thing that made him attractive to girls, other than his physique, possibly, was his confidence. Aside from when he was around Anton, who made him flinch at times, he had charisma. He made Gaia laugh, often very loudly. This was probably more noticeable to me as, often, everyone spoke in Greek when he was about. His English was good but not to the highest level of conversation. Having said that, he had been trying more and more to speak English around me. I think he secretly wanted to go to university in England, or maybe stay with Gaia when she would inevitably go. Perhaps I was wrong, but I could tell he had been making a concerted effort to improve. His accent was particularly good. I stood up and took Anton back to the garden to let the pair have a little time alone.

'Shall we go for a walk around the garden?' I suggested.

Anton nodded and took my hand in his. We made our way up to the swing chair and sat down. It was my favourite place to be, sitting on the chunky, navy cushions, curled up under Anton's arm as he slowly rocked the chair with his feet. We quietly chatted, rocking back and forth.

'I like your crazy pink window frames.' I laughed.

'Our crazy pink window frames,' he corrected, and squeezed my shoulder. It was a hot, late afternoon but I still enjoyed having him pressed up against me. 'What do you want to do on your birthday?'

'It depends on Gaia. If she's up to it, I'd like for us all to go to Yiannis Restaurant for orange cake and then for drinks after.'

'What if you are pregnant?' He bent down and kissed my head and a refreshing breeze rolled by, giving me goosebumps.

'I can't live thinking about it all the time. It's always there in the back of my mind, but I think just relaxing is more likely to have better results than being uptight.' I shifted my weight away from him and pointed my feet on the floor, as I looked up at the window of the spare room that might one day belong to our child. Anton's hand appeared on my jawline and he gently tilted my face up to his. My lips were met with a soft kiss from his. 'Should we invite Michail and Basil to my little get together? They're basically family too.'

167

'I happen to know they are away that weekend visiting Basil's brother in the south of the island.' There was a long silence before Anton continued, as though no time had passed at all. 'I have enjoyed spending time with them again. The pandemic separated us all. I think we have all got used to not spending time with the ones we love. I wish you could have known Iolanthe. I think you would have liked her; she definitely would have liked you.'

'Just based on Basil and Michail, I imagine I would have. Why do you think she would have liked me?' I looked down at the grass lightly moving as a breeze rolled past.

'Because you are smart and caring. You are a good mother to Gaia. She always hoped I would find someone. She nagged me like my mother.' He exhaled a laugh but as I glanced up at him, I could see his eyes were etched in loss. 'Come, let's go see what the kids are up to.'

I'd been surprised that Anton had managed to leave them alone for a full thirty minutes, with Gaia looking so dreadful. Although he had accepted Finn into his life, there was still some way to go. Mostly he was worried he would break Gaia's heart by breaking things off with her again. I was dreading telling him that they had taken the next step together to solidify their relationship and had taken a huge step towards being adults. I tucked my hair behind my ears, and my palms started to sweat thinking about it.

As we made our way back to the house, a thought occurred to me. 'If Gaia has an allergy, if something she is eating is making her ill, maybe she should only eat plain food and water. I mean really plain. Maybe only chicken, potatoes and simple veg. What do you think? Until the results arrive.'

'I think that is a very good idea. We have chicken in the

fridge. We can start tonight.'

We came in to an almost-silent house. The only sound was that of tiny, mewing noises. Coming in through the back meant that the lounge corner was obscured by the stairs in the centre of the room. Anton didn't let go of my hand, but I quickly felt like I was almost being dragged along by him. Finn was still on the sofa, but I couldn't properly see what was happening right away. Finn's face was a little rosy. It was only as we drew closer that I realised Gaia was fast asleep with her head on his lap. Finn whispered to Anton, shrugging his shoulders and chopping the air above Gaia's head to indicate what was already obvious.

'He didn't want to wake her and couldn't work out how to move her,' Anton said to me but didn't look at me. Instead, he folded his arms and tilted his head to one side assessing the situation. 'I think we will just have to wake her. She needs to eat anyway.'

Then Finn whispered something else and gestured towards the TV nook. He and Anton both looked in that direction so I joined their gaze to see a kitten pooing on the rug.

After waking Gaia, sorting the cat poo, finding the kitty litter tray and generally getting organised, we eventually had dinner together. Gaia agreed to plain chicken and potatoes while the rest of us had some moussaka from a batch Anton had frozen a month or so before.

This was the first meal where Finn had been determined to chat almost exclusively in English. Gaia only translated the odd thing. I had to compliment how well he was coming along.

'Thank you, Melodie. I hope to spend time in England one day,' he replied, then turned up the corner of his mouth in

Gaia's direction.

This made the muscles around Gaia's cheekbones lift, although she did her best to hide it and didn't look back at Finn.

'Maybe you could come along next time we go to visit Gaia's grandparents in Essex.'

Almost halfway into my suggestion Anton started to choke and had to pick his red, spotted paper napkin up to hide his face – although the bits of him I could see were going rather purple. Gaia, on the other hand, had stopped pushing her chicken around her plate and was doing a million tiny nods looking between Finn and me.

'Seriously, Melodie? I would love that! Yes please.' Gaia dropped her cutlery and hid her smile behind her knuckles before turning and grabbing Finn's hand.

'I would love this. I– I–' Finn went into Greek with Gaia. His cheeks began to flush a little too and I wondered what the problem might be. Gaia's hand went limp in his and her whole face took a nose dive from its position on cloud nine.

'He can't afford it. He doesn't think his parents would pay for the trip. They've promised to buy him a motorbike and he hasn't had his job long enough to save much money.' Gaia gave a despondent smile to match Finn's.

'That's okay. Anton will pay. Won't you?'

I didn't even turn my head to look at him. I just took a mouthful of food and waited. I was trying to use the excited and confused expressions of Gaia and Finn, who were sitting opposite me, to gauge what Anton might look like. I could only imagine that he had become more red. After a moment, I did turn and he was looking at me with his eyes wide and one eyebrow lifted to the ceiling.

I placed my hand on his stubbled cheek. 'Won't you?' I smiled.

His expression melted, and he kissed the palm of my hand. 'Of course. I think my mother took a liking to you when she was here. I'm sure she would happily see you again.'

It was worth putting Anton on the spot to see how Gaia and Finn were. Finn couldn't stop thanking us both. When dinner was finished and the plates were being moved into the kitchen, Gaia began to look more feeble than ever. All the excitement of the day was taking its toll. Finn decided it was time to go home.

Gaia was already asleep in bed and I had just finished loading the dishwasher. Anton was very quiet and happily agreed to go straight up to bed.

Lying down next to Anton, I decided I couldn't put off telling him about the pregnancy test a moment more. When I had known that Gaia was going out with Finn, and had not told him, he had been so furious with me that I nearly lost them both. I wasn't about to make the same type of error again.

'I need to tell you something.' His face didn't move. He was almost as still as a possum. 'I was going to empty Gaia's bin, but I didn't.'

'That's okay. She can do it tomorrow if she hasn't already.'

'Yeah, I know that, that's not what I meant. I meant that there was a pregnancy test in the bin.'

His mouth began to open and his eyes became slits, menacing, in the dim light of the room.

I stepped up my pace. 'It was negative! Before you worry. It just ... It means she thought she could be too. But obviously, when the blood test came back, and assuming what she told us was true, it was negative.' I realised I'd been as rigid as Anton had been still. The muscles between my shoulder blades began to release, and I let a shiver roll through my body to free my muscles further.

Anton pulled me in and pressed me to his chest. My nose was tickled by the tuft of curls there. He gave a trembling exhale and buried his face in the hair around my ear so that I could almost hear his thoughts in my mind. His tiny noises, the snuffling and puffs through his nose, told me more than the words I could imagine rolling around his brain. He was worried, that much was obvious, but there was also the fact he was being faced with his daughter growing up and taking more steps away from the child he had been guiding through the world. She was on her way to independence and likely to an education in England – that's what he wanted for her. He wanted to cling to the idea of his daughter as a child and clung to me instead.

Chapter 24

The day before my birthday, Keres came back with Akis in tow. Gaia had been doing exceptionally well on her new diet and was starting to gain back a little bit of weight, and her skin was back to her normal bronzed-olive tone. It wasn't all shadows and grey. She hadn't even vomited since the day Finn had come over. Anton called the restaurant in advance and checked they'd be okay with something very plain for Gaia. Unsurprisingly, they were more than happy to help. Having had time being well meant that she'd been able to enjoy getting the kittens to settle into their new home. Donnie was a complete softie, but all Looper, or Loopy as we would call her, was interested in was jumping on things and sharpening her claws, ready to try to scratch the side of the leather sofa. Every time she tried, Ant would give me a *this was your idea* look then pick her up and cuddle her. His attempts at being mad at the kittens were feeble at best. Whenever Anton fell asleep on the sofa now, it was always with one or both of the cats tucked under his chin. It turned out he was the biggest softie of all.

It was good to have Keres back in the house. Gaia's eyes were often so wide whenever Keres spoke that her thick, black eyelashes would almost stand up on end. She even asked me what sort of thing I thought Keres might wear to go out for my birthday meal. I had no clue and suggested she ask her. Gaia shrugged it off. I found it endearing and loved that Keres was already becoming an established member of the family. Now and then, Nico's words and his smug, pretty-boy face would catch me out though. Sometimes I'd think about the fact that, if he were telling the truth, I didn't know Keres that well. The argument felt as though it were happening between both my lungs, as each opinion caught in my chest and made my breathing quiver. My heart would step in between the squabbling pair and reassure me that it would in fact all be okay. She was my sister after all. Nico must have been lying to me. Keres was seeing Akis, and likely Nico was just jealous.

Keres had told Gaia she was "seeing" her uncle. I'm not actually sure of the term that was used as I wasn't there, and anyway they would have been speaking in Greek. Either way, this was the first time Gaia would have seen them together. It was interesting to watch. Gaia could be a straight talker, asking questions inappropriately at times, but she was being more cautious. There were a few times that evening when I caught her watching Keres and Akis, and her mouth would open or she'd snatch an inbreath like she was about to speak. All that would come out was the same air that she'd taken in. No words were spoken, not outside of her mind.

We passed the time from lunch through to dinner eating salty, dark-purple olives and telling stories. Many came from Akis about what he remembered of Anton growing up. Being the youngest, his perspective differed from Ant's on many

174

occasions. Not that Anton said much. Often, he just shook his head at the stories. Akis told us all about a time when Anton was about sixteen, making Akis only eleven. He was hanging out with Katerina. Akis made it clear that they were just supposed to be friends, but apparently everyone knew Katerina only had eyes for Anton. There was another girl, Angelina. The three of them would hang about the house after school.

'Ant thought he had it all. Two of the prettiest girls in his school were following him about and I tell ya, if he said jump, they wouldn't ask how high, they'd just do it.'

'Akis, is this story going anywhere?' Anton began to moan, but he was soon shushed by Gaia who desperately wanted any details of her mother's younger years.

'One day, the girls were following him about in the garden and they started squabbling about who was going to get Ant his book – or something stupid—'

'Pencil case. It was my pencil case.'

'Ha! Yeah! Course it was! I was basically invisible so I just watched from my open window. Dad saw me looking. The crazy bugger was watering the plants. He just looked at me, looked at them and did a little …' He made the action of moving his wrist. ' … just a little flick of water. A sprinkle, if that. They couldn't stop screaming.' Akis fell about laughing at it. Anton rubbed at his face behind his hands. 'Dad only did a little, you know, almost nothing, a little …' He gestured again with a pulsing hand and made a *tss* noise. 'But he got them right in their eyes.'

'Yes, but then what happened, Akis?'

'I may have fallen out of the window from laughing.' We all gasped, but he was still laughing. 'Luckily, Dad saw me go and saved me from hurting myself, but he left the hose to soak us all. Not Anton though. He was too cool and had walked off all embarrassed.'

'Can I do the same now?' Anton asked, with a half-smile in jest at his brother.

'Was Mum mad at Grandad for soaking her?' Gaia piped in.

'Nah, not for long anyway. Think they were both more embarrassed about arguing over a pencil case. Plus, after I fell out of the window it all changed a bit. That wasn't long before we moved back to England for our *education*," – he put on a mock posh accent for "education" – 'leaving Anton behind who refused to leave Corfu. He was determined he could make a life here for himself. Dad said he would be back in England with his tail between his legs in no more than a month. Bugger still owes Marty money for losing that bet.'

Then Keres told a story about her dad, her adoptive father. How he had picked her up from school after lunch one day and hadn't told her mum about it. They'd gone all the way to Anavyssos beach, an hour or so away from their home near Athens. When she didn't come home her mother had worried and called all her friends and family.

'Was she not worried about your father too?' Anton asked, before discarding another olive stone. He leant his weight forwards and tapped his finger on the table. Keres's little face tilted to the left filled with a frown. She glanced at Akis before lifting her feet onto his lap.

'No. Why would she be?'

'Because he didn't come home either,' Anton said, turning his hand into an open palm, almost in place of a shrug.

'Oh, I – Well, he, he worked away. She wasn't knowing he was back.'

Anton accepted her answer with a low grunt. His fingers then began to trace the mosaics on the table, and we all became caught up in the moment of silence. Eventually, Gaia broke it by announcing that Finn had been able to get the night off work and would be coming out with us for my birthday meal. It was nice to see her green eyes bright again, full of questions and wonder. Akis leant towards Keres, took her hand and kissed it. Gaia's mouth opened and closed like one of those bins that open with a sensor; Keres and Akis's interactions kept setting her off to no purpose.

After dinner, Gaia went off chatting to Finn on her phone, while Anton and Akis cleared away plates and loaded the dishwasher. Keres and I went for a walk up to the swing chair. I sat with my right foot tucked underneath me so I could twist to face her and appreciate her company.

'How are things going with you and Akis?'

'He is a lovely man. I do like him. I have enjoyed staying with him.' Her face broke into a broad smile, so broad the little creases in the corners of her eyes appeared and the apples of her cheeks stood out from her face. 'He has been very kind to me. He wants me to live with him. I think maybe it is too soon. But I do like him.' She diverted her eyeline to her swinging feet, but the smile lingered on her lips and in the corners of her blue eyes.

'You deserve to be happy. Akis is a really lovely man. I know he seems all loud stories and confidence, but underneath he is a sensitive one,' I said, while studying her face.

She nodded in rhythm with the swaying chair. 'Yes. I have been very lucky to find you all,' she said, 'but I do worry about Gaia. I do not know what I should say and what I should not.'

'What do you mean?'

'With Finn. I worry. That is all.'

'What's there to worry about, Keres?' I stopped the swaying by kicking the ball of my foot into the scorched grass and dirt below. 'Keres, you're safe talking to me. Gaia is a fourteen-year- old girl. If you know something is wrong, you should tell me.'

'Finn, he wants to …' She tapped her fingers together and I began to nod.

'They've had sex?'

To my surprise she shrugged, making the strap of her top slip out of position. She didn't make a move to replace it which slightly bothered me.

'She told me they have. He had been begging her. I think, demanding. At first, I think she is pregnant with all the vomiting. She told me she can't be pregnant. It can't be Finn making her ill?'

'No, don't be ridiculous. She hadn't seen him for ages, before she got ill again. Plus, how could he make her ill? Poison her? I think that's a bit farfetched, Keres. He's only a kid. Plus he hasn't even seen her while she's been ill.'

'You are right. I like Gaia and I worry for her. That is all.'

'We all are. I can't believe she said that about Finn. That he was demanding.' My fingernails dug into my palms as my hands scrunched into tight balls.

Keres agreed, telling me Gaia hadn't wanted to disappoint him, but that she didn't know much else. The conversation continued, although not along the same lines. It was about something else, something I couldn't invest in and grab hold of because I was considering when Gaia had seen Finn and how lovely he had seemed. How could he have been demanding with her? I knew he had broken things off once before. She said it had been because of Anton. Was that the real reason why? Or was it because she hadn't been ready? I let Keres keep talking while I, under the guise of listening, was working like a human calculator. Numbers and statistics related to human behaviours online was something I could deal with, such as when people were more likely to react to social media posts and what styles could catch certain people's eyes, like trending colours and trending words. But faced with individuals in real life, I was useless, unable to add up the facts as I made them out. My main conclusion was to ask why. What reason would Finn have to do such a thing? As far as I could tell, Gaia had given him what he had asked for, and they both seemed happy. I recalled his face when he had seen her for the first time in two weeks – the worry; the love. Unless that was all fake? Unless he was some brilliant actor?

As we made our way back down to the house, I could hear Anton whistling and other funny noises. I could see them through the trees: Gaia with one hand clawing her scalp through her hair, eyes darting from side to side, and Anton meandering about whistling.

'Have you two lost Akis again?' I laughed as we got closer.

'Someone left the back door open and Loopy got out.' Gaia's eyes were pink at the edges and brimming with tears.

I quickly put my arms around her and reassured her.

'It is a cat,' Keres said. 'It will come back.'

'It's not that simple, Keres,' I said. 'Kittens need to settle into their new home before they're let out or they might not come back.' I turned my attention to Ant who was still whistling. 'Where's Akis?'

'He is running along the … He is there!'

We all looked in the direction Anton was pointing. Akis was

walking through the metal gate at the side of the house. Gaia pulled away from my arms and ran towards her uncle who was shirtless – he was holding little Loopy in his T-shirt. Gaia bounced from foot to foot as she thanked him and carefully took the kitten from him. Keres seemed more distracted by Akis's sixpack and edged over to congratulate the hero.

We had made sure to tell Keres and Akis to keep the back door closed because of the kittens. I caught Anton frowning in their direction, before he followed Gaia into the house. I'm pretty sure he knew as well as I did that Keres had been last out of the house. She had rushed back in to the loo before we went for our little walk around the garden. But it was a mistake that could have happened to anyone.

It wasn't too much later that we all called it a night. Apparently, there were big plans for my birthday and I had been informed we should all get some rest. It made me a little anxious, but I played along. Mostly I was looking forward to spending time in Anton's arms. I'd stayed downstairs to help Gaia with the kittens and he had already gone up without me. I assumed he would be waiting for me in bed, but the light was off and the en suite light was on, with its door open a crack. I edged round the bed towards the door.

'Are you all right?' I called in the direction of the light. It wasn't the usual white light of the main fitting. An orange glow was creeping into the bedroom, flickering.

'Come in,' Anton said in a husky, low voice. There he was in the bathtub full of bubbles. 'Room for two.' He smiled, with one eyebrow raised. My hands fell to my hips, with a little laugh. 'That is a very nice dress,' he said. 'I would not want you to ruin it, so maybe take it off? Before I start blowing bubbles at you.' His grin became uncontrollable, and he sat forward into the bubbles.

I didn't say anything. I just slipped off my clothes and carefully joined him in the very full bath.

'The day's been too hot for this, really,' I said, as I let my foot run along the length of his torso.

'I put the air conditioning on high to try to help,' he said, as I sank down into the bubbles, letting the ends of my hair swirl around my shoulders. Anton's large, firm hands began to rub my feet. 'You know, when I saw you at Yiannis Restaurant last year, after walking Gaia up to Natalia's, I nearly didn't come over to you. I saw you when I was walking with Gaia and spent the whole way back questioning if I should or shouldn't stop.'

'You've never told me that before.'

'If I hadn't gone up to you, we would not be here.' He gave my foot an extra squeeze. His eyes were lowered, hidden behind his thick black lashes. 'I know some people have said we have rushed into marriage. Mostly Katerina's parents, but some others too. I do not care what people think. You make me happy, and Gaia too. I wouldn't change a thing.'

'You know their hearts are in the right place. They miss their daughter, and in I come replacing her. It must be so hard, and they are so kind.' Under the water I smoothed the little hairs on his calf to reassure him.

He pressed his lips together and gave a short nod. Thin lines of sweat, or water, ran from his forehead, past his throat and along his pecs.

'My meaning is: I love you. I see your birthday as our first date, the best one I ever had.' He moved, pulling his legs towards himself, tucking them under to climb towards me.

'You'll get stuck!'

'No, I will not. This bath is big enough.'

'You're getting water all over the floor!'

'So?'

As water sloshed over the edge of the white porcelain, he managed to manoeuvre himself between my legs, pressing himself against my wet breasts, his arm around my waist as he began to kiss me. His tongue tentatively teased mine. I arched my back to press myself harder against his lathered skin, only to make his arm that was holding our weight slip, pressing his body down on mine. Suddenly, I was submerged with no air in my lungs and bubbles in my eyes. In a moment, Anton pulled me up as if I were a rag doll and pressed me spluttering to his broad chest.

'I can't see!' I coughed. 'I've got mascara bubbles in my eyes.'

I couldn't open them; I didn't dare try. Anton got out of the tub, lifted me out and wrapped me in a towel.

'What do I do?'

'I need face wipes,' I spluttered. 'In my top drawer.' I pressed my fingers to my stinging eyes, desperately wanting to rub them but knowing it wouldn't go well if I did.

'Can't you just use water?'

'No, I can't just use bloody water Anton. It'll make my mascara even worse, please, I need makeup remover. Just get my wipes.' I could hear him jumping over the bed.

'It's an empty packet,' Anton called back to me.

'Shit! Look in the big bathroom under the sink. I keep loads there in case Gaia needs any.'

I could hear his feet pad along past the bed, then he crept out of the bedroom into the sleepy house. It seemed to take him much longer than I expected. I had to just stand there, dripping and blind. I was afraid to move in case I slipped

182

or bumped into anything. I had no idea which way he had even faced me. At least it didn't hurt as long as I kept my eyes closed.

When he came back in, he led me to the bed where he sat me down and helped me to gently wipe away the mascara and foam residue. It stung to open them and left me with pink blood vessels throbbing in my eyes. Once the make up was gone I went to the sink and splashed them with water to ease the stinging.

Eventually, I was able to see his slightly blurry face. His eyes were deep-set beneath his heavy brow. I couldn't work out if he was sad or angry.

'Don't worry. I'm all right.'

'Hmm? Yes. Good.' He lightly kissed me on the head and sat down next to me. He looked like a soldier ready for war, with rock-solid posture and an unmoving expression that could frighten even the most daring warrior.

'What's going on? You look like you're about to kill someone.'

At that he stood up and began to pace the room, muttering in Greek. Every so often he ran his fingers through his hair to set it back in place. I tucked the fluffy navy towel under my armpits and in on itself to secure its position before standing up to interrupt his little rant. Which, by that point, had included having his hands tap his forehead and the air around him.

'Anton, what's going on?'

He stopped everything, hesitating. All that could be heard was the clock ticking and his heavy breathing through his nose. He sat on the white chair next to the en suite door, which I'd suggested would look nice there. It was a small, shell chair that made Anton seem even more enormous. Air puffed out of the cushion as he sat on it.

'Now, Anton …' I snapped, folding my arms across my chest.

He leant his elbows on his knees and placed his large hands over his face so that only his nose protruded between them, and began:

'When I left the room. I could– I could hear something. It was your Keres.'

I shook my head, waiting for more information, completely missing his meaning.

'So?'

'I mean … I could very clearly hear her, with Akis. Their room is next to Gaia's, Melodie. And your Keres is in there … screaming.'

It suddenly hit me what he was getting at. Why he felt so angry and confused as to what he should do, if anything.

'Yes, they are adults. Yes, I am not a fool. I know what goes on. But in the room next to my daughter, being so … loud. It is that or he is killing her.' He shrugged, almost as though that would be preferable.

'It's not like we don't have sex when Gaia's here.'

'Yes, but you don't make sounds like … like that!' I couldn't help but let a smirk fall across my face as a small laugh burst from my lips. Anton gave an impatient exhale. 'You know what I mean!'

'Well, that will be nice and awkward for poor Gaia tomorrow. But, it's not a big deal, and it's too late now, isn't it! Let's just get some sleep and you can talk to Akis in the morning about being more sensitive.'

Anton grunted in agreement, but he clearly wasn't overly satisfied with the resolution. At least he let me lead him to bed. I felt the tension between my shoulder blades creeping back in as I wondered about Gaia and her experiences and wished they could at least be healthy and happy ones.

Chapter 25

The next morning, I came downstairs to a chair full of gifts. It was a stark difference to the year before, when I hadn't even opened a card on my actual birthday. Gaia was sitting on the sofa next to the chair, still in her neon-green-and-black Rick and Morty pyjama shorts and T-shirt, with fluffy pink slippers. I wasn't actually sure who Rick and Morty were – the pyjamas displayed exceptionally ugly cartoon figures. I had been assured it was a hilarious TV show and Gaia's favourite genre – sci-fi. She jumped up and gave me a hug. In Greece they mostly celebrate name days, but Gaia, being part British, loved birthdays as well as name days. Keres and Akis didn't come downstairs until much later.

On one hand, Anton was being attentive and loving. He passed me gifts and watched me open them, then made bacon sandwiches and coffee. On the other hand, I could see his jaw was clenched tightly shut and a small vein on his temple had begun to show. Gaia hadn't said anything; for all we knew, she had been asleep and missed the whole Keres-and-Akis escapade. When they did emerge, they brought with them a

small, perfectly folded square of purple tissue paper. I carefully
unwrapped it to find a silk, dark-green scrunchie and a Greek
phrase book of rude words.

'The scrunchie has a zip. Look! You can hide things in.
Good for when we run or for hiding money or anything.'
Keres grinned. It was a very sweet idea and I thanked her for
the unique gift. 'And I take it this book is from you?' I looked
at Akis who gave a silly bow.

Soon after, Anton asked Akis for help with the bins outside.
It took some doing – Akis really didn't want to help with
Anton's made-up problem. We girls sat around the coffee table.
Gaia became quiet, without making her usual eyes at Keres. I
started to think she had heard the whole thing between Keres
and Akis, and maybe she did feel awkward about it. It was
her uncle after all. Gaia kept most of her focus on me and
told me to get ready for a day of fun. I wasn't quite sure what
that meant and not knowing made me feel a little sick. So
much so, I began to hope I was pregnant and that it was very
early-onset morning sickness.

Anton took Gaia and me, and, Akis and Keres went in his
hire car. I sat tapping my knees and watching olive trees out of
the window. I had my mama and papa on my mind. My mum
too, but Mama and Papa more so. They'd brought me up when
she couldn't, and every birthday it was they who had made it
special. Mama always made me her fudgy-sludgy chocolate
cake. I'd named it that when I was little and it had stuck. It
was the gooiest chocolate cake I'd ever eaten. Sometimes I'd
help her make it, but it was never the same if I made it myself.
As I sat, jiggling my knees, I thought how I wanted to make
the cake with Gaia. I loved cooking with her and it would be
nice to pass on the recipe.

'You're quiet,' Anton said to me, as he reached across to place his hand on my vibrating knee. Perhaps the tapping and jiggling was getting annoying. I just gave a blank nod. He said, 'I spoke to Akis.' I quickly glanced over my shoulder at Gaia who was absorbed in her phone and had put her earphones in. 'He won't be staying over again. I told him he wasn't welcome.'

'You didn't!' I slapped Anton's hand.

'I did.'

'What else was said?' I shifted in the leather chair to face him. He was glancing in his mirror, back at Akis and Keres who were following behind.

'Nothing important. He did apologise and said he wouldn't drink as much next time. If he were invited round again.' His lips pulled into a tight line.

I didn't feel like pressing the matter. I didn't want to know. I ran my fingers through the hair on his arm like a cat pawing a cushion. He was wearing a fine navy shirt and dusty-pink shorts that I'd got him for Valentine's Day. The girth of his bulging arms almost didn't fit in his shirt. I was a little afraid that if he moved too quickly the whole thing might rip. Because he was so broad and tall, it did make finding the right-size clothes for him a little problematic. I'd often order things only to find they were much too short or narrow in the arms.

'I want to go home. I don't think I like the idea of doing anything exciting.'

'You will like this. I promise.' He brought my hand to his lips as he cruised along with his left hand on the wheel. 'Do you trust me?'

'Of course, I do.'

The car paused in Anton's usual central spot in Agios

Stefanos. He stopped the engine and kissed my head and said in a heavy put-on Greek accent, 'You are my Greek girl now. But we come to your beatz to play tourist with you.'

'But we are back later on?' I said, looking from Anton to Gaia in confusion.

'Nope. We will get ready here!' Gaia said. 'Dad hired a couple of rooms in Barras for the night so that we can get ready after our day on the beach.' Her pretty little face popped between the two chairs, very pleased with herself.

'What about the kittens?' I looked between them, pangs of worry about leaving the kittens slipped through my chest.

'Finn's parents will have them tonight, and Finn, when he gets home.'

We got out of the car and made our way to the hotel. Anton had a chat with the owners, shaking hands and laughing before organising our keys and our rooms. Luckily, Anton had brought along enough swimwear and evening wear to last me a week. I put on my favourite lime bikini, a black kaftan and a black straw hat then we all made our way to the beach. Finn was already there waiting for us. His sweet face lit up when he saw Gaia looking so much better. She ran to him, the first time I'd seen her run in weeks. Her gangly legs kicked up sand, making an elderly lady on a sunbed flinch behind her Kindle. Gaia knocked Finn off his feet. I'd never seen them have such a public display of affection before. Usually, it was just hand-holding and bashful looks. I couldn't imagine him being forceful with her. I really hoped that Keres was wrong or confused. They looked so happy together. I needed to try and suss it all out, maybe even talk to Gaia about it somehow. I hadn't wanted to tell Anton, but I knew I would have to, as I always did.

I scanned the beach. My home from home. Not even that really, since I'd moved to Corfu. It was just home. Rows of bodies adorned sunbeds with thick cream cushions and large wooden parasols. Almost all of the sunbathers were spread out to avoid the shade of the parasols, and instead were angled to take in as much sun as possible. Masses of bodies went from not seeing the light of day for eleven months to golden-brown in minutes.

That is, everyone except for us, as Finn had brought a ball. We played beach volleyball, which turned into water volleyball when I tripped over Gaia's foot and went face first in the sea. Luckily, I was wearing a solid, waterproof mascara and the sea's foam wasn't the same as copious amounts of bubble bath. Keres refused to join in, stating that the sand would ruin her bikini and she wanted to tan. I felt a little saddened that she didn't want to run around with the rest of us, but I had to accept the fact we were different.

Once we were in the water, we just got sillier. Anton put Akis on his shoulders and I had Gaia on mine. To say Akis looked like a sea monster would be an understatement. He swayed about as he clung to Ant's hair and even poked him in the eye once or twice. Gaia and I couldn't stop laughing at the bizarre duo. We made sure to compose ourselves when we began the game of "topple" though. Of course, the boys let us win. I don't think Akis would have really tried to topple Gaia in the water given the way she had been over the past weeks. Finn had been the referee, making sure the matches were "fair" before the next game was invented. We were the source of all the noise on the beach. Not the three-year-old chasing his toddling sister, or the man with his fruit calling for customers. Us; we were the noise.

Keres didn't look up from her sunlounger. Not that I could tell, anyway. Then, halfway through playing "who can hold their breath the longest" with Gaia and Finn, Akis looked across the beach and saw that Keres was gone. He went off to Barras Hotel but couldn't find her there either. Eventually, he found her drinking a cocktail at Mango Bar, sitting in her white, string bikini that he had got her on one of their shopping trips in Corfu town. He left her there chatting to the bar staff and joined us back in the sea. I decided I would go and get dry and relax on the beach for a bit. Anton followed me, leaving Akis to be goalie as Gaia and Finn kicked the ball at the sea.

We lay down on our sunloungers, facing each other. Anton's long arm stretched across and his index finger ran along the line of my leg.

'Thank you for this. It's perfect.' I smiled.

'I know you have been thinking about your grandparents. I wanted to bring a part of them to you. This was the only way I could do that.' How did he know? I hadn't said anything about my nostalgia for birthdays with my grandparents, I was sure.

'Your eyes, your beautiful round eyes make you easy to read, Melodie-Mou. You ask questions with no words, and sometimes I read stories too. With the wedding, your birthday and wanting a child, of course you think of your grandparents. Sometimes, I see sadness shadow your face, and I know you're thinking of them, or Liliana.'

'It has been more of them than Mum. I feel so much pain not to have known more of Mum, but with my mama and papa – I just miss them.' Anton swung his legs off his sunlounger and knelt in the sand to kiss my head. 'I wish you'd been able

191

to meet them, that's all.'

A fake cough broke through our little moment and we looked up, squinting into the sun, to see the outline of Maria standing over us.

'Hello lovebirds,' she grinned.

I jumped up from my sunlounger and ran round it to grab her, squashing her arms to her sides. 'You're here!' I bounced.

'Don't press yourself against me again, please. You'll smell the baby sick, or worse, get some on you.' She looked down and there was indeed a big white stain across her grey shorts. 'Don't say anything. I know what it looks like.' She could hear Anton sniggering as he sat on the sunlounger. 'I can't stay long, girl. I wish I could, but Harry and Noah are in the car. He just fell asleep and if the engine stops, he'll wake up again.' She lifted a little pink paper bag 'I wanted to give you this, before I go and sleep in the car next to Noah. I'll be social again next year, I promise.'

'You're too lovely, Maria. Thank you.' I put my hand in the bag to find a beautiful pair of silver earrings shaped like leaves.

'I hope you like them. I saw them and thought they were you.'

I pressed them to my chest. 'I love them.'

As Maria made her way back up the beach, I couldn't believe how lucky I was. I'd suffered so much loss, but it had brought me love, family, friendship and a sister. That was the best birthday gift of all. I wasn't alone anymore.

Chapter 26

Luckily, Anton had packed the outfit I wanted to wear that evening. I was grateful he had actually been paying attention when I'd been trying clothes on in front of the mirror earlier in the week. It was a black, jersey maxi dress with slits to just above the knee. It was one of those dresses that could be dressed up or down. I put on yellow, strappy, high-heeled sandals, which tied up the length of my calves, and the necklace that Keres had got me. My hair fell into perfectly thick uniform waves about my shoulders and down the middle of my back.

Putting down my eyeliner, I turned to Anton, who was lying on the bed, scrolling through his phone. 'Finished!'

He looked up and threw the phone down. 'You are perfect. Come here.'

'No! You'll ruin my make-up, and we are meeting everyone at the bar in' – I pressed a button on my phone – 'ten minutes.'

'I should get dressed then.' He sauntered past me in just his pants, and I couldn't resist tapping his bottom as it went by.

'No, no, we only have ten minutes,' he said, and shook his

index finger at me. He grabbed the one shirt he had brought along, black with white abstract roses all over it, and black chino shorts. Then we were off to the bar to wait for everyone else.

We sat sipping drinks; mine, of course, was a cocktail, a Sexy Greek. Anton had a straight ouzo. We were chatting, and giggling at someone who had just tripped down a step and sort of danced as they fell, when Keres and Akis came into view. I saw them first and Anton clutched my hand, asking what was wrong. I can only imagine that my mouth hung open a little too wide, or perhaps my eyes became rounder than usual. Either way, I was being too easy to read again. I shook his hand a little as I pushed back my chair to stand.

Keres strode forward with long steps to reach me, grabbing my shoulders and kissing my cheeks. She wasn't normally affectionate in that way, but I was too taken aback by her outfit to notice much. Her dress was also black and her heels were also high. Only, her dress barely covered her bum cheeks and was exceptionally low in the neckline. It was the sort of dress I wouldn't bat an eyelid at in my twenties clubbing, but going for a family meal – it just seemed so out of place. She seemed out of place. Her hair was pulled up into a high ponytail and it was only as she grabbed me, I realised she had put in a long extension that really did look like a pony's tail. It was as straight as an ironing board all the way down her back. As I was taking in her red lipstick and green shoes, Gaia and Finn appeared. Gaia had been begging Anton to let them stay the night together in the room, but he only said they could get ready together in the knowledge that Anton had a key too. Then, after the meal, Finn was to go home.

Gaia's delicate black eyebrows nearly joined her scalp as she came up behind Keres, and Finn's face went pink and blotchy under his normally golden complexion.

'Keres, you look—' Gaia started, but Keres soon interrupted, leaving Gaia standing there with her mouth open and one limp hand hanging in mid-air. I wondered if that was what I looked like.

'Akis bought it.' She did a little spin as we all formed a circle around her and the table we'd been sat at. I could feel everyone's eyes on us. Under the layer of music from the bar there was silence, or at least hushed talking as people muttered. I told myself we were all entitled to wear whatever we liked, and even though it wasn't my personal taste, Keres seemed happy and so did Akis. In fact, Akis looked glazed. His smile was glued onto his face in a way that didn't sit well with me. I couldn't put my finger on it. He commented on how beautiful Keres was – and she really was; that much was undeniable. The sweet angelic face, and bright-blue eyes framed by flicks of false lashes, and a body that was designed to wear a dress that fits like skin.

Eventually, we were all sitting with a drink. Gaia had shrunk down and kept looking at her dress then back at Keres. For all that Gaia could be outspoken, it was more a case of saying what was in her head without thinking rather than a deep-set confidence. Keres was perhaps the opposite; she clearly had lots of confidence. Gaia looked wholesome and lovely. She wore a short, pale-blue, fitted dress with a sweetheart neck and little cap sleeves. Normally, she liked to wear trainers or slides, but she was wearing silver high heels that we had picked out earlier in the year. They had tiny silver bows on the front. She started to almost hide in her long, dark hair which had been perfectly curled for the occasion but was now being used as more of a blanket. Finn only had eyes for Gaia though. I liked that, no matter what Keres had said. He kissed Gaia's hand and whispered in her ear, making her show a small smile behind her hair blanket.

As we wandered along the main street on our way to Yiannis, a whistle came from across the road. It cut through the air, a well-practised whistle, like a dog owner might achieve after years of dog walks. We all looked around, apart from Keres, who held her head high and kept on walking. The noise came again, and I managed to bob my head to look past Ant, only to discover Nico jogging across the road. Foolishly, I thought it was to say happy birthday to me, but he skimmed right past me and stood in front of Keres. For a moment he just stood there, so close to her, looking down across her body, biting his lip. He had a lit cigarette cupped in his hand. Without moving away from her, he took a deep drag letting the smoke pour from his nose like a pyroclastic flow and filling the space between us all with the smell of it.

He started to speak. All Greek, of course, so I had no clue what was being said. It was only as Anton yanked my arm to pull me away, because Akis had stepped up into Nico's face, that I knew it hadn't been well received. Nico slipped the cigarette into the corner of his mouth. Keres didn't flinch. She had been looking past Nico the whole time, as though he were a puppy in training and ignoring his bad behaviour was the only option.

Everything fell still; even the evening air seemed to be in suspense. Nico's smoke sat over us in a humid cloud, making it hard to breathe. My eyes were fixed on Nico. From my angle, his nose was almost touching Keres's, while Akis's nose was aimed at Nico. In some kind of farce-like moment, I realised the bar had started playing "Crazy In Love" by Beyoncé and I began to wonder if it was someone's practical joke or just a matter of coincidence.

Nico's head moved, only his head, in what seemed like slow motion. I saw his mouth move, but I was a good two steps away and I couldn't hear what he said. Not that I would've understood anyway. Within the same moment, he threw the cigarette, only missing Keres's toe by an inch. Whatever he had said caused Akis's whole body to tense. He pulled his weight back in his shoulders and rebounded like a dolphin playing in the sea. His forehead aimed itself towards Nico's nose, only marginally slowed by Anton grasping for his shoulder. Anton pulled at Akis, and credit to Finn who stepped forward and started to talk to Nico whose nose was leaving a trail of blood down his crisp, white T-shirt. Finn pulled him away. Not that Nico was going towards Akis. He was laughing, with blood trickling into his mouth, catching around his teeth. Just laughing.

Akis shouted, 'Kíta éna maláka,' which just made Nico laugh more. I knew that maláka meant wanker. I wasn't sure of the rest. Akis was not laughing.

They'd chosen a prime spot to entertain everyone – right where the road bends and splits – the perfect place to be seen. People at Silver Star and Tasty Corner watched from a high vantage point and someone at Barras Bar stood up to look across at all the commotion.

Gaia followed after Finn, almost trotting next to him in her heels. Only Keres and I remained unchanged. I think at least my face had moved throughout; Keres, on the other hand, had become as still as one of those street performers who pretend to be statues. I wanted to say something, but each time I tried, my jaw seemed to hold itself tightly shut. She broke her skin of stone to crush the cigarette that lay on the floor with her green, pointed shoe. Smoke had been floating up from it as it had remained ignited throughout – but she ground her foot into its papery body until all that remained were ashes. Then it was over, almost like nothing had happened. Everyone buzzed away in Greek around Keres and me. Nico was back across the road, presumably going back to the bar from where he must have spotted us, and Akis had his arm draped around Keres's neck. I was only lifted from my trance when the back of Anton's index finger stroked my check and he pulled me into his chest.

Nothing was said about it over dinner. Nothing. I could've asked, but I didn't really want to. I sort of felt like everyone had forgotten I couldn't understand. Or perhaps they didn't really want me to know what had been said by Nico. I kept wondering if he'd had a change of shirt with him. I didn't hate Nico; I couldn't. Underneath it all, he wasn't a bad person. He was a product of his reasonably good looks and a disproportionate ego, an ego that was fed into every single day by working behind a bar in a small resort. Of course, he was able to gain and hold women's attention. I was pretty sure that underneath it all he wanted something real. But he could so quickly become a caricature of himself and hide what he really wanted. Part of me wanted to give him a hug and the other part wanted to give him a slap.

I found myself waiting for my dinner with a faint, absent smile lingering on my lips. One I'm sure that was much like the way Akis had looked at the start of the evening. I would nod here and there at the chatter around me, and sometimes I would watch people walk past or couples eating at other tables, whose lives seemed so simple. The warm night filled with the smell of thick-cut pork and juicy moussaka as plates were passed across our table. For a moment, I just looked down at my blue-and- white plate, filled almost to the rim with salad and meat. Anton squeezed my knee under the table, triggering me to pick up my cutlery and put on my vacant smile once more.

Unlike the year before with a lonely slice of cake, that night I had candles on a whole orange cake that had been arranged by Anton. There was singing and clapping, and I almost ran away from the attention. Quickly it died down, and the sticky, sweet cake was devoured. Keres and Akis wanted to go for cocktails at Little Prince, whereas I felt like walking. To make the most of being together before Finn was picked up, Gaia and he went to the bar with Keres and Akis. Anton and I walked hand in hand in the opposite direction to everyone else, promising to meet them soon. We made it past our hotel before I spoke, barely audible above the pounding beats from the bar.

'What did he say?'

'Nice heart.' He answered so quickly his words almost overlapped mine. Like his words had been sitting in the back of his mouth waiting for me. He didn't look at me, he didn't flinch away from our meandering as we passed the glow of bars and restaurants along the dark night.

'Nice heart?' I bleated back at him. I didn't look at him either. As though we were together and completely separate. Our feet were scuffing along the concrete. I stopped looking into the restaurants and watched my feet. I couldn't understand Nico or Akis, or Keres for that matter. 'Do you know what he meant? That doesn't sound like a reason to headbutt someone.'

199

'I did not ask. It didn't feel like the right time.' Neither of us spoke again; we just kept walking. We were surrounded by laughing and cheering, by karaoke and live music. Everywhere fizzed with noise but not us. We were locked in our minds. It wasn't like us; when things happened, we would talk, give each other knowing looks, lifts of eyebrows and little giggles. This felt different. Maybe because it was my sister and his brother. It was all too close.

We reached the shop where Keres had got my necklace. I opened my mouth to say, 'Perhaps we should turn back', but a young woman I didn't recognise came out of the shop with her arms moving like the blades on a fan, whizzing about in all directions. Her voice was loud and confident. At first, I looked behind me, thinking she must be talking to someone nearby, trying to gain their attention. Her dark curls bounced as she took a step towards me. Anton then started talking to her. They were both talking so quickly I had no hope of understanding even a word. With another lunge, she grabbed the necklace around my neck, making me stagger backwards. Anton managed to catch my arm then thrust his finger close to her face. She didn't seem bothered by him towering over her; she did let go of the necklace though. Another woman, one I did recognise, came out of the shop and assessed the situation, eyes hotly darting over us all. She butted in like a schoolmarm and took my arm from Anton and led me carefully into the shop.

'Sorry for the problems. Please follow me,' she said, and I did as I was told. She walked me through to sit on a stool in a quiet, white corner of the shop with all the shoes. Anton and the young woman hung over us as she knelt down next to me. She took the disk of the necklace in her hand looking at it. Her eyes pulled into slits as she studied the yellows and golds. Her thin fingers clung to it, making me feel like a lost dog having my collar checked. Then she spoke calmly, still holding the necklace as she spoke.

'This necklace was stolen. Taken from here. Where did you get it?'

My breathing became shallow. The cool air from the air-conditioning unit almost made my teeth tingle and my throat close up. I went to say something, but again I was interrupted, this time by Anton.

'I gave it to her. I found it on the beach.'

'On the beatz?' The young, curly-haired woman chimed, in her heavy Greek accent. 'The beatz?' Her mouth pursed, her arms fastened around her chest and her hip swayed out in my direction as her eyes stayed fixed on his face. She was probably very attractive when she smiled, but the frown on her face creased it in such a way she became like a stubby gargoyle. Anton's head was rising and falling in a slow nod. He didn't turn to look at her; he was talking to the kind-looking lady, with soft curls and delicate freckles on her ageing skin, whom I'd spoken to many times before in the shop.

'I had no idea it was stolen. I'll pay for it now. Melodie likes it. I'll make it hers.'

The woman by my side carefully laid the disc back on my chest where I held onto it, pressing it into my skin where I was sure it was burning a hole into my heart. She turned to me before she stood, placing one cool hand on my face, beautiful eyes slanting up in the corners. She said something in Greek with a gentle smile to which Anton said *Efharisto* – thank you. The three of them made their way to the till. They only took half what it was worth as Anton insisted on paying something

201

for it. Everyone was kind. Everyone agreed. I felt like my belly was full of fire ants, crawling around nipping my flesh from the inside out as the reality of it all crept through me.

Walking from the shop into a cloud of heat was actually comforting. My skin had risen into millions of tiny bumps from the cold of the shop, or the cold rush and sweat I'd had. The humid air soothed me.

'We need to talk about Keres,' Anton said. His feet were dragging me along now; I had to occasionally skip to keep up with his strides. 'I had not wanted to say it, Melodie, but I do not trust the girl. This, this *gromto*, this just confirms it.' He stopped and turned to me, taking my face in his hands, his thumbs in front of my ears and his fingers melting into my hair. 'This is your birthday – your day – and I am so sorry. But I need to protect Gaia from her influence. I am sorry.' He kissed my head and began to walk again.

I didn't follow, not right away. 'Hey!' I cried, and ran to catch up with him. 'Hey! What happened to giving someone the benefit of the doubt here? Firstly, she could've found it, just like you said. You have no idea. What do you mean you "do not trust her"? You can't just say that and march off.' My voice seemed to be coming out an octave higher than its usual pitch.

Anton dipped his head to look down at me, exhaling heavily through his nose. People's feet slapped on the concrete in our direction; we parted to let them through with smiles and laughter and thanks before we stepped back to face each other. I grasped my waist, digging my fingers in to control the ants from making their anger come out of my mouth.

'*Na 'cheis ta mátia sou dekatéssera,*' he muttered.

'And what does that mean?'

202

'Just ... you need fourteen eyes with her.'

'What?'

'You should watch out, or beware. It's a common Greek phrase. It's not just this, Melodie. I spoke to Gaia about the pregnancy test.'

'So?'

'So, she told me she only took it because Keres bought it for her. Keres has been pushing her to take the next step with Finn. Gaia was embarrassed and eventually lied to Keres about it. Saying she had done things she hadn't.'

'Why would Keres care what Gaia was up to with Finn? It makes no sense. Keres told me Finn had been pushing Gaia into things.'

'Why had you not told me that?'

'She only said so yesterday. I wanted to speak to Gaia—'

'Gaia said it is Keres putting pressure her. Not Finn, Melodie. I trust Finn more than Keres. First the photo, then pressuring Gaia, and the test. Now the necklace. And let's not forget the cigarette. Gaia told me after the party it was Keres who encouraged her to go! I didn't want to tell you or upset you. Something is not right with her, Melodie! I don't even dare be alone with the girl for fear she might touch me!'

'What? Start again. What do you mean the photo? She explained about that. And you spoke to Gaia? You didn't tell me that? And what do you mean "for fear she might touch you"?'

'Melodie-Mou, you lost that photograph before she had looked in the box with you. I did not want to point it out, not when you were happy. But this' – he waved his hand in the direction of the necklace that had become a lead weight around my neck – 'this, stealing ...' His voice dropped to a whisper and he bent his knee to bring his face into mine.

I stamped my foot. 'You don't know that! And what do you mean "touch you?"'

He turned away from me with a growl and carried on walking.

'Anton!'

He stopped, but he didn't turn to face me. 'That first night. You asked me to drive her to your mother's. When the car stopped, she kissed my cheek and put her hand on my knee. I know it sounds stupid, I know. You had to be there.'

'It does sound bloody stupid and bloody arrogant if you ask me. And why didn't you tell me you were going to talk to Gaia? Shouldn't I have been there too? I was the one who found the bloody test!'

'I needed to talk to my daughter and so I did.'

He didn't mean to be hurtful. Gaia was his daughter and not mine. She was turning into a grown woman and I'd only been in her life for one short year. That didn't stop me from wishing she could be mine and loving her as though she were. It was like having a tiny hole in my heart and sometimes something would tug at it and tear it. Wishing that Gaia was my daughter was pointless; the sad little hole would always be there. I just hoped that with time it wouldn't so easily be tugged and torn. I swallowed the feeling down.

There was nothing I could say on the subject without crying, so I just nodded and whispered, 'It's my birthday and I don't want any more arguing.' My voice dropped to a whisper and Anton edged towards me so I could be heard. 'I know Keres is odd. I'm not bloody stupid, Anton. She's my sister. We don't know what she has been through, and she's a kid. I want to help her. Please, help me to guide her. Please give her time. She's my flesh and blood. Tomorrow. I'll talk to her tomorrow.'

Chapter 27

I didn't sleep well. I think I slept at points. Even when my eyes were closed, I would dream I was awake and lying with my eyes open. I could no longer tell what was real, other than the looming anxiety. I didn't toss and turn; my body felt rigid, unable to relax. Occasionally, my legs or my whole body would convulse and that's how I knew I must have been asleep. Sometime in the early hours I went to sit on the balcony of our room, tired of trying to rest with such a heavy mind. I sat in a dark corner looking out across the pool. A couple of round, frosted bulbs sat on the top of concrete posts to light the way for anyone getting back late at night. They weren't bright; just a golden glow trickling over the swimming pool.

A dark figure appeared silently from out of the shadows, feet moving quickly, but their arms didn't really move. They slowed down as they reached the dark corner that led to the back of the hotel. Another figure stepped out, with blonde hair reflecting in the light. I leant back into the darkest spot of the balcony, hoping not to be seen. The couple began to kiss, the blonde girl pressing the man to the wall next to a

"No Diving" sign. They stood still for a moment, presumably words were exchanged, and the girl kissed him once more before turning to leave, retreating into the shadows near some of the rooms and the stairs to the rest of the apartments. Before she completely disappeared, the man pulled her hand and I caught sight of her face in the light. I knew the round face to be Keres's. My eyes shot back to the man, but she quickly pulled him into the shadows.

I was sure the figure hadn't been tall enough to be Akis. He was broader and much taller than Nico, but they were both quite slim and dark. It could have been Nico, or someone else perhaps. I argued with myself that there was a chance, albeit it a slim one, that it was Akis. Perhaps she had sent him off to get something in the middle of the night. I wasn't really sure anywhere would be open at that time, but that wasn't to say it wasn't the case. Perspective is also tricky from a distance; maybe they were taller than they seemed.

I walked back into our room and lay on the bed like a zombie returning to its grave after a hard night chasing people. Anton's heavy arm stretched across me and pulled me in.

'I love you Melodie-Mou,' he breathed in my ear.

I closed my eyes again. *She's your sister*, I chanted over and over in my mind. *She's a teenager. She needs you.* Eventually, I was dreaming of shadowy figures circling me like trees with arms. However much I wanted to move, I couldn't. In the haze, I could hear Keres crying for help. Perhaps she was on the other side of the shadows. There was nothing I could do. I just didn't know how to help her.

I didn't want my dream to be a reality. Keres was to be given the benefit of the doubt, and either way, I wanted to bring out all the lovely things that I could see in her. She could be fun, interesting and confident, and I was sure there was much more to be found along the way.

Late in the afternoon the next day, Keres was lying in our garden sunbathing, Gaia was with a group of friends and Anton was helping Basil and Michail with some prep work for the pool. I knew this was my time to say something to Keres, but I had no idea where to begin. She had got one of the sunloungers out of the main outbuilding. It was to the left of the garden and masked by a row of bushes and trees. She was completely still, palms facing upwards, with her white bikini on and black sunglasses. I wasn't sure if she was awake, until she suddenly spoke out of an almost unmoving mouth, making my shoulders strike upwards in a panic.

'Are you all right?' she said again, this time bringing her weight up on to her elbows and peering at me above her round glasses. I made some noise, some kind of agreeable sound that lacked commitment. She pulled her glasses down a little further and curled slightly onto her side. 'Melodie?' Her fair eyebrows dropped as she questioned me, seeing through me.

'I was wondering … my necklace … Do you have a receipt? Only the clasp has broken and I was thinking of seeing if the shop could exchange it.'

Her legs swung round to plant her feet firmly onto the ground.

'I think, no. I can fix if you like. I am very good.'

'No, no, that's very kind, but the way it has broken, it's a fault, I think, so I'll take it back into the shop. I'm sure they'll remember you buying it. It's quite a distinctive piece.' I could feel my hairline begin to grow damp. It was a hot afternoon, but it wasn't that. I was standing in the shade of a nearby olive tree. Lying was not something I enjoyed to the point that I sort of wanted to go and break the necklace to make it less of a lie.

Keres's fingers pulsed and contracted into the squishy cushion before she stood up as tall as the tree behind me and told me she had found the necklace on the floor in the street and kept it because she knew I liked it. Instinctively, I hugged and reassured her. She dipped her chin in embarrassment. I reassured her as best I could while holding in all the rejoicing I felt from her innocence. She might play the boys, but at least she wasn't a thief. As she lay back down, I turned to leave her in peace, quickly checking we were on to run before dinner. Then in my excitement, I decided to find out about Nico and Akis.

'What did Nico mean? "Nice heart"?'

'I do not know,' she shrugged. 'He is a bad man.'

Her voice hit a tone I hadn't heard in her before. It was deep and mean, almost menacing. I walked away back to the house just as Gaia was coming in the front door.

'You're back early,' I called, as I strode across the expanse between the back door and the front. Gaia threw her pack down next to the stairs and leant on the banister. I followed her back towards the kitchen where she pottered about, moaning that she wasn't allowed to eat anything she liked anymore and explaining to me that's why she had left early because everyone wanted to go out to eat and she was too frightened to. She picked out a slice of cooked chicken from the fridge and a leftover potato and devoured them before they even saw a plate. She hopped up onto the work surface and sat swinging her legs as we talked. I'm not sure if she brought it up, or if I did, but the night before and the Akis-versus-Nico nonsense came to the forefront.

'Have you spoken to Keres about what happened?' She leant forward and lowered her voice.

I shook my head and slid my hands into the pockets on the front of my denim miniskirt and leant back against the fridge. 'You?'

'I don't really need to. It was very obvious.' Her vibrant, green eyes glistened in the sunlight streaking in through the window at the side of the house, and her nose wrinkled in a mischievous smile. Her body was leaning so far forward, I began to worry she might topple right off the edge of the worktop.

'Really?'

'Yeah! Nico said about her heart tattoo, you know, the one on her— *Kalispera*, Keres!' Gaia whipped back upright, and my head spun to the left so fast I nearly gave myself whiplash.

'What are you talking about?' Keres enquired as she turned on the cold tap so hard its mist touched Gaia's hand, which was resting next to it. She filled her glass and watched us as she drank.

Gaia looked from her to me; I opened my mouth, but Gaia came in with all her honesty. 'I was just saying about Nico and your tattoo.' Her voice came out quick and thin, like the unravelling of thread when a bobbin breaks on a sewing machine. 'Just that, I guess he said it to upset Akis. Well, it did upset him, didn't it? I mean, he did get angry, at least.'

'Men can be fools.' Keres gave Gaia a pleasant smile then spoke in Greek.

Gaia's cheeks went pink, then almost a hot red. She gave some short, sharp nods then the most insincere smile I'd ever seen on her pretty, round lips. The corners of her mouth were tiny and pointed into the kind of smile that can easily be found on many girls' Instagram accounts when they have taken three hundred selfies trying to get the right smile then settle on the beautiful but very fake-looking one. Then off Keres went, narrow hips swaying as she returned to the sun.

'What did Keres say to you?'

'Nothing,' Gaia muttered, and hopped down from the work surface. She folded her arms across her chest, making her navy NASA T-shirt that Anton's parents had sent screw up so it looked like it said AA instead. Her long, thin legs set off across the expanse of the room. I called after her, but she said she had homework and vanished around the corner. I was left to hear her stomping up the stairs.

I turned to look out of the window. Most of the back wall was taken up by kitchen cupboards, but near the back door a long window stretched above the worktop. I could see Keres talking to Michail. He was very still and clutching his folder to his chest. Keres on the other hand was very animated, laughing then leaning towards him to touch his face. The poor man edged round her, likely needing to make his way to the van. I debated whether or not to save him from my sister or to watch it play out. I was too tired from the night before to do anything other than watch as he scuttled away from her all on his own.

Keres hadn't said much on our run. She had admitted to me that she had a tattoo of a heart. She said it was very small, almost unnoticeable, but that she had shown Nico, and he was making it out to be much more than it was. I'd seen her in a string bikini and not noticed a tattoo. So, it was either very small or somewhere only a bikini would hide it.

When we got back from our run, Anton was in the kitchen chatting to Michail and Basil over a bottle or two of beer. We went straight over to them to grab drinks for ourselves, and in my presence everyone shifted into English.

'How's all the pool work coming along?' I smiled and slipped my arm around Ant. I could feel the tension in his body as he looked over at Keres who was reaching up and across Michail to grab two glasses. Poor Michail shifted, almost trapped between her and the cupboard behind. She laughed and said, '*Sygnómi*' – sorry.

As soon as she made her way to the sink to fill our glasses with water, Michail muttered something to his father and put down his beer.

'But Michail, we have not finished our drinks. Anton and Melodie welcome us in for a drink, we stay and drink it. He is – what do you English say? – all work and no play this one! Uh?' Basil laughed and elbowed Michail in the ribs.

'Poor Michail. He is shy. Aren't you, Michail?' Keres had passed me my water and was leaning against the sink opposite where Michail was standing. 'Michail tells me he has a girl. I'm not sure. I think he is too shy to talk with girls.' She proceeded to sip her water and watch him, her blue eyes unblinking, waiting for a response as his cheeks flushed.

'Sophia! Yes, yes. Lovely girl. I met her not so long ago. Pretty thing, no idea what she sees in this one!' Again, Basil laughed and nudged his son affectionately. 'He has done well.' Basil reached across and gently patted his son's blushing cheek.

I looked back at Keres whose mouth had flattened into a

thin smile. I don't know why she enjoyed toying with men so much. It was like it was her hobby. Michail drank his beer quicker than I'd seen, before hurrying his father along too.

Unsurprisingly, dinner had been quiet too. I'd tried to strike up conversations once or twice. Keres had been keen to converse with me, but Anton and Gaia had made every attempt feel like I'd got my foot caught in a black hole. Every cell in my body wanted things to go back to a few weeks before when we had all been laughing and joking. Not accusing and confusing.

At least one positive thing had been agreed. To extend my birthday celebrations, Keres and I were going to go for Chinese food in Sidari on the Friday night to have some sister time. It seemed like the perfect opportunity to have a drink or two and to straighten things out a little.

Anton cut huge oranges into slices at the table and combined them with Greek yoghurt and honey for dessert. The largest one spritzed the air as the knife pierced the skin and the table filled with its fresh, zesty scent. As it did so, Anton's eyes met mine. Perhaps he could see the desperation behind them, because he suddenly decided to talk.

'I was thinking the DNA tests sound very interesting. I might buy some for us all. Keres, where did you buy your test?' He looked down at her where she sat opposite me and to the left of Anton.

Keres pulled at the sleeve of the pink shirt that Akis had bought for her. 'The internet.' She turned her head up at him and smiled.

Ant let out a short laugh as he placed his knife back on the wooden board and passed her a full bowl. 'Yes, but what is the site? Which one did you use?' he said.

Keres put a large spoonful in her mouth and we all began to eat as we waited for her response. She began to shake her head.

'I will send to you on your email. So I am not getting it wrong.' She then took another large mouthful.

Gaia started to quietly tap the side of her bowl. Anton had only put oranges in hers, just in case. It was obvious she was getting fed up, but we were hopeful to have the more detailed results back within the coming days. Anton nodded his head.

'What do you think, girls?' He looked across at Gaia and me with a smile. 'Would you be interested in finding out where you are from and who you are related to?'

We both agreed, but the conversation only lasted until the end of the oranges.

When Anton and I went to bed, we pottered around each other, getting in each other's way at every turn. If I wanted to get to the cupboard, that's where he would stand. If he wanted to go to the loo, I would step in front of him. Each time, one of us would mumble an apology, but not a lot else. We had basically managed to avoid each other all day. Eventually, we were in bed with just the little lamps glowing behind our heads, making false halos around our overworked minds. It was Anton who broke the angelic spell.

'I need to tell you – I was not helping Basil and Michail this afternoon. That is not right. I did help a little, then I did something else.'

I rolled to face him. His hands were resting on the expanse of his chest and he was staring at the ceiling. With a little hum of encouragement, I indicated he should continue. He hesitated, but he did continue.

'It is about Keres,' he began. I let the air that'd been waiting

214

in my lungs free itself in one sharp hiss. 'Don't be that way. Just listen to me, Melodie-Mou. I called the orphanage. I asked about Keres – if there was anything they could tell me. If she had been adopted on the island or elsewhere—'

'And?'

'And they could not tell me anything. They are not permitted to give out anything. I did talk further to the woman on the call. She said if a baby is adopted often their names are changed, particularly a name like Keres that is so distinctive. Sometimes that is because the adoptive parents want to name the child themselves and sometimes it's to protect the child from being found.'

At some point in his little monologue, he had begun to turn to me. I heard the rustle of the sheets and felt the gentle shuffle of the bed. I didn't look at him though. I had closed my eyes, fighting back the tears that were clumping together and trying desperately to escape the corners of my eyes.

'So, wait, all babies' names are changed?'

'No, I do not think all, just—'

'So, you haven't actually found anything out. You just think her name should've been changed because you don't like it?' I snapped my eyes open to find Anton's face only a few inches from mine.

'If she was adopted as a baby, in those circumstances it is very likely her name would have been changed. The woman thought it was highly unlikely she would have been given the name Keres. Did she tell you that was her name?'

My temples were beginning to throb and I hated that Anton was inches from my face while feeling like he was miles away. I searched the folds of my mind to remember if she had told me her name or if I'd presumed it was Keres. I couldn't be

215

sure. Akis had said Jones, so she knew her name was meant to be Jones.

How could Anton go behind my back? Talking to strangers and coming to conclusions without evidence. It was bad enough with the necklace and thinking a kiss on the cheek was anything to worry about. Which made me realise I hadn't told him what she'd said.

'Well, perhaps she was adopted when she was older. And she hadn't stolen the necklace, by the way. She came out and said she had found it. She was embarrassed to tell me, but she didn't want to lie.'

One of Anton's thick eyebrows twitched slightly, and his jade eyes seemed darker and duller than usual. Other than that small twitch, his face remained unchanged as if it had been hand-carved out of bronze.

'Okay, Melodie-Mou, maybe ask her what age she was adopted. Maybe she was older. I do think you need to find out more before telling her about any inheritance you think she might be entitled to, at the very least.'

'I'm so tired of defending her, Anton. Can't you just, please, try to help me guide her instead of always judging her? We've been over this. I know she's odd. I bloody know, okay? And it's too late. I've already mentioned Mum's place. She knows it's half hers. I'm not going to lie to her, no matter what conclusions you keep running to.' I paused, waiting for a response. For the longest moment I wondered if he would ever reply, or if he had decided to just ignore me.

'How about this then? We speak to our solicitor. Get them to do it all properly?'

216

'Okay. Yes, I think that's a good idea.'

His lips found my forehead before he rolled away to turn off his halo.

Chapter 28

The Chinese restaurant in Sidari was my absolute favourite. We sat on the veranda at a wooden table with a crisp, white cloth, surrounded by a healthy mix of locals and tourists. I always think the food must be good if you get locals going there too. It was nice to be surrounded by chatter in Greek as well as in English. Keres and I were getting a lot of attention that night. One table of lads had drinks sent over to us and the waiter, whom I'd never seen there before, seemed almost too attentive. It wasn't surprising as, yet again, Keres had dressed to kill. Both of us had high-heeled shoes on, and as the average man is five foot nine in Greece, we both towered over everyone. I was wearing the dress I'd worn on my birthday the year before, bright purple that wrapped around, with thin straps – it had become a favourite of mine. Keres was wearing a tiny black bandeau and black-and- white miniskirt. With her slim frame, hint of a six pack and toned arms, she almost looked like a professional swimmer or dancer. All the running had toned me up again too, but it would take a decade of training for me to look as athletic as she was.

Our conversations had been mostly superficial. It was my fault really – I kept avoiding certain subjects for fear of the answers. But eventually, the subject of our father came up. I wondered how Keres had felt after discovering that her father had been such an evil and manipulative man. I knew how it had haunted me. The idea was always lingering as if someone were reading a book over my shoulder. I might not be looking directly at them but I knew they were there. That's what it felt like to me being related to a monster yet never meeting him face to face.

'He cannot be *all* bad,' she said, nibbling on a prawn cracker.
'Really?'

'Yes. No one is *all* bad.'

'Mum did say he was good at maths, I suppose.' The sizzle of aromatic duck went by with the rich smell of hoisin sauce, making me bite my lip in regret at not having ordered some for myself. 'But from what I know there wasn't much more.'

'You did not know him.' Her voice snapped a little.

My eyes met hers, as round and as blue as his, or perhaps as Mum's. Maybe seeing her face in his made it hard for her to see him as bad. No one wants to find out they're related to someone like that. I shook my head and dusted my fingers along the starched, white napkin on my lap.

'No, you're right. But I did meet Mum, and she was lovely.' I lifted my face and tilted my head, trying to offer the reassurance that at least one of our parents was normal.

Keres clenched her jaw and her lips fell into a thin smile. Her eyes quickly diverted from mine as the waiter came back. They spoke in Greek. Keres delicately rested her chin on the fingers of her right hand and giggled as he placed down another drink. He asked something and looked at me as I sipped at my straw like a one-year-old lost in an adult's conversation. Keres waved her hand at me dismissively and sat back into her chair. I had never seen this waiter before. He was either very new or just helping out the way Nico did if a place was understaffed. His name was Yiorgos. He was reasonably good-looking. His black hair was waxed firmly to his skull, and he brought with him a strong undercurrent of aftershave that I'm sure hadn't been there the last time he'd appeared. His eyes were almost as black as his hair. Something Keres said made them widen above his short, turned-up nose. His mouth opened to speak, but before he did, he glanced at me. When he did let his words out, his voice was lower and his eyes had sunk into a frown.

Keres shrugged and laughed, then said, *'Ta léme argótera'*, which I understood to mean "we will speak later".

He smiled at me, looking me over with a slightly raised eyebrow and then turned and walked away in some kind of trance.

'What did you say to him?' I put down my drink and picked up my chopsticks to tackle my rice.

'Not very mutz.' She took a long sip of her cocktail. 'Just that you were married to a very big man and he would be jealous of him talking with us.'

'Is that really what you said?'

'Yes. You do not trust me?'

I nodded. I wanted to trust her; she was my sister. It was hard knowing that Anton didn't trust her though. It was as though he were there telling me she couldn't be telling the truth all the time, yet he knew as much as me – nothing. Yes, she was odd, but she was a teenager with every reason to be odd. I had to keep telling myself that with the right support and influence she was a good person underneath it all. I didn't want to lose her without knowing her. She was all that was left of my mother and my grandparents. My only link. Anton couldn't understand that. He had lots of brothers and both of his parents were alive. I loved him for wanting to protect me but overreacting to situations wasn't helpful.

'Did you trust Liliana?'

My forehead may as well have answered for me. All the muscles pulled together in confusion at such an odd question.

'Are you sure they are not running off together?' Keres said. 'Maybe she wanted you to like her? With Father gone she could say what she want. Maybe?'

My head slowly began to shake as I considered her words. She continued to spoon rice and little pieces of fried pork into her delicate mouth as though she had just said something everyday like "funny old weather".

'She had scars on her face and the baby's grave in the garden.'

'Scars?' she repeated slowly. 'I do not know this one.'

'Marks, scars from injuries.' I pointed at my skin, looking for a scar, and remembered one on my elbow from falling on a patch of ice as a child. I'd caught my elbow on a short, brick wall on the way down. Papa had scooped me up, pressing the flap of skin back down, kissing my head and cursing me for running outside after him in my pyjamas. 'Scars like this,' I said, indicating my elbow, 'but worse. On her face.'

'Oh. I have scars, but no man beats me.' She shrugged before taking another spoon of food.

I didn't really know what to say. I had no reason to doubt my mother. Her diaries backed her up too. It would be ludicrous to think she had faked all that as a backstory to prove to me our father was bad and she was good.

'She wrote about it in her notebooks after his death when

221

she was looking for you. She wouldn't lie in those. She had no reason to. She didn't know I would ever read them,' I snapped, and Keres's face changed. She carefully pulled up her slipping little top before waving her hands like wipers at me.

'No, no. Only, you did meet her only a little and I want to know what you really think.' She shrugged. 'You are very right. I was silly.'

I gave a sharp nod. Of course I was right.

'Speaking of Mum, I have something exciting to tell you. Ant and I were talking last night and today he called our solicitor, our *dikigóros*, to get things moving with your half of the inheritance of Mum's house. I'm not sure what you want to do. If you want the house and will buy us out or if we pay you for your half. I don't think I'm ready to sell it to someone else. Or we could go on a joint venture and rent it out to someone together. What do you think?'

'Maybe you pay me. I think I need money more than house. What is next? When will this happen?'

'So, the solicitor said we will need to verify your identity – who you are – so you'll need to take in some ID. Like a passport or something. You might also need the DNA stuff and adoption papers too.'

'I do not have these things. Not here. This would take so long – if my brother has kept things. Is there another way? Maybe I just go and speak to this man, the *dikigóros*.'

'It's actually a woman. The solicitor.'

'*Dikigorina*, for a women. It is *Dikigorina*.' There was a pause as Keres tapped her fingers on her lips in deep thought. 'I cannot get these things, Melodie. Do we need solicitor?'

'It's okay. We'll find a way to get the paperwork together. If you call the orphanage on Monday that'll be a start. We'll get there.'

The air conditioning in our bedroom had gone off and Anton had rolled and slithered his way across to my side of the bed. One of us must have accidentally put it on a timer instead of continuous. Somehow, I'd got wrapped in the white sheet, making me look like a Halloween ghost. The heat was unbearable, and I'd forgotten to bring up a glass of water. Unravelling myself carefully from the mess, I slipped out of the bedroom. As soon as I stepped through the door, I could hear whispering downstairs. At first, I thought perhaps Gaia and Keres were talking and giggling. Taking small steps to reach the thick, wooden banister, I peered over into the darkness below. The only light was coming in through the front door that was half-open, and Keres and Yiorgos from the restaurant were standing there. My eyes adjusted to the dim light puddling in from the moon and our lanterns outside just in time to see his hand groping her backside as he kissed her. A moment later, she pulled away and he left. I had Nico's words in my head about picking her up in the dead of the night, then the thought of Akis's face if he knew what she was doing behind his back. The raw fury at Nico knowing about a tattoo was enough. I edged backwards, pressing my back into our door while silently trying to open it and slip back in. I had no idea if she saw me as she breezed up the stairs. I stood on the other side of the door. My skin felt on fire from the closeness of the room, but I was too afraid to leave again to do anything about it. I sprinted on tiptoes to the en suite and splashed water over my face and arms at the sink, and gulped down handfuls. I caught sight of myself in the moonlight. My face was pale and dripping, but it was the deep line between my brows that stood out to me. I rubbed at it as though it were a dirty mark I could erase rather than a physical reaction to a situation I was lost in.

I wanted to talk to Anton. She was cheating on his brother with a total stranger. And not only that, bringing him to our home where Gaia slept peacefully in her bed. My skin rippled with goosebumps at the fear of what Keres's stupidity could bring with her. Should I tell her what I'd seen? Or speak to Anton? Or Akis? My mind was darting about like a wasp at a picnic. I paced the floor until eventually Anton walked in without turning the light on, scratching his belly.

'*Gromto*! I didn't know you were in here! Why are you in the dark?'

'I– I don't know.' My face screwed up like an old tissue and hot tears ran down my even hotter cheeks. Ant's arms were immediately wrapped around my shoulders as he quietly shushed me in the dark.

'What's wrong, Melodie-Mou? Don't hide from me.' His words pressed through my hair and trickled at my ears. I was hiding, or at least trying to. I shook my head as my chest began to shake under the strain of my sobbing. 'Melodie,' he said, in a low and stern voice.

My knees didn't want to hold me up anymore. They gave way under the weight sitting on my skull. Strong arms held me together and eased me down to the floor like a child trying to prop up a rag doll. The only thing in my body that held itself firm were my lungs as they juddered and pulsed, choking on each inhalation of tears. Anton's lips found my damp cheeks, accidentality pressing my hair against them, sticking it to the hot salt on my skin.

224

'Calm down now, Melodie-Mou. You are making me frightened. Talk. Talk to me.'

'I don't know. I don't know!' Gently, I pushed out of Anton's embrace and stretched for some toilet roll to smother my misery in. 'There was a man, downstairs—' This was the wrong choice of words.

Silhouetted by moonlight in the bathroom, Anton sprang to his feet and began to hiss questions as to the man's whereabouts, eyes skipping along the lines of the room like stones on the sea.

'No, no. Stop, listen! He was here to see Keres. It was a man from Sidari. The waiter in the Chinese. He's gone.'

'What?' His head shook silently in the dark. 'Why was he here?'

'How– how would I know? I just s-saw him at the door talking to Keres. I'm pretty sure it was him.' My chest still shook, but at least the tears had subsided. 'I think she is cheating on Akis. Maybe with Nico t-too,' I stuttered.

Even in the shadows I couldn't look at Anton's face. In my mind's eye I knew how it looked. I'd spent most of the past year enjoying his expressions, his idiosyncrasies. Instead of watching his brow descend on his face, I looked at his hands and his fingers closing in around his thumbs in a stranglehold. A small noise of acknowledgement jutted out from somewhere behind his nose.

'So it is what I thought.'

I'm not sure if he could see much of me but I nodded anyway.

'"Heart" is a tattoo. Gaia told me. We have both seen her in a bikini and I've never noticed a tattoo, so it has to be somewhere—'

He interrupted me with a *tsss* noise like an old-fashioned

kettle.

'I do not like this girl, Melodie. I do not trust her. I want her away from my brother and my daughter. I want her away from you.'

'Now, that's not fair,' I wailed. 'She's only young and she is acting out!'

'Is she? She told Akis she was twenty-five.'

'That's exactly the sort of stupid thing a young girl would do! We don't know what's going on! It's not fair to assume. That man might have followed us back here and she might have been telling him to go away – we don't know!'

'And Nico?'

I hesitated, remembering our night at Barras. It could be that on their one and only date, he had seen the tattoo and then never again. Maybe it wasn't her or wasn't him. I couldn't be sure of anything. It was much too dark to know for sure one way or the other.

'It could've been from their one date. We don't know. I don't want to shut out the one relative I have left.' My voice began to sound like a whistle in the back of my throat and my lashes gathered up tears again the way bees gather pollen.

Anton took me in his arms again and shushed me once more. He rocked me gently and kissed the top of my head.

'Please don't say anything to anyone. Not yet. Akis might work it out on his own and we might be able to help Keres to find herself. Please? Please, Anton?' My words hung in the air until Anton eventually agreed to stay silent. For me.

Chapter 29

I promised Anton that I would at the very least get Keres out of the house until things died down. There was no need to argue because it was what I wanted too. I didn't want to lose her, but I'd had enough of lying to myself about her too. After breakfast, I would sit her down and speak to her about what I'd seen. What I knew. I would say that there was no judgement or anything like that, although, in my opinion, she should take into account how it might all play out and who might be hurt in the end. It was planned in my mind, and I let sentences spiral in practised conversations as I brushed my teeth, knowing I couldn't actually stomach breakfast. In fact, even my toothbrush made me feel a little sick, and I started to question if I'd had too much to drink the night before. Did I even see her with the man? I shook my head, making strands of hair stand up in all directions around my face. I just needed to talk to her.

'Bye!'

As though she were stealing thoughts straight from the pockets of my mind, her voice carried along the landing. I

227

quickly splashed water on my face and patted it with a thick, white towel before running towards her voice. By the time I'd made it to the top of the stairs, she was gone. I didn't know where and I didn't know with whom.

I sat working in the office for the whole day. Anytime there was the slightest noise around the house, I'd be calling her name. Each time it would be Gaia or Anton. I'd got absorbed in looking up content ideas for one of the restaurants I was working with when Keres's head popped around the door.

'Do you want to run?' she said.

'How long have you been home?' I looked at my watch. It was five fifteen, our usual running time. I decided it would be the perfect opportunity to talk to her so I quickly went to put on my crop top and short leggings, ready to run. I pulled my hair into a ponytail with the scrunchie she'd got me for my birthday.

She was at the bottom of the stairs bouncing from foot to foot. I kissed Anton goodbye, who gave my hand a little extra squeeze before I began to jog after Keres. As we began, I thought that I should wait until the quiet of the olive grove to talk to her. It would be a safe place to stop and rest for a chat. We were just about to turn off the road and into the olive grove when Keres squealed.

'My earring! It's fallen in my top!'

I offered my help, but she said I should keep running and she would catch up. In my head it was perfect, I could sprint ahead and wait for her. Because I would be stopped, she could stop too and talk to me. The route became quickly quite dense with trees, outside of the dusty path we followed. It was not a formal path in any way, just a route that had been carved out over time. Soon I was deep in my own thoughts, running as fast as my legs would take me, pressing on as quickly as I could so that there would be plenty of time to stop and think at the high point of our route.

Running between the trees and the shadows gave light relief in the thirty-four-degree heat. When I made it to the top, I was drenched in sweat. I grabbed at a tall, old olive tree to lean on and stretch out my calves. I knew I had some time before Keres would catch up, as there was no reason for her to be sprinting.

Then a branch, or a twig, or a bone crunched to my right. I turned, expecting to see a sweet lizard or a bird. A hooded man jumped out, knocking me to the ground. His fingers were quickly on my mouth, pressing my face, squeezing my bones. As I hit the dirt path, all the air left my lungs empty, and his fingers clasped over my lips. Lactic acid gripped my muscles; they were stiff and frozen. My body needed more oxygen. Not less. Not none. I twisted, my lungs convulsing, my fingernails desperately trying to find his skin. But I had no energy, and the sun was streaming in my eyes. I couldn't think and I stopped being able to feel anything other than the throbbing of my skin and my bones beneath it.

When he removed his hand to tug at the thick strap of my sports bra, it gave me time to pull in thin, sharp breaths. My mouth opened in desperation as my lungs jolted like hiccups dragging in what little air they would allow. Not much. Just enough. There was no hope of screaming.

Every muscle was weak from lack of oxygen. Adrenaline went to my head, making me dizzy. All it seemed to do was tire me more, give me more lactic acid to seize up my screaming body and my silent mouth. I tried to twist away as he grunted in frustration or anger that my sports top was so tight it was almost impossible to pull down over my shoulders.

Then he was off me. Standing over me, with his head obstructing the sun. I couldn't see his face. Only his black eyes. He was wearing a medical face mask. I tried to scramble towards him and reach for the mask as he hunched over me. I was still clumsy and he grabbed my wrist and began to pull me along, my feet scrambling to stop him dislocating my shoulder. Twigs and dried soil dug into my skin as I slipped and was dragged along. He dropped me behind the olive trees, laughing. Then there was a noise. Like a dull thud. Hollow. The man stumbled towards me, crushing my ankle under his boot. I gasped – the first proper breath I'd managed to inhale.

Keres's voice came from the path, with that low aggressive tone. Squirming at the pain of my ankle, my eyes caught her. She was holding a thick branch the way someone might hold a baseball bat. She shouted at him, but he didn't react right away. In one vicious move, she leapt forwards and struck him across the back again. Then he turned and staggered away, waving his arms at her, saying the same words over and over again. She came at him again as though she might strike his head, and he jolted back before shaking his head at her. Her mouth barely moved, but I'm sure she muttered something, edging closer to him.

Then he was gone.

It was only once he was well out of sight that I cried. Keres threw the branch to the ground and held me. She rocked me and chatted to me in Greek and then English. She scooped me up from the floor, bleeding and bruised. She called the police and they had arrived at the house before we did, as I limped along the road. Anton was running down the driveway as we turned in. He pulled me close, scooping me up and enveloping me, making me flinch. He asked more questions than I could ever answer. All I could manage was, 'She saved me.'

Keres stayed by my side and answered the questions from the police officers. They asked for my account of the attack too, as I sat and had my grazes dressed and cleaned. Keres reassured me that it wouldn't happen again and that they would catch the man. All I could say was that he had black eyes and eyebrows with tanned skin. I sort of felt like I recognised his voice but with a face mask on, I couldn't be sure of anything much. Dark shorts. Keres said they were black. A grey, sleeveless hoodie. Keres added a brand name. And he kept saying something.

'Keres what did he keep saying to you? Over and over?'

'*Fÿge*? It means "go away".'

'No. It was more than a word. Maybe one had a shh in it? I'm not sure anymore.' I touched my head at the back only to find a small patch of dried blood. They wanted to take me to hospital for tests and X-rays.

I let them.

Chapter 30

I wasn't broken. I had to keep telling myself that. I wasn't broken. I wasn't broken. The hospital had told me so. All I needed was rest for my badly bruised ankle and soul. But I was not broken.

Keres and I had gone running around the same time most days on and off before the attack, so the police didn't think it was random. They thought the attacker had likely seen us running before at the same time and was waiting for the right moment. But we hadn't seen his face, and dark eyes were pretty normal in Greece, so there wasn't much hope of catching him.

That stupid man had shaken every last bone in my body. But he hadn't broken them, and I wouldn't let him break me. I stayed in bed for as long as I could. It was like being back in the thick of the first two waves of the pandemic all over again. Just after losing my grandparents I'd spent all my time in bed. It was all I could do.

I slept for twelve hours straight the night after the attack. When I woke up, Anton was sitting on the bed next to me, fully dressed, scrolling on his phone. Anton had lain with me for a long time. He had tried to ask questions, but I didn't feel much like answering so we just listened to the clock tick time away instead. Eventually, he disappeared and came back with a breakfast I didn't eat.

Overnight my body had picked up new aches, with their echoes of mistreatment. Every muscle in my neck and back was pulled taut. The thin fibres of my muscles felt torn and bruised. I'd been lucky. I was mostly just scraped and bruised. If it weren't for Keres being so brave ... It didn't bear thinking about. I pulled my eyes tightly shut and sloped the sheet back over my head.

A week after, I had Gaia, Keres and Anton around me, making me feel like a fraud. I wasn't broken. Eventually, Anton had to take Gaia to Natalia's to help at the taverna. Keres stayed sitting on the bed with me. I had seen her less and less as the week progressed and I'd started to think she couldn't bring herself to be alone with me anymore. She did her best to reassure me, stroking the hair around my face.

'Why didn't you just run for help?' I looked up at her from my pillow as her lips curled in a soft smile.

'I would never leave you. You are my sister.' Her fingers glanced away from the sore, purple bruise on my wrist where he had pulled me, and she settled on holding my hand.

'Melodie, I need to tell you ...' Her voice was low and she was much scruffier than she normally was, with unbrushed hair and a long-sleeved, baggy T-shirt. 'Anton has not let me see you. I am sorry, but he is bad man, Melodie. Look ...' She yanked up her sleeve and thrust her wrist at me. There was a big, red-purple mark. Only a large hand could have made such a statement.

I shuffled to sit higher in the bed, taking her hand in mine to examine the injury. It was so similar to mine, only now mine was more blue and purple with yellowing edges.

'Are you saying Anton did this?'

'Yes.' Tears fell across her cheeks and clung to her dark-blonde lashes. 'Last night he pulled me away from your door. Pulled me to my room and threw me to the bed. I was afraid what he will do. He is different when you are not here. Please help, Melodie. Please protect me.' That's when she began to really sob in my arms.

I didn't know what to say or think. I just sat for a moment with my mouth open. My instinct was not to believe her. I couldn't imagine Anton being that way. It seemed impossible, but the mark on her wrist was undeniable and I knew he didn't like her. Anxiety tugged low in my gut. Directly after the attack I'd struggled to let him near me. The idea of any man so close made me feel too vulnerable. In the past days we had held each other more and started to be a little normal again. Although what had happened to me made it hard to trust people, I still trusted him.

He said he didn't trust her, that he wanted her away from me and Gaia. My mind began to vibrate with questions as to how far he might go to keep her away from me. After everything that had happened in the olive grove, I owed her the benefit of the doubt that perhaps something happened to her. Every part of me wanted to scream at her for lying but then I looked down at how distraught she was and the mark on the arm that was clinging to me and I had to reassure her. I had to find out the truth.

'I need to talk to him. This doesn't make any sense Keres. It'll be okay, shh. I won't let anyone hurt you again.'

'No, please no! Do not tell him I told you. He say to me if I tell you he hurts me more. He tells me you will never believe me. He has always been hating me.'

'Listen to me, I'll get to the bottom of it, okay? It has to be a misunderstanding. Why don't you stay with Akis? Get your things, get ready now and call him.'

'I cannot leave you.'

'I'll be fine, Keres. Do you feel safe with Akis?'

She nodded. 'But he cannot get me until tomorrow, Melodie.'

'Stay in here with me until then.'

So, she did. She sat with me, and when Anton appeared and asked for her help with dinner, we declined, saying we were watching a film on my tablet. I got myself up and dressed for dinner. It was time to stop sulking and time to work out some answers. Keres hadn't wanted me to speak to Anton about it. There was a small part of me that was relieved. As soon as her lie was revealed for what it was, I might lose her. I kept trying to work out why she might lie or what circumstance might have caused such a misunderstanding. Nothing could wash away the mark on her arm. What choice did I have other than to talk to him? I needed to read his face when I asked him to truly be sure.

Everything seemed normal. Like it had been before the attack. Like it had been before the questions. Dinner. Chatting. Maybe even more smiles as Gaia and Anton were so happy that I had actually left the bedroom for a meal. There was no way I could stay for long after though. I gave Anton a come-with- me look after dinner. Keres squeezed my hand as she kissed my cheek goodnight.

When we were alone in our room, Anton held me and began to kiss me. It was the first time he had properly kissed me since the attack. My lungs squeezed and I pulled away, clutching his thick arms in my hands. I opened my mouth to ask him why, why would he hurt her? How could he? But I didn't. There's no way to explain my actions other than the desire to escape the reality of the present and disappear into the past. Our shared past. A past where I could believe we were going to live as one happy unit together.

I pulled him back towards me, kissed him fiercely, almost biting his lip, and dragged him down to the floor on top of me. We pulled at each other's clothes as if we had an unquenchable thirst; we needed each other. I needed him. It was only when our skin was pressing together that he stopped and pulled his face away from mine. He gently brushed hair from my eye, then pressed his soft, freshly shaved cheek to mine.

His long fingers ran the length of my leg, carefully placing it around his torso as he eased himself towards me, gathering me up like a soft quilt as he tenderly caressed me, confused me, loved me, hurt me, teased me, tormented me. Mostly without even knowing.

I went to bed that night wondering what tomorrow might bring. I would have to ask Anton about his supposed violence towards Keres once she was safely out of the house. Would that be the last time he would love me? Would it be the last time Keres was allowed in our house? Or was she telling the truth about his hatred for her running deeper than I could possibly imagine? Was it in fact Anton causing all this upset from the start and making things up about her? My love for

Anton wasn't something I'd ever been able to control. From the moment I met him he had left an imprint on me and I couldn't shake it. I didn't want to. I just wanted to be a part of his little world and to live in it until the day I die. The idea of cutting him out, or a sister because of him, dug into me and hurt me deeper than any stranger ever could. But I had only known him just over a year. I would be stupid not to at least ask him for his side of the truth, even though trapped air that was sitting stale in my lungs was there because I'd only known Keres for a matter of months, and however much I wanted to trust her, I couldn't. I didn't.

In the darkness, his hand felt for mine.

'Melodie-Mou, I would do anything to make sure no one hurts you again.'

And that's what I was afraid of. I squeezed my eyes tightly shut and silently cried into a dream world of nightmares where I was screaming *I'm not broken* until my lungs crushed my heart and there was nothing left that could be fixed.

Chapter 31

Keres lugged her new, much bigger case down the stairs.

'Akis is here. I will call you soon, yes?'

I nodded, clutching her hand as she kissed my cheek. Akis was at the bottom of the stairs holding Gaia's face, squeezing it playfully and laughing. Anton was there too, with a smile on his lips but also the line between his eyebrows. He looked locked in place, with his broad shoulders tall and square and his arms crossed over his chest, which made his biceps look like they might pull his milk-coloured T-shirt into threads. It was clear he still didn't want Keres anywhere near his brother either. As soon as Akis saw Keres, he skipped up the stairs two at a time, in the same way Anton and Gaia always did, ready to take her case for her. Kisses brushed everyone's cheeks, and then she was gone. No conversation. Nothing. Anton closed the door and hovered near it, with his large, right hand resting on it. Deep, slow breaths made his shoulders rise and fall, and I could almost hear his gritted teeth.

The phone started to ring, making the three of us twitch round to hone in on it. Usually, it only rang twice a week.

Once was Anton's mum and once was Katerina's mum. Gaia and I didn't move even though we were nearer to the phone. Instead, Ant marched between us to the left of the stairs and towards the wood burner where it stood on a thick, wooden shelf that looked a bit like driftwood. Whoever was on the other end of the phone was doing all the talking. Anton only interjected with short bursts of questions that left Gaia standing at his feet, tugging at the edge of his T-shirt as though she were a small child. Eventually, he pressed the button to hang up the call and replaced the phone.

'The doctor does not know what was wrong with Gaia. All the tests came back negative. They said start to eat normally but add food back slowly, and you must keep a food diary.' His finger pointed at Gaia who had begun to bounce on her heels at the idea of eating normally again.

'Can I start today? Finn will be here soon. Does this mean I can be normal again?'

Anton gave a singular downward nod that was enough to make Gaia jump at him like a deranged frog, clumsily leaping into his ill-prepared arms. This was followed by cheering and skipping up the stairs. I followed suit – not with the skipping – just up the stairs to make myself a little more presentable for the day and to prepare myself to talk to Anton.

He followed me, which stupidly I hadn't prepared for. When we were in our room, I hesitated and didn't know what to do with myself.

'What's wrong, Melodie-Mou?'

'I– I'm not sure. Sit down. Here, next to me. Listen. I need you to tell me the truth, no matter what the truth might be, okay? Because if you don't, I'll know, Anton Greenwood, and if I don't know right away then I'll bloody well find out. Do

239

you understand me?'

He was perched on the edge of the bed with his hands clasped together in his lap, nodding and frowning, waiting to hear what truth he had to tell.

'Have you been stopping Keres seeing me this past week?'

His head twitched to one side and he pouted a little as though he wanted to ask a question but didn't know where to begin. 'No.' The "o" was elongated as though the "o" in itself were a question that I had to answer.

'Did you pull on her arm the night before last? At all?'

'What are you talking about, Melodie? Of course not! Why would I? I can't believe this is even a question. Did that girl say I hurt her?'

I nodded, silently hoping his voice wouldn't gain in momentum.

'That lying bitch.'

'Don't talk like that, please.'

'If she is telling lies to come between us then she is worse than a bitch! No, I did not hurt her, or even see her that night. No, I did not stop her from seeing you. Every day she comes up to talk to you after lunch, to be alone with you. I have let her! She wanted time alone with you and I didn't stop her. I do not like her. I do not trust her. But she saved you when I couldn't and I am grateful for that. So, I agreed to it.' He continued to rant, only in Greek. Then he held his face in his hands.

I wish I could read people. Anton and Keres both seemed to be telling the truth. The difference was, Keres had a track record of lying and Ant didn't. Not as far as I could tell. The real problem was that Keres had no reason to lie. No reason to get between us. Anton did have a reason, a very deep-set

240

dislike for her that he had openly admitted.

'Well, she has a bruise like mine on her wrist, and she said it was you who caused it.'

Both our phones buzzed. It was Akis in a group chat he had made that had Keres in too. The text read:

Are you still in? We are on our way back now.

Anton:

Ok. C u soon.

'We should go downstairs,' I said. 'I think we should all sit down and talk about this. Akis too. Shit! Finn is here. Look, once Finn has gone, we'll sit down and sensibly discuss it all. It's the only way we can get through this. If you truly love me, you'll do this for me.'

He began to shake his head, making my stomach squeeze and the back of my throat burn with rising acid. Then he whispered under his breath.

'Yes. I love you enough to do anything.'

Gaia and Finn were intertwined on the corner sofa in the TV nook. Ant gave a cough to announce our arrival downstairs as they clearly hadn't noticed us, and Finn almost threw Gaia and Donnie to the other side of the chair. She just let out a little puff, blowing hair from her face, and lay down pretty much on top of him again. Gaia had her own ideas and what her father thought about them was becoming less and less of a factor for her. Finn at least was polite enough to say hello and to ask how we were, leaving poor Donnie to jump down and rub himself along Ant's ankles. When we sat down, we

241

were the polar opposite to Gaia and Finn. Firstly, we sat in the opposite corner of the house, on the brown sofas, and rather than cuddling or kissing, we sat apart. Waiting. Eventually, Donnie jumped up to rub around us both, giving us a little light relief. When Akis and Keres burst through the door, we re-enacted Finn's reaction to Anton, jumping up, making Donnie dash towards his bed near the kitchen.

'We have news!' Akis announced. His smile was so broad the little scar on his cheek had completely disappeared into its dimple status.

Gaia and Finn picked up their drinks and came across to group around the couple. Keres put her phone on the coffee table in a childlike, over-exaggerated manner, then, when nothing was said, she wiggled her hand above it.

Akis said, 'I asked Keres to marry me!'

'And I say yes!' Keres thrust her right hand towards me to more directly display a gold band with a large – presumably diamond – round solitaire.

No one said a word for a good few moments, but the room was far from silent. It was filled with gasps, foot shuffling, loud exhales and the almost-but-not-quite start of words, like *Wha—* and *Bu—*. We all had too many things to say and ask, yet nothing was able to penetrate past our teeth. Eventually, I managed to kick off with an easy cliché.

'Con– congratulations!' I squeezed out, then Keres grabbed and squeezed me.

'We are sisters twice,' she breathed in my ear.

'We must celebrate! Who wants champagne?' Anton said, and clapped his hands together. His words were light, but his face was dark red. There was a general round of nodding, before Ant led Akis outside to choose a "nice bottle" from a fridge in the outhouse.

'Can we have champagne?' Gaia bounced on her tiptoes with her cheekbones high on her face. She hadn't reacted with more than a gasp to the engagement but the idea of champagne had her almost jumping.

'You two have milkshakes that you've barely touched!' I pointed at their glasses on the coffee table.

'Have champagne,' Keres said. 'Don't worry about milk-shake!'

'It's okay.' Gaia grabbed their glasses and passed Finn his. She said something in Greek then they both gulped back the milk.

'Now can we have champagne?' She laughed as she wiped her mouth with the back of her hand.

'I was going to say I can't see why not, anyway.'

The playful moment was splintered by Akis exploding through the front door. He may as well have left shards of woodchips across the floor. His palms were waving and thrusting towards Keres. Greek words spilled from his mouth like an overflowing *karáfa*. Ant slipped in behind him and hovered near the door. Akis was barking more than shouting. Growling. Spitting almost. I mouthed at Anton, but I could read his face. I didn't need his words. He had told Akis what he knew. Perhaps about there being multiple men. Perhaps about the morning's accusation. Akis turned back towards the door, chased by Keres. Finn had gone bright red and Gaia's mouth was wide open.

Before anyone could say anything, Keres's phone began to vibrate and a name popped up onto the screen. We all looked from one to the other.

'I guess I should answer it,' I said, pointing towards my chest.

As I answered it, I realised I couldn't actually converse in Greek but managed, 'Hello, I mean, *kalispera*. Keres *tilefono*.'

'Hello?' snipped the women on the line. 'Wrong number.' Her accent was strong, much like Keres's, but her English was good. As quickly as she'd said "Hello", she was gone. The phone was still in my hand when it began to ring again and the letter "M" flashed up again.

'Gaia, you answer it!'

'Me?'

'Yes, at least you speak Greek!' I thrust the phone at her and she answered.

She'd only said a handful of words before she stepped across me and sat down, burying herself in a frown. Anton came out of his not-so-hidden hiding place where he was clearly listening to the arguing on the other side of the door.

'Melodie,' Gaia said, pressing the phone to her chest, 'she says this phone isn't owned by a "Keres". She says it's her daughter's phone. She says it's Evangelina's phone and wants to know why I have it. What do I even say to that?'

'That doesn't make any sense. Ask her to describe her daughter.'

My palms began to sweat, waiting to hear that the phone was yet another item Keres had stolen. I thought it looked new, but I hadn't dared to ask. Gaia was nodding and saying something, but she was looking at me.

'Five foot eight. Blonde hair. Slim. Runner. Blue eyes. Round face. Twenty-five years old. Heart tattoo. She is demanding to speak with her daughter.'

'Hang up.'

'What?'

'I said, hang up!' It was the closest I'd ever come to really shouting at Gaia. I wasn't intentionally shouting at her. In fact, I wasn't really shouting at her at all, I was shouting at the situation.

She quickly hung up and placed the phone on the table. Finn was still lurking on the other side of the coffee table like a bucket without a spade. His shade of red was tinged purple under his sandy skin.

'Can you send me that number, Gaia? Now, please,' I said, and carefully tucked the wild, wavy strands of my hazel hair behind my ears. Smoothing down the soft ends was a way of distracting myself, or perhaps it helped me to think.

'Melodie-Mou, I do not know what's going on here, but it is not Gaia's fault. Your sister – if she even is that – she is to blame.' Ant's words rushed past me in the slipstream of my thoughts.

I sat down on the chair behind me to study Gaia who had picked the phone back up and pressed the screen. 'Mou-mou, her phone is locked. I'm so sorry, I can't.' Gaia's voice trembled and her eyes became as shiny as Keres's engagement ring. I nodded, and reassured her. My eyes fell back on Finn.

'Are you okay?'

On cue, he ran towards the loo under the stairs where we could all hear him vomiting. I looked at Gaia whose skin had begun to gather tiny beads of sweat like tiny ticks clinging to her flesh. She picked up her milkshake glass and vomited straight into it. In an instant, Anton was the other side of her catching her hair to stop it falling in the vomit that had curdled in the glass.

'What have you had?' His voice was quick, desperate to solve the puzzle.

She wasn't able to answer as she hovered over the glass

245

gagging, her stomach visibly contracting with the strain. Eventually, it momentarily settled.

'Milkshake.'

Anton took the glass from her and scooped her into his arms, just as he would have done when she was a baby, and carried her up to her room. Poor Finn was still locked in the downstairs loo. Alone for a moment, I begun to almost vibrate. Every muscle in my body had began to pull taut under the strings of Keres – Evangelina – whoever she was. The creature I'd let into our house, into our lives. My green nails unconsciously dug into the flesh behind my knees and I didn't need a mirror to tell me the veins in my temples were throbbing.

Just as she crept across my mind, Keres – Evangelina – crept in the door. Mascara coloured her cheeks instead of her lashes. She came towards me, arms outstretched, begging without words.

'Oh Melodie,' she cried.

I stood up. I walked. I went to her. Cradling her head. Rocking her. '*Shh*, it's okay, Evangelina.'

She yanked away from my constricting grip, eyes narrow and wild like a grass snake's.

'Your mother called.' I took hold of the sleeve of her top as she tried to slither free. 'Yes, that's right, your mother. You disgusting creature. I don't know who the hell you are, but you stay away from my family or so help me god there will be nothing left of you!' As I spoke, I bundled her along, thrusting her towards the door.

She didn't say a word. I hadn't drunk any of the milk, but as soon as the door closed, I vomited into my hands.

Chapter 32

After days on end of staying in and hiding in work, Anton booked for us to go to Manthos Restaurant in Agios Stefanos. It had been beautifully refurbished in recent years and was quickly becoming a favourite place for a special meal.

My bruises had healed. I knew Anton had been the one telling the truth about Keres too, other than just instinct, Akis told us that she had asked him to hurt her a few nights before it all happened. Apparently, she had been sneaking around with Akis as well as behind his back. She said it was for fun but he refused. Clearly she had found someone else to help her create the mark on her arm.

Gaia was going to stay over at Finn's for a birthday movie night. It had been her birthday the week before, and we'd thrown her a sci-fi-themed party. Gaia had been a little too excited to be allowed to stay at Finn's and Anton nearly changed his mind. Ever since Finn had sat down with him and spoken about Gaia, Anton had completely changed with the boy. He now welcomed him like a son. Since she stopped using the milkshake powder, Gaia had been fine. No more problems, only smiles. Which had just meant smiles from Anton too. We had kept the powder and had been trying to find out where we could send some to have it tested to find out what was wrong with it.

I had been dressed and ready for ages. I wasn't sure how long it had been. I just sat on the shell chair in the corner of the room thinking about how dark the man's eyes had been that attacked me. Black. I could almost taste the blood in my mouth again. I didn't mean to think about it. It just crept up on me sometimes. Then it was Anton who crept in and sat down on the bed facing towards the chair.

'You look beautiful, my Melodie-Mou.'

'Isn't that like saying "my Melodie mine?"' I didn't look up, but in the corner of my eye I could tell he was nodding and smiling.

'Yes. I was being Greek-lish.' He gave a gentle laugh. Not a real or solid laugh. Just a nod to the fact he was trying to make me smile.

'I'm ready. Other than shoes. I think my orange heels to match my lipstick. Could you grab them, please?'

As Anton left the room to get my shoes, I quickly stood up and positioned myself in the full-length mirror that I could see in the bathroom. I'd straightened my hair, something I rarely did. I smoothed the soft ends between my fingers and told myself that it was my life and it should be lived. I was not going to let some nasty prick dictate my ability to leave the house. Not him and not Keres. With that thought still pulsing around my mind like the blood through my veins, Anton passed me my burnt- orange heels with the thick straps. I slipped them on and we left.

When we arrived at Manthos, a blonde woman was having

her photo taken in one of their beautiful white, wicker swing chairs that hung like cut open eggs ready to cocoon and look after the inhabitants. I always wanted to sit in one, but by the end of every meal we had there, I had forgotten to.

The owner of Manthos had given us the perfect table to watch the beach and the sunset. Anton had booked it all in advance. A bottle of champagne was already waiting for us in an ice bucket that hung off the edge of the table like a lobster claw holding a clam. Being the perfect gentleman, Anton pulled my chair out and tucked me in. He was almost ready to pour the champagne, but the waiter beat him to it. He made a toast. To me. To his Melodie. To us. To being out. To living. That's when I had to stop him.

'You need to stop. It's starting to feel like you're pressuring me. Or in some strange way you're bringing it up again. Please, just be normal. I don't want to think about her and the damage she caused. That I caused.' He looked so hurt. That wasn't my intention and I became irrationally annoyed about it, snapping at him further. 'Please don't make that face. I just want to forget about it all. Please.'

'Of course, Melodie-Mou. I am just happy it is just the two of us.'

'I'm sorry. It's me, not you. No, it's not me. It's him, it's her. It's the past few months of unanswered questions constantly dancing about in my head.'

'I keep thinking where was she in the first place?'

'Not this again.' I put down my glass before I'd even managed a sip. So many times Anton had questioned how it could have taken so long to look for an earring. Each time Keres – Evangelina – had explained the same thing. It fell down her top. She couldn't find it. Eventually she found it on the floor. That was all. I explained how I had sprinted ahead so I could find time to talk to her. It was the one thing that hadn't been her fault. 'I can't go over that again. I know she lied and cheated, but she still saved my life. Whoever she really is, I can still be grateful for that.'

'I'm sorry. You are right. Let's just look at the menu and talk about something wonderful.' His fingers settled on top of mine, slipping his thumb into the hollow of my hand. It wasn't fair to keep taking it out on Ant. I knew if he got his hands on the man who hurt me he would kill him. But it was nice to know he never put his hands on Keres ... Evangelina.

We decided to start again by just having a quiet drink overlooking the sea and the orange-and-gold glitter that was forming as a decorative reflection of the sun.

We had beetroot dip and fresh, crusty white bread. We followed it with the catch of the day – sea bass – all perfectly presented, zesty and fresh. The waiter came over with a broad smile on his face, as full as the curls on top of his head. He began to speak, but I quickly had to interrupt.

'What did you say?' I looked between him and Anton, and pointed at the waiter. 'Anton, what did he say?'

Both of them tucked their chins to their chests and frowned. 'I say, did it go as plan?'

Anton said, 'He was just asking if the table and champagne went as planned. Why?'

'Say it again.' I thrust my open palm at the waiter. 'In Greek! Say it again! Please.'

The waiter slowly said in Greek, 'Did it go as planned?'

'Oh, my Christ. We need to leave. I need to leave.'

'What about dessert?'

I didn't care. I had to leave. We were sitting outside, but the buzz of people still crowded my mind and I needed to think. I marched under the whitewashed, concrete "Welcome" arch, pausing to lean on it and remove my shoes before turning right, up the hill. A minute later, Anton was running after me, shouting at me to slow down.

'I think I just left a thirty-euro tip! What's going on? Stop!'

He managed to get in front of me, but I was afraid that if I stopped then I would hyperventilate. Marching was the only thing regulating my breathing.

'Stop,' he whispered into my face, as he bent forward and held my shoulders. 'Melodie.' He pulled my chin up to look him in the eyes. Each breath tugged shallowly into my chest and my shoulders punched upwards with every attempt to breathe.

'He, he …' Gulps of air came in as I tried to speak, reminding me of the struggle to breathe on that day. 'He said that. To Keres, to her. What the waiter said. *Schédio*. The word for "plan".'

Anton pulled me into his arms at the side of the road. It didn't matter that people were walking around us, staring, or that cars needed to slow down to pass us. My whole body shook as though I was cold, and I let myself cry at his shoulder. At some point, he scooped me up and I didn't argue or care what anyone thought. My arms clung to his neck and I let him cradle me all the way to the car.

'Why would he say *schédio* over and over to her? She– she knew him, didn't she? I'm, I'm such a fucking idiot. I let her into our home. I'm s-so, s-so sorry.' My words blurred to nothing, much like my make-up. Anton was still holding me across the gear stick, but his body had become a concrete wall that I couldn't penetrate.

251

Chapter 33

'What are we going to do?' I said to Anton, as we sat down at Taste Me for a coffee. We didn't have long as Anton had promised to help Basil and Michail back at the house. They needed to discuss some issue with the swimming pool, and I had arranged to see Maria and baby Noah.

After our beautiful but broken meal at Manthos, I'd been a mess. I had tried my best to sleep on it so that we could talk about what to do in the bright light of day. We agreed that a coffee at Taste Me – with the beautiful view across all the trees and then further below out to sea – was the best place to gain perspective. I was watching Anton as he sat forward on the low chair. He had one leg stretched out to the side of the coffee table and the other hairy knee was being used to lean on, as he tapped his phone repeatedly on the glass tabletop. It had rows of elegant white stones underneath the pane of glass and I was beginning to worry about the safety of the table.

'I think we tell the police. We know her name. What she looks like.'

'But she didn't attack me and the evidence is thin at best.

I think perhaps we just move on with our lives. Forget that horrible woman even existed. Have you spoken to Akis today? How's he doing now he's back in England?'

'I think Mum will have driven him back to Corfu with too much coddling. Even with all this Keres stuff putting him off, I think he would be happier here. I'm not happy to ignore what that girl has done. But perhaps we have no choice.'

'Do you think she put something in Gaia's milkshake powder? I couldn't have imagined it before, but now...'

Anton froze with his espresso halfway to his mouth, before putting it back down without managing a sip. 'Why would she—?'

'Why would she have someone attack me? Lie about you? None of it adds up. Not really.'

He muttered to himself in Greek, I couldn't really hear him let alone understand him. He exhaled and ran both of his hands over his perfectly sweeping hair.

'Sometimes people are born evil, Melodie-Mou. Some people grow into it. Let us just be happy she is gone.' I let the cool frappé take the edge off the heat that was pressing on my shoulders. I usually loved the frappé at Taste Me, but with the stress of the past month or three, everything felt off. I put it down and looked towards the sea in the distance. The curves of Corfu had formed a perfect 'V' to frame it like a beautiful painting. I deeply inhaled the strong scent of Anton sipping his espresso from across the table. 'How are you?' He stopped drinking and actually looked at me.

'Yeah, I'm all right, I guess. No more off than is acceptable for someone who was betrayed by their deranged sister... Why?' His lip curled at the corner of his mouth, and he let his face soften at the sight of me.

It was a relief to know it wasn't all falling apart, to know that he was still there by my side no matter what crazy things went wrong or insane people I unleashed on our life. Then he changed from the soft, loving eyes to leaning his chin in his hand and his eyes moved as if he were counting the little white stones in the table. He slowly leant towards me, and instinctively I copied him until our noses were only a couple of centimetres apart.

'Melodie-Mou, are you late?'

For a small moment, I wasn't sure what he meant. I didn't say anything. Not right away. Then I probably looked like I was counting the stones too, and Anton slowly started to smile. My periods weren't perfectly regular, but he was right. With all the crazy goings-on, I hadn't realised just how far away I was from my normal cycles.

'Maybe.' I whispered so quietly even I wasn't sure I'd actually spoken. The strap of my linen top slipped off my shoulder, and Ant reached across the table to push it back up, giving me a sharp static shock, as though the tension and excitement between us was creating something out of our own control. 'Please don't get excited. Let's go and buy a test now so we don't have to sit around thinking about it all day.' With that he was up, paying the bill and dragging me toward the car to head to the local pharmacy.

'Wait, stop. You need to get home to Basil and Michail. You drop me off at home, and I'll go get a test. Then I'll let you know the result when you're done with Basil.' I tried to keep my lips still, but I desperately wanted to giggle.

'No! You wait for me before you take the test. I did not know about Gaia until long after Katerina knew. It is not fair. Wait for me.'

'Okay then. How about I go to see Maria and we can go together to pick up a test? To be honest, that makes more sense because who knows what I might accidentally buy. As if I know the Greek for "pregnancy test". I know I'm getting better but that is a little... specific.'

Maria was already at the taverna – Olympia – waiting for me when I arrived. I could see her as I walked up from where I'd parked. She was jogging the bundle in her arms while walking around the garden, circling their ceramic pots and stones. When she saw me, she made her way back to the table next to the grass on the decking. I knew it was our table because of the navy pram that was next to it.

'I thought I was meant to be late. I'm the one with a baby, after all,' Maria said, as she stepped forward to kiss me, almost whipping me with one of her two little fishtail plaits poking out from behind her ears. Noah was wailing in her arms, and she bounced on her tiptoes to get him to stop. He was bright red, with tufts of black hair like wild grass springing from his scalp. The white short-sleeve bodysuit had a bright yellow ring around one leg pressed to Maria's arm.

'I think perhaps he needs changing,' I said, pointing to the leak.

Maria began to curse in Greek.

'Let me hold him while you sort yourself out. Please?'

'Don't get shit on your nice top. I don't think it needs a yellow patch.' She looked down at herself as she passed him over. 'Unlike mine. And all my clothes. Noah told me all mine need a splash of yellow today.'

'Perhaps pale pink wasn't a good idea for Mummy? Was it Noah?' I cooed and bounced the little red ball in my arms.

'You might have to wear black more.' I laughed.

Once Noah was changed and fed, he fell asleep in his pram without too much fuss, leaving us to enjoy lunch and a catch-up. When my prawns with chilli and garlic were placed down in front of me, a little panic rippled from the base of my spine to the roots of my hair. Was it okay to eat prawns if I were pregnant? I didn't know. I tugged at my short linen top, considering it, and biding my time as I inhaled the subtle fresh chilli scent of the sauce.

'What's wrong with the prawns?'

'Nothing. They smell beautiful. I just ...' I looked up to see Maria poised with a forkful of bacon and freshly made potato skin halfway to her mouth. One thin eyebrow cut through me at a slant. I didn't know what to say. It was likely fine but somewhere in the back of my mind I knew there were some types of fish – and maybe shellfish – that were advised against while pregnant. 'I'm not sure I made the right choice. I'm not sure I'm hungry.'

Then both of her eyebrows gathered together in a thin line and she shook her fork at me as though it were an extension of her head. 'No, girl. Don't talk shit. You love prawns and you love these prawns. Talk.'

I hesitated, knowing how red my face would be, knowing if I told a lie she would just keep calling me out. 'I, I might be pregnant.'

Her fork dropped from her right hand with an excited clatter, and in the same moment Noah let out a moan from his pram. I'd never seen Maria jump up so quickly, hands on the pram to gently rock and soothe the little red creature within. 'What do you mean "might be"?'

'We're going to get a test later today. I think I'm late. Can I eat prawns though? I suddenly had a panic that I didn't know.'

Her blue eyes had pushed her eyebrows almost off her face, they were so wide. So much so I had to laugh a little. 'Oh, bloody hell, they change their minds on that stuff all the bloody time. Do you trust Olympia to give you fresh, well-cooked prawns?' I nodded frantically. 'Well then, you should be fine.'

'Good! I'm starving. I've felt off all morning.'

A smile tickled across her mouth as she sat back down to eat what remained on her fork after its descent to her plate. Carefully placing her fork back down, she proceeded to make fast but silent little claps and tapped her toes under the table in some kind of dance. 'Please stop. I might not be. And even if I am, it would be so early!'

'Okay, I'll stop. Either way, you'll get there. You're already a wonderful mum to Gaia. Have you told Gaia? Or Keres,' she managed, through a mouth half full of food.

'That's something I wanted to tell you. I didn't want to worry you, not with Noah – you have enough going on.'

'Worry me with what? Tell me now!'

'It's a long story. A very long story. But Keres wasn't Keres. She's not who she said she was.'

'Shit! I knew it! Girl, I bloody knew it! As soon as I saw her my hormones told me: no! Don't trust that one.'

'Well, your hormones were right.'

'It's your star sign.'

'What is?'

'You're a Cancer. Too empathetic and trusting, Melodie. I swear you would believe any story.'

'I'm not that bad.' I began to chew a perfectly fresh, fat king prawn, not wanting to tell her about the attack, about any of it, but I knew I had to. She sat there with a look on her face as though she were at the cinema eating popcorn, utterly engrossed by some horror film waiting for the tragic ending where the screaming lead gets eaten alive. It was funny, I told the whole story, all of it – Akis, Nico, the man from Sidari, the attack, almost giving her my inheritance, the accusation, the possibility she was poisoning Gaia, the lies, all of it as though it were a shopping list. Maria might have been on the edge of her seat gasping, but I wasn't bringing any drama to it. I had detached how I felt. Like a broken iceberg sliding away into the sea.

'Do you really think that bitch poisoned the milkshake? She's clearly capable of it! If I ever see her again …' Maria just shook her head and looked off in the distance towards the slice of sea that was visible at the bottom of the road.

'I honestly can't even think about it. If it was her then it's like I hurt Gaia because I let that woman into our house. Why would she do something like that? I can't get my head round any of it.'

'She's a nutcase that's why. I mean look at your evil father. Evil father, evil daughter.' I couldn't help but wince. 'Sorry.' I looked across at her as she pulled her lips into a line across her face.

'It's not your fault he was a sadistic prick. I can't rationalise him. The thing is, she isn't my sister is she? Her name wasn't Keres and her mum was the one calling her phone. I don't know who she was.' I paused watching holidaymakers laugh as they carried towels down the road to the sea. 'Why poor Gaia though? All the rubbish about Finn and painting her in a bad light. What was there to gain?'

'Divide and conquer?'

A wasp whipped round at me and I knocked it with the

back of my hand leaving it thrashing on the table. *Divide and conquer?* The idea bounced about in the same way the wasp did on the table until it eventually righted itself and flew away. I felt a little envious of its ability to escape.

'Maybe you're right. I don't think we'll ever know why though.'

'You can't reason with someone who had no logic Melo. You just can't. Honestly, I think she must be mentally ill, or something. If you see her again call the police.'

'You're right. We're just better off without her.' I audibly exhaled through my teeth. 'I don't want to talk about her anymore. Tell me more about you and this beautiful little creature. I need to focus on what's good in the world.'

As Maria told me about how much fun it was to pick little clothes out and not so much fun to dress herself, my body tingled at the idea of being where she was in a year's time. I didn't want to get my hopes up, but I knew it was too late, they were already up.

When tiny Noah woke to be fed again, we decided not to push our luck. As Maria put it, we had actually managed a whole hour of uninterrupted talking and that was as close to a modern miracle as things got. My tummy was in knots on the drive back, churning the fat prawns as though they were still swimming in the sea. I was desperate to find out if there were more than just prawns floating around in the pit of my stomach.

Chapter 34

As soon as I stepped out of my car, I could hear the belly laughs coming from the garden. Instead of going through the house, I went down the side, through the tall, metal gate and under the bougainvillea arch to find the reason for the laughter. There was Anton, hand slapping at Basil's back, scrunched over with tears streaming down his face. There was Michail, hovering, clearly the one who made the joke.

'*Kalispera*,' I called out as I made my way towards them.

'Was this your idea or the big man's?' Basil said. 'We need to fetz more supplies now you want to change the design. But do not worry, we can still work today.'

'Wait? Change the design?'

The three of them glanced between each other. Michail had been looking between us the whole time with his wide eyes, but now Ant and Basil had joined in.

'I have said the wrong thing. Anton will explain!' He gave Anton a hard slap on the shoulder before he and Michail made their way up to the clearing.

'Well? Why are you changing it? I thought you weren't

bothered?'

'I'm sorry. It occurred to me that it might be nice to have a shallow section.'

'There is a shallow end,' I snapped.

'No, I mean, a little addition. A safe area where we could sit and the baby could play. When it is a toddler, I mean. I'm sorry, I'm excited.'

'Well, I guess we had better find out in that case.'

Both our phones buzzed. We paused our smiles to simultaneously pull out the phones, Ant from his back pocket and mine from my handbag on my shoulder. It was Gaia:

Can one of u come and get me? I've finished early. Can u drop me at Finn's please?

'Well, that's okay,' I said. 'We can get the test on the way then get Gaia.' Looking up at Anton, he wasn't smiling as I had expected. In fact, he was baring his teeth in a grimace. 'What?'

'I need to mark out the new pool area that is being added on with Basil to see if diggers are needed again. If you can get Gaia, I'll get the test once I've finished. Yes?' His face relaxed into its normal, handsome features. The sun's rays caught the tips of his eyelashes and made the green of his eyes look almost a pretty, clear-mint colour. He bent forwards and kissed me. Not our normal brief goodbye kiss as I would have expected. He gathered me into his arms and pressed his soft full lips hard against mine.

'*Se agapó*'

'I love you too.'

Then he was off up the garden, almost running to catch up to Basil and Michail. With the touch of his lips still on mine, I walked in a daze around the house and under the bougainvillea arch. When I made it to the drive, there was an unfamiliar car there with a very familiar face behind the wheel. Keres/ Evangelina.

She stepped out of the car, dressed in black like the grim reaper in hotpants. I clawed into my open handbag to get at my keys, not knowing what to expect. She edged towards me with her hands on her chest, as though I were the one to be wary of.

'Melodie. I need to explain it all to you. I could not stay away anymore. I am your sister. But only half. Please listen to me.' She had edged along in front of me as I'd made my way to my Mini. She had managed to get in between me and the car and press her back against it.

'Don't talk to me. Don't even fucking look at me. How can I believe you? You set up that attack, didn't you? Didn't you?' My heart was pulsing like I'd just been on one of our sisterly runs through the olive grove. The afternoon sun was pressing down on my skin like a straitjacket.

'Yes. I will not lie anymore. I want you to know I was worthy of you. You were not in harm.'

'Not in harm! The prick almost broke my ankle and nearly pulled my arm out of the socket!'

'He thought that was what you like. I told him it was a sex game. This was stupid idea. I want you to trust me. That was all.' The faster she spoke, the more disjointed her English became. 'Melodie, I am sister. Your sister. I love you. I am stupid, yes. A fool. Please listen.'

The palm of my hand met the soft cushion of her cheek, causing a noise cleaner and more satisfying than a solitary clap in an empty house. I'd never hit anyone before. Not that

I could remember. Not like that anyway. Not the kind of hard slap that starts with a twist of the spine and uses every muscle in the shoulder too. Evangelina was left with her face glowing and turned to the right with her eyes tightly shut.

'Please listen,' she whispered. 'My father was Adam Jones. He was good to me. My mother did not know of Liliana. I did not know of her, or you. He was not around and she realised he had someone else and told him not to return. He did not visit after my mother sent him away. When I have money, I look for him. I found you.'

'What? Well then, why lie to me and say your name was Keres? None of it makes sense! Why wouldn't you just tell me all of this from the start? I'm sure you are his child. You're an evil witch! You're just like him.' Every muscle in my body was contracting harder than I could imagine possible and each short hot breath left me feeling dizzy with rage. 'Tell me why you lied.' She shrugged and rubbed the lines on her cheek when my hand print throbbed in the sun.

'I did not know you. I did not trust you. I needed to find out who you were. If you were lying to me to take Daddy's house from me. You call me this name, Keres, I know this evil name but not why you give it to me. So, I try to find out. I played along.'

'Did you poison Gaia too?'

'No, no. Why would I do suttz a thing?'

I dropped my bag and keys and grabbed the scruff of her neck, overcome with fury. I pulled her into me. I'd never had a fight with anyone. Then again, I'd never been more angry in my life. The thought of her hurting Gaia made me want to pull her apart with my fingernails.

'Tell me the truth, Keres!' I shook her with each word. 'It

was you, wasn't it? You did something to her milkshake! If you tell me what it was, I'll let you go.'

'Yes! I did.' She wriggled and screamed Greek words I was yet to learn before she pushed me away. She stood very still, visibly shaking before wrapping her arms about her and clinging on to her own elbows.

'I am sorry. Please, forgive me. My brother, he would torture me and I would give him *Ipecac* to make him sick, make him leave me alone. I only want time with you. Gaia was not hurt.'

The moment seemed to drag on with no words only the sound of electricity in the air. I had no idea what *Ipecac* was but I said it over and over again in my mind to keep hold of it before managing to react.

'How can you say that?' I exhaled the words through my teeth. 'How can you know that? That poor girl was whittled down to a bloody toothpick and you have the audacity to say she "was not hurt". What's wrong with you? I opened up my heart, my home and welcomed you in. What's wrong with you?'

'You love her more than me. Even now *what is wrong with me*. Blaming me! I just want you to myself. How is this bad? When Gaia is ill, you cook with me. You talk to me and run with me. We are sisters at last. This is a good thing. I do not hurt her, no, I am helping you. Making life easier for you, without these people taking you from your only sister and having them, having them,' she looked around searching for a word, 'manipulate you.'

'What are you talking about? Gaia and Anton are the best thing that ever happened to me... wait, is he my brother too? Is Andreas Adam's son?' She shook her head and I couldn't help release a breath of relief.

'No, do not worry. No more unwanted siblings for you. Only me. Send me to be homeless. This is what Anton and his precious girl wants all along.'

'Are you fucking kidding Keres, Evangelina, what-ever- the-bloody-hell-your-name-is. Love isn't some cake that you use up and can't share. You're completely unhinged just like our controlling father.' I pressed my hands over my eyes, desperate to hide from what I'd done in letting her into our lives. 'I can't believe I ever let you into our home. I don't want you near any of us again.'

'Do not say this Melodie, we are sisters.'

'So? All you've done is try to destroy everything I have. And for what? Money? I said you could have half of everything I have? Was that not enough for you? Or was it exclusively just to control me? Perhaps for the fun of tormenting people?'

'Not half of everything.' Her voice was quiet and her blue eyes became blackholes.

'Is that it? It wasn't enough money for you? You wanted the whole bloody lot? Kill us all off one by one and you get the bloody lot?' It was then I was sure I saw something. Just a twitch in her cheek, almost like she was suppressing a laugh. She began to talk, denying that it was money, saying all she wanted was me in her life. My mouth went dry and the sweat on the back of my neck left me with a chill even under the burning heat of the sun. *She wants to laugh.* That's all I could think. *This is a joke to her. I'm a joke to her.* She was still talking when I cut in.

'It's time to leave.' She didn't move straight away, and when she did her eyes were pleading and I could feel the lies about to pour out of her as she opened her mouth. 'Just leave! I'm not letting you poison any of us again. Get away from me, now!' I yelled and stamped my foot.

That's when she showed herself. Maybe she could see she would never win. She took off her Keres mask and became Evangelina. She hissed at me in Greek, *'Na, Na'*, as her open palm and outstretched fingers thrust towards my face – the moutza – a worse gesture than two fingers from the English at the French. Then her index finger was thrusting into my chest. Her mouth was moving so fast and so close to my face, I instinctively stumbled backwards as she spat her words at me. 'Daddy was good. *Skatá ston táfo sou.'* I knew that one from the rude phrase book Akis had given me: "Shit on your grave".

'Póso malákas íse?' I said in return – in an oddly sassy tone – as the only other phrase I could remember. Basically, asking her how much of a wanker she was. Not perfect Greek by any stretch, in fact I'm sure the gender was wrong, but she was momentarily stalled by it.

'Stupid Melodie. You and big house and big man. Stupid man, never looking at me. It should be mine! Daddy's house, Daddy's money is mine! Yes, I give your girl poison. You care for her – your stupid girl – and not me? Not your sister?! Do not worry. It never damaged my brother. Only shut him up for the day. Like your sick princess.'

'What? You did this to your brother too? You're insane; a pathetic lying bitch, no wonder your brother wants nothing to do with you. Assuming that's even true?' I took a breath as a cascade of words and thoughts poured over me. 'I'm going to make sure you don't get a single thing. Adam was long dead and that house was my mothers. You deserve nothing.' That's when she laughed but her eyes clouded with tears. Through everything, it was the idea of being left with nothing that caught a nerve. She placed her hand to her mouth and laughed as a tear streamed down her face.

'You would never give me what is mine. I see this now. You never loved me. I was right to hide being your half-sister. You are uncaring, only loving them,' her index finger whipped towards the house even though neither Anton or Gaia were inside, 'you wouldn't give me half. No, no.' She began to pace. 'He didn't want me to have anything. He wants me to show passport and take everything from me! He controls you; I am your family. He tells you what to do, him and his brat and you follow. Never listening to me. They have everything. I have nothing. All I have was you and now you take this.' She began to sob again, desperately clawing at the façade of Keres. Perhaps genuinely feeling sorry for herself.

'Leave now and never come back or the police will be the least of your problems.' I didn't recognise my own voice. It was as though I had been taken over and a low, dark shadow of me had appeared from the depths of my guts. Anton had been right; he had seen through her from the start. What had he said? *Ta matia sou dekatessera* – the fourteen-eyes thing. I could see her now and I wished I'd had fourteen eyes on her from the start. Instead of blinded by the idea of one big happy family. I picked up my bag and got in my car without another word. I let my Mini's wheels spin, throwing up dust and stones at her as I left her standing, sobbing.

I had to consciously make myself slow down as I drove to pick up Gaia. The blood was still racing around my body, making my toes tingle and press the accelerator. I kept trying to make sense of it all but there wasn't any. Not really. She clearly wanted money, that much I was sure of, but why she wanted to divide me from Gaia and Anton I couldn't work out. I would have shared anything with her. But then, why did she really poison her brother? Was he really dreadful to her or was she just evil? Mum had told me about Adam, how controlling he was and how he wouldn't let her out and didn't even want to share her with a child that was theirs. I could only imagine that Evangelina was like him. She wanted money and power and to separate us all. She broke my heart. Adam, my stupid father broke my heart with every ripple he caused in my life. Every touch of information that brought me close to him was like a fatal blow to my heart.

When I picked Gaia up, she went straight into a rant about boys and how Finn was desperate to see her but also wanted them to hang out with his mates – or something – something about his friends. I wasn't sure. My mouth was dry and all the thoughts and words that weren't about Evangelina had evaporated into the Corfu heat. Eventually, she stopped and looked at me, hair blowing across her face.

'Mou-mou?'

That was enough. Enough to make my face crack and crease and pour with tears. Enough to make me beg for her forgiveness. Enough to make my stomach churn and contract in hard desperate breaths of sorrow. At despair. At anger. Anger at being a part of Adam's legacy. Being related to him and to Evangelina. I had to pull the car over and vomit at the side of the road while my poor, beautiful Gaia reassured me, although she was utterly confused by the outburst. We drove slowly and on the way to Finn's, I told her everything.

When I arrived back home, Keres's car was gone and the house was empty. I called for Anton, but the only sound was the breeze from the air con churning round. Just in case he was in fact still outside talking to Basil, and not at the pharmacy, I walked through the door and straight out into the garden. As I stepped out, I was blinded by something reflecting on the table. Momentarily shielding my eyes, I stepped towards it and realised it was Ant's phone. The screen was rippled with cracks like the roots of trees that had taken hold and destroyed everything that was once contained inside. I ran across the garden, through the olive trees to where the pool was being built. There was no one there.

There was no point in worrying about a broken phone. It happens. I took myself back into the house and sat down in Anton's big armchair, my thighs sticking to the leather. I placed my hands over my lower abdomen and wondered how long it had been since he left for the pharmacy. It wasn't far, only to the centre of the village of Karousades. Our house was on the outskirts, but I knew it couldn't be long until he was home.

Six hours later, Gaia was home, but Anton wasn't. I had contacted Basil. He had been the one to find the phone as Anton left before him. It had been in the driveway. He thought perhaps Anton had dropped it and ran over it without realising.

Gaia was calling everyone we knew, but no one had seen him. I had to tell her he was going to the pharmacy, although I didn't say why. She called there too, but he hadn't been seen. It's not as though he were hard to miss. I desperately needed air and had escaped to the garden. I stood behind the olive trees, not quite as far as where the pool was going to be. I couldn't bring myself to go all the way up to our swing chair and look back on our empty home. We were meant to be laughing or crying together while looking at a stupid bit of plastic that would tell us if our child was in my belly or not. There was no point looking at my phone, but I still held it tightly in my grasp, checking as though Anton's number might appear.

Leaning against a tree, my mind slipped to the last time I'd seen him. The way he pulled me in and kissed me. I replayed it again and again, how it felt like more than our usual goodbye. He had seemed excited, so much so he was making changes to the design of our swimming pool. I felt as though my tight grip was around my own throat, not the phone in my hand. With each second Anton didn't come home my pulse seemed to gain speed and acid burnt the back of my throat, seeping into my lungs. Surely, he would just walk through the door with a hilarious explanation at any moment. Surely?

A note from the author…

Thank you for reading *Behind The Olive Trees*, the second book following Melodie's story. I'm so sorry about the cliffhanger ending. I hope you understand this had to be the ending of this book… The characters made me do it.

I wrote my first novel, The Little Blue Door, during the 2020 lockdown just after having my second child. I've always been one to create my own version of freedom, and that book was the ultimate way to create freedom during the first wave of the pandemic.

I love to read what you think about my work. So please remember to review (reviews change lives - trust me) and come and have a chat with me on my social pages. I'm on **Instagram Facebook Twitter TikTok** and my Amazon Author Page

Before I sign off, I'd like to say a little thank you to my husband, Samuel, who actually has a small role in this book! (Yes, the parkour/cat story is real - my husband saved the little beauty). Check out his parkour talent over on his Instagram @samtheparkourguy

Francesca x

Milton Keynes UK
Ingram Content Group UK Ltd.
UKHW04101722O524
443072UK00004B/120

9 781915 208040